My Nightingale

A LOVE STORY BURNED IN THE HYMNS OF INDIA'S GREATEST STRUGGLE

notionpress.com

My Nightingale

A Love Story Burned In The Hymns Of India's Greatest Struggle

Arun Bhimavarapu

notionpress
.com

Notion Press

Old No. 38, New No. 6

McNichols Road, Chetpet

Chennai - 600 031

First Published by Notion Press 2016

ISBN 978-93-86009-27-2

Cover design: AB Core Design. Hyderabad

Cover Illustration: Thirupathi Sambe - thirupathisambe.blogspot.com

To Bose

To Gandhi

To Independent India

The Point in Thanking

If you have already read my first novel, you would have known by now that I don't thank my friends. That already makes you my reader, and my readers are also my friends. If you are not my friend or reader, any of both is same again, and you are not reading this, then what's the point of thanking you?

But if you never knew me and still going to read on; then welcome aboard buddy. We are going to have a roller-coaster ride back into time. We are going to love, laugh, cry, think, question and realise things… And at the end of the day, end up with a new friend.

However, there was also this group of guys, without whom the novel would never have taken shape; my producers – Priya Pandarinath, Raja Surya Pradeep Dakamarri and Sudheer Ippagunta (No priorities, just alphabetical order). I still don't want to thank them for spending their hard-earned money on me, but I would love to thank them, along with all my 'friends', for that one gift a human can ever gift another, *Trust.* Thank you all for trusting me on this. And finally making a point to thank…

Hope you will enjoy the read.

Special Note

(Not the kind you usually skip)

Mack Wright. Esc., I.P.

17th July, 1942

When I arrested Sarat Chandra Bose, he left instructions that all his political correspondence should be dealt with by Suresh Mozumdar, the Editor of the "Hindusthan Standard." It was the "Hindusthan Standard" alone of all the newspapers of Bengal which appeared definitely to discredit the news of the death of Subhas Chandra Bose in an air crash. In the editorial column of its issue of Monday, 30th March, 1942 there appeared in heavy print only the following notice:

"SIR SUBHASH CHANDRA

'REUTER' ANNOUNCES THE DEATH OF SIR SUBHAS CHANDRA ON INFORMATION GATHERED FROM LYONS AND VICHY RADIOS. WE REFUSE TO WRITE AN OBITUARY NOTICE. LONG LIVE SRI SUBHASH CHANDRA!"

It struck me at the time that this group was in wireless communication with Japanese occupied territory.

Yours Sincerely,

W. Mack Wright, Esc., I.P.,
Intelligence Bureau, Home Department,
Government of India,
New Delhi

The above shown is a letter that I found in a classified report that was one among the documents which were recently declassified by Mr. Modi's government. These are the top secret government files of the time when Subhash Chandra Bose fought for our independence through his INA (Indian National Army). There were many more interesting facts I came to know through these files, but none excited me as this letter did.

Thanks to the management of Calcutta Police Museum for treating me so well. That day which was spent reading those files over and over again was the best day of my life, to say as an Indian. I never knew how to react after getting to know what happened to the real hero because of whom we are living our lives today in respect and freedom – the born rebel, his Excellency, Netaji Subhash Chandra Bose.

He and his men were officially called 'Terrorists' in the letters that went to Viceroy's offices. His transmissions from Berlin were forcefully stopped, and civilians who were caught listening to him were punished. His soldiers, the Indian National Army soldiers, were left to die in unemployment and hunger after the independence. And his ideas of fighting the real war making his country take steps towards the real progress were murdered by the so-called "mass-leaders" of that time.

At least, they thought that they did, but no.

"It's the activities of Netaji Subhash Chandra Bose and the INA forces that weakened the very foundations of British in India, and the impact of Gandhi's Quit India Movement was minimal on us," said Lord Attlee, then Prime Minister of England.

The files I went through, not just reflected the ideas and struggle of Bose, but it also took me to the days of our independence movement. I came across a handwritten page by Mr Bose himself. I saw a stamp of half-ana on a postcard and read the story of an African Black soldier who fought for our freedom.

There were also tales of uncountable number of soldiers among the common man then. There were fighters, there were activists, there were leaders, there were teenaged martyrs and to my surprise, there were dangerous spies, ruthless assassins and also path breaking intellectuals who mastered the subjects of data tapings and signal interceptions, here in our own country.

Don't know if it's going to turn out good or bad, but it changed the plot. A major plot of "My Nightingale" changed while it was in the making.

Besides the intriguing love triangle between Prudhvi, Sanjuktha and Emily, now it's going to talk about the intriguing course of events that is beyond our imaginable limits. It's going to talk about why the then Dum Dum Airfield is now named Netaji Subhash Chandra Bose International Airport; it's going to talk about why the Germans feared to transmit their signals to Japan through Indian airs; it's going to talk about how the Indian National Army made the British bleed internally; and most importantly, it's going to talk about why they say that Bose hadn't really died in that crash....

However, to remember all through, this novel is just a fictional representation based on historical facts; but not to offend or disgrace any political party, community, religion or an individual. Please take it that way. And forgive my flaws.

-Arun Bhimavarapu

When you witness situations, you never imagined you would see

You will turn into a person you never thought you would be

Chapter 1

03:16 am

3rd November, 1938

British Council Estate. Narsipatnam, Madras Presidency.

"Come on. Nothing is going to happen. We will make it back, alive," whispered Prudhvi, lying flat on the ten feet wall, stretching out his hand for Saleem.

If it wasn't for Prudhvi, Saleem would never have been even close to that wall. Like never. But now he was going to climb past it and intrude into a British building, in the middle of the night. That was more than plain suicide. He knew that Prudhvi won't listen even if he tried to hold him back from going and also he might die today. But Saleem was not letting his friend go alone. It was also a full moon day, and the moon was brighter than usual making shadows of everything around - bad day to plan intrusions.

Finding no other way to make all this turn back, that too at this point of time, Saleem stretched his hand reaching him, and Prudhvi pulled him up with all his strength. In the next second, they were on the ground on the other side of the wall.

Prudhvi turned to look at Saleem, who was breathing heavily, may be out of fear. He always wondered how he managed climbing things with that dhoti on. And why he wore a dhoti in the first place? He's a Muslim.

"I don't dress according to religion. I dress according to comfort," he says.

"Comfort and dhoti?" Prudhvi never understood the relation. He was quite happy with his cotton trousers, linen shirt and leather suspenders. Sometimes he also wondered if that was the distance between their economic statuses.

"What now?" said Saleem turning to Prudhvi.

"Wait for the signal," he said as a matter of fact, and they moved towards the dark shadow of a bush.

On the high lands, to the left of the council building, Suryam and Rudhra waited behind a tree, until their friends made it past the wall. Suryam was a typical Indian-faced boy who was dressed in a dhoti and a sleeveless kurta made out of cheap fabric and with a cloth tied around his head like a turban. Rudhra too was in his dhoti and kurta, but ones that were made out of a fabric of comparatively better quality. He too had a cloth tied into a turban on his head. They use that cloth to clean their faces when needed, lift any hot vessels when their mothers ask them to or sometimes roll-up into a pillow when sleep overpowers them away from home.

They both stared at the building that too had cast its long shadow on the ground. Prudhvi and Saleem waited in that dark with baited breath. From the place where Rudhra and Suryam were hiding, they can see the whole aerial view. It was the only construction on that entire plane with the vast barren lands behind it meeting the horizon. And from the distance, they were at, the guards on the side of the building that they planned to enter from could be easily identified. Suryam had an eagle's eye and could even tell if a guard was sleeping!

"Shall I?" enquired Rudhra turning to his friend who was perching like an angry hawk.

He hadn't moved. Not even his head. Rudhra tapped his feet restlessly as his hand clasping a cardboard, in front of the burning lantern, shivered.

Suryam might never have been to an actual school, but he was very good at patterns. Even human patterns and Rudhra knew that. He knew that his friend was as good with patterns as he was with signals. But to Rudhra it seemed like the guards on the night shift were not following a specified pattern. Or may be only the one who was familiar with patterns could see through. Rudhra offered his god a quick prayer to provide their friends with a gap to get inside and then back again; as Suryam still stared as if he was sleeping with his eyes open.

"Now…" he said on an impulse, and Rudhra, at once, started cutting the light of the lantern with the cardboard in specified intervals of time. He prayed again while doing so. This time to let the message be right and clear. Even if it was not, he knew that Prudhvi will read his mistakes. He was the master in data signalling.

"What does that mean?" Saleem said, staring at the blinking light from the high lands.

"You want to know?" Prudhvi said smiling after a long, intense stare at the light. "It's show time."

While they ran towards the building with deft steps and a slow pace, bending to their hip levels, Saleem started imagining how he was going to be tortured by Sir Charles Canning and then hanged till death. Their long and thin shadows ran along with them.

As they neared the building, they heard a guard talk to his mate. They were discussing the recent Salt-Satyagraha. They ran as fast as they could, and once they reached the outer hallway, they pressed their backs on a huge pillar each, beneath which they seem like miniature dolls. Prudhvi leaned to the other side of the pillar without loosening the grasp, to see if the hallway was clear. It was, and they took the chance.

Past the hallway, they climbed the staircase made of long and vast marble stairs, bending to the floor level. There were the two sentries they heard talking, standing in the hallway on the first floor. The topic of their conversation had switched to speculating whether Congress had intensions of killing Bose for being a threat to their grip over India. They were dressed in red and black sentry suits with double barrel shotguns hanging from the shoulders. Prudhvi took a step backwards fearing to be seen, and Saleem suddenly saw the light from the highlands flashing again.

"What is he trying to say?" he said, and Prudhvi turned to take a look.

Prudhvi squinted his eyes to stare while Saleem feared if the sentries would notice the blinking.

"S – E – M," Prudhvi started decoding the light to letters from the number of seconds it flashed for, "T – R – Y – C – P – M – I – N – G," and the light was gone.

Saleem took his time in arranging and reading the words.

"Sentry coming?!" he almost screamed.

"Damn..."

In the next split second, they started descending the stairs as fast and as quietly as they could. The stairs were so broad that it took two steps to cover each stair. They took the turn in the middle of the staircase and Prudhvi made an abrupt stop. Saleem knocked into him as he hadn't expected the sudden halt. Prudhvi somehow controlled himself from falling, and Saleem lifted his head up from the stairs immediately, to see a sentry walking in the dark, towards the stair case. The sentry was coming from the ground floor. Suppressing the panic, Prudhvi slowly moved back without much physical activity, and Saleem followed what he did. They went back to the bend in the staircase and slid themselves down, panting with fear.

"What if he sees them?" shivered Rudhra.

"Say 'Kill'," ordered Suryam turning to him at once.

"What? Did you go mad? How could they?"

"Why can't they?" Suryam started shouting. "You see any other way to get out of there? Prudhvi can kill if he should."

"How can you be so sure?"

"Do you know what clan he belongs to?" Suryam was raging with anger. "Alluri Sitaraama Raju... I think you know what he did to the British. Prudhvi Prathap Raju also had that in him. So say 'Kill'. Now..."

"But these guards are not British. They just work for-" he said turning to the bungalow and stopped at once. The sentry almost reached the stairs now.

Rudhra turned to look at Suryam, who was staring at him desperately, stared back for just a second and picked up the lantern and the cardboard.

"Kill," said Saleem, making a word with the four single harmless words his friend just uttered.

Prudhvi just stared at Saleem as if hoping for some support. Behind him, he saw a bronze statue of a medieval Chinese knight near the wall at the bend. It had a detachable double-sided naginata in its hand.

"No…" Saleem whispered turning back to Prudhvi from the statue, "they are also Indians like us."

"I don't care. If we don't, we don't see another sun rise," he whispered back.

"But we shouldn't."

"Now don't start being a kid again," he said holding him by his shoulders. "You always wanted to die for your country right?"

"This is not called dying for the country."

"Yes… This is called 'killing' for the country." Saying so, he went on to pick up the naginata.

The sentry who knows that Prudhvi was the son of an Indian-British general and who will leave them unharmed, if caught, started climbing the stairs. He was a man in his late forties, dressed in his sentry uniform and had no one even to cry for him if he died. He lost his wife, his two daughters and their families in a bomb blast last year. He had fought for freedom once, but now had no strength left in him. He was just counting his days and working for his everyday meal.

Prudhvi tried to detach the naginata from the statue's hand. He aimed to throw it on to the sentry even before he could see him. If he made a sound while falling back, he would run fast to fetch it back and kill the others too hiding near the bend in the stairs. The lethal weapon got almost separated from the statue when suddenly a raging fire broke out on the high lands behind the wall.

They exchanged glances and went to hide behind the railings again. The old man just stopped midway noticing the sudden fire in the middle of a calm night. Without a doubt, the sentries on the first floor might also have seen it. In the next few seconds, they too would cross this way.

"Hey..." shouted the sentry, who had already climbed up few steps, turning back to descend. Prudhvi and Saleem followed him like swift wind – calm and fast. They reached half the way and suddenly heard footsteps from behind. The sentries from the first floor were coming, and they weren't so far from them. Getting hold of the railing with both hands, Prudhvi lifted his body up jumping over the railings and landed on the ground floor.

"Come on... Jump..." he shouted in a whisper to Saleem, who was shivering with fear. "Saleem jump. Or you'll die."

With his hands still shaking, he got hold of the railings and jumped, taking his hands off the bars just before the sentries turned at the bend. He fell on to the floor as if he jumped off the stars. Prudhvi pushed him towards the dark area under the stairs and rolled along with him. The sentries ran down the stairs to join their mate in investigating the issue.

"You have the courage. But it should be pushed," Prudhvi smiled.

"Let's get the hell out of here." He could hardly see his friend in that dark corner.

"Ya. Once we are done with what we came for."

"Are you mad? They'll be back in no time."

"We'll be back in half of 'no time'," said Prudhvi, dragging him by his shoulder and they climbed the stairs running with all the energy remained. Prudhvi knew that once they reach the top, there was no coming back in the same way again.

"What the hell?" said Rudhra making a halt. They were in the midst of absconding after setting up the fire. Suryam too stopped to look back at what Rudhra saw.

"Son of the gun," he exclaimed, as Rudhra stared at him with anger pouring out of his eyes.

"That was supposed to be a code to abort the mission. What did he think of himself?" he shouted, being on the edges of turning back and running before the guards reached them with their loaded guns.

"Blame the clan," Suryam shrugged with a smile.

With Rudhra still blaming the clan, they escaped, jumping into the lake and swimming to the other side.

Prudhvi pushed one of the huge wooden doors in front of which the sentries were standing a few minutes earlier, making a narrow gap between them. They squeezed their bodies through and closed the door behind. The room was not as dark as they thought it would be. The moon light piercing through the ventilator lent some visibility.

They walked across to reach another door that led them to the main hall. The hall was so spacious and so big that Prudhvi was led to believe that he was in an auditorium for a second. Saleem's thoughts weren't even close to Prudhvi's. He had never seen an auditorium. He just opened his mouth wide to stand still and watch the beautiful and flexuous roof that seemed like a second sky. The more than smooth marble on the floor was reflecting the moon light on to the ceiling adding much ambience to it. In the middle of the ground floor, there was a statue of an Indian woman with a pot on her hip, out of which some colored water was overflowing into the pond beneath her feet. The two stair cases on each side of the hall that lead ways to the floor they were standing on are built in perfect curvatures making them seem like the tusks of a mighty African elephant. Out-taking all these, there was a huge crystal chandelier hung from the middle of the roof in its complete grandiosity, glittering like diamonds studded all over its mighty metal surface.

"Can you please close that tunnel?" Prudhvi said pushing Saleem's chin up and grabbed him by his shoulder to run towards the door that led them to the dome. Saleem kept on looking back at the hall until it finally disappeared from the limits of his eyesight.

"Fast fast fast..." Prudhvi repeated the same word as Saleem pulled out a cloth from the folds of his dhoti that he had tucked into by its edge. They were on the dome of the building with the heavy winds from the north trying to push them off of it. But they stood tight with all their weight concentrated on their legs. By the time Saleem took out the cloth, Prudhvi had pulled down the rope with the

British flag tied to it. The cloth that Saleem brought was a flag too.

From the other side of the lake, drenched from head to toe and shivering from the cool midnight breeze, Suryam and Rudhra saw the British flag being dragged down and two sixteen-year old Indian boys tying knots to hoist their flag. A flag with saffron on the top, white in the middle, green at the bottom and the 'Charkha' (spinning wheel) at the center of the white color.

"How did they do that?" said Suryam trying to stretch taller than his actual height to have a clear view.

"Do what?"

"Climb the dome."

"That's not the point. Ask me how they are going to get off it."

"How?" exclaimed Suryam. Rudhra just smiled in response.

Prudhvi pulled the rope as fast as he could, as the sentries who were at the wall, shouting out to the empty lands could turn back at any minute. While the flag rose towards the vast and clear sky shining with stars all over its surface, Saleem stood there watching it with pride in his eyes. To him, it felt as if India had really become a free country – free from the ruthless rule of the British, free from the hundreds of years of tyrannical slavery; free as a bird, free as the flag.

But it was not. Many struggles were yet to come… Many battles yet to be fought…

Saleem saluted the flag as Prudhvi tied last few knots on the rope at the bottom of the pole. Suryam and Rudhra did the same standing on the other bank of the lake. It was this love towards their country that always united them more than their friendship. But Prudhvi never fully agreed with them. He somehow developed some repulsive ideas towards freedom.

Prudhvi turned to look at Saleem saluting the flag and smiled while rechecking the knot.

"Enough patriotism… let's go," he said standing up carefully, as the dome was slippery from the fog, which made the climb difficult earlier.

"What's the plan?" said Saleem, once he was contended with the feeling of saluting his country.

"Why say it? When I can show it," smiled Prudhvi. That smile felt familiar to Saleem. He knew that smile. And something way crazier than ordinary happened every other time after that smile.

The building they stood on was a palace-type of construction, with the dome located to the rear end of it. From the front view the dome will be in the center of the building's length, but from the side view, the edge of the dome was the edge of the building. And there was a thick clump of trees just after the narrow backyard.

Prudhvi slowly moved towards the rear end side and turned back to look at Saleem. "When you complained about the fog while climbing, I said it will come handy later. Do you know why I said that?"

"No...," he said trying not to think about what looks likely to happen.

Prudhvi turned back slowly, sat on the dome, took a deep breath and all at once he glided over the curvature of the dome. When he reached the small horizontal slab at the end of it, he took the inertia from sliding and ran as fast as he could to jump off the roof with all the force he had. He spread his limbs as he flew on to the trees. Saleem shivered with fear of missing them. But he didn't. He folded himself close in mid-air as he reached the trees and went piercing into them like a cannonball. Saleem stood there watching with disbelief as he disappeared into the trees.

"Sanjuktha... I hate you," he murmured with his teeth clenched and followed him.

The sentries returned to the building, deciding that the fire might just have occurred due to a lantern that the local fisherman accidentally forgot on the highlands. Some of them are very strong about their conclusion that they even started discussing stories about how once a whole village got burned to ashes due to an unattended lantern. But none of them have observed that the flag that was flying high on the dome was not the same anymore.

Rudhra and Suryam watched with smiles on their faces as Prudhvi and Saleem swam towards them. They helped their friends out of the lake and then hugged each other patting their backs.

"This is the last time; I'll never come with you idiots on suicide missions like this," said the angry and shivering Saleem. The other three laughed.

"But this is not the last time. You'll say that again," said Rudhra circling his arm around his friend's neck and teasing him. Saleem struggled to get free.

"Back home?" Suryam asked Prudhvi, who was laughing out loud encouraging Rudhra.

"What's the hurry?" he said turning to him. "Let the sun rise."

Resting on the bank of that lake, they enjoyed the sunrise that two of them almost missed.

Chapter 2

09:30 am
Same day
Same place.

A considerably big group of locals who were dressed in their dhotis and kurtas with turbans tied on their heads; and few women, in their sarees with the pallu draped over from behind to cover their faces, waited near the main gate as a Model-T Ford went in passing them. It's Sir Charles Canning, for whom they were waiting since the last one and a half hour. He was the acting president of the Board of British Deputies which covered almost thirty villages around, and also the head of the Irrigation and Drinking water department - the most callous ruler that ever walked this land. He never considered himself anything less than god. Brimming with ego, pride and violence, this British officer was a nightmare to many rebel forces.

But the man who was leading this group was no rebel. A man in his early forties, he was a devout follower of Mahatma Gandhi. Chakradev was his name, and he was the president of this Un-British-Official panchayati raj.

"Even today, he's not going to see you, sir. Why do you waste your time standing here for hours every day?" pleaded the guard of Indian origin at the gate.

"No problem, sir. We'll wait until he comes out," Chakradev said with a smile.

"But he won't meet you. Forever."

"Then we'll wait, forever," said Sanjuktha, daughter of Chakradev.

She too wore a saree with the pallu on her head and was probably the cutest Indian girl in her teens; whose looks and age never suited her acts. She followed her father to every protest he had been to; sat with him in every hartal, walked with him to every meeting and will fight for freedom even after him.

In her childhood, when her mom was alive, she had never known what *slavery* and *freedom* were meant at least. But when she lost her to a massacre at the age of eight, when she saw her mother cut in halves lying on the verandah in a pool of blood, something in her changed forever.

They stood for hours in front of that gate as the scorching sun tested their will. Many of them sat on the dusty ground unable to stand anymore. Even Chakradev took the weight off his feet leaning on to the wall. But Sanjuktha and few others remained standing.

The clock ticked 05:15 pm and the sun slowly decided to test the other side of the globe. Another day passed. It was at 06:00 pm they usually headed back every day, but today they decided to leave early, as the hardship of the last few weeks had taken its turn on their bodies. At 05:25 pm, when they finally decided to leave, suddenly the guard opened the gates for the Ford that was heading out. The group gave way to it standing on the sides of the path. They never tried to stop it or talk to the man inside while it passed through the gate twice a day.

"Father!" said Sanjuktha staring at the car that just passed them and Chakradev turned back to see what it that made her daughter break into a shock.

The Ford took a halt few meters from the crowd that was clubbing back into one again. The car door opened with a squeak and Sir Canning stepped out.

Six feet three-inch tall, broadly built shoulders, more than fair complexion, athletic body and the British officers uniform with so many medals over the pocket. A leather belt with a holster and a handgun in it around the hip that made the lower part of the suit to bulge a little, another belt that went across the chest from the left side of the first belt on to his right shoulder and the officer's cap that made him look even more dangerous. He came walking towards the group, banging the baton in his hand on the side of his thigh.

"It has been weeks since I last saw you Chakradev," he said in his British drawl. The silent protest did break him at last. "What are you doing here with your friends? Want any donation for your little village?"

Most of them hadn't understood what he said. Actually all of them, except Chakradev and his daughter. Sanjuktha raged with anger. All the others except this filthy pig are Indians here. They can easily beat the life out of him with their bare hands and throw him in to the lake. The same lake from which he denies to supply them some drinking water. But she controlled her anger. Her father always taught her this: *Ahimsa paramo dharma*, which means 'Non-violence is the ultimate dharma.'

"Just water sir," said Chakradev with due respect. "All we need is some water to drink."

"I believe that you do have some water reserves in your area," he said as if they were in an official meeting.

The water resources he was referring to are the drainage pits that were formed due to pipe breakages and no matter how much they cleaned it, a new batch of sewage came flowing every day. The pipes too were laid by the government to dispose waste from their locality into the dumping yards beyond the village land.

"No sir. I fear that they are not portable," said Chakradev voicing the same respectable tone.

"Then filter it. You might have some of your old Indian techniques to do so. You're the one who invented flush toilets right?" smiled Canning, as if he was enjoying a great old-buddy-chit-chat.

"But we haven't come up with any technique yet," Sanjuktha said, and her father spun to her with fear in his eyes, "to get rid of the waste that got accumulated on our land. So until then, please consider," she said with anger in her tone.

Canning looked at her just in anger, but in the very next moment he did that, he found himself regretting his fate of not seeing her until then. Though he couldn't see her face clearly from inside the pallu, the raging anger in her eyes provoked him.

He had always enjoyed tasting Indian women; rewarding them with gold and money if they accepted his offer in the first go, or rape them in his farmhouse when they denied sleeping with him. This was his way of working with them. But this time, he wanted to touch her right away. The thought of her pure and smooth teenaged skin that was flowing like a river on uneven lands inside that saree made him thirsty.

"Why do you want the water?" he said inching closer to her. "To drink? Or to cool down your burning body? I think all the water that falls on your skin will evaporate."

"Sir please," said Chakradev obstructing his way, jumping between his daughter and the monster, "this is not the way you treat us."

Canning turned to him in sudden anger. "Don't you teach me how I should treat you, you filth," he said pushing him aside and went back to Sanjuktha. "You are so desperate for water? I'll give you a bath with my very own hands miss."

Sanjuktha stepped back in fear as the white-skinned race that once came on their knees to India begging for a trade now approached her as if it was his country into which she migrated. By then the villagers around also understood what was going on, but no one dared to stop Canning. He went on to her as she walked backwards and past the gate. He got hold of her by her shoulder and started laughing like a sorcerer.

"Leave me," she wiggled trying to get free.

He tried to pull her close and kiss her when suddenly something he saw through his peripheral vision grabbed his attention. All at once he went numb lifting his head high to the dome but did not loosen his grip on her. All the others too turned, to look at what made him go star struck. Sanjuktha still tried to break free.

For the next few seconds, silence prevailed. Even Sanjuktha stopped wiggling now, and she started seeing smiles on the faces of her people.

"Guards..." Canning shouted at once and let her loose to run past her. The guards at the gate followed him and the remaining ones in the building came out hearing the shout of their officer. Sanjuktha turned back panting, to see what was it that saved her. She looked up to the dome, to find an Indian flag fluttering in the evening wind. And that was on a British building.

It came as more than a shock to her. She gaped in surprise. Chakradev came running to her daughter and started pulling her back to leave. "You're not coming with us from tomorrow," he said in a shivering tone.

"I thought he's joking about the bet," she thought to herself smiling out of shock while they left the place.

She knows exactly who did that. Her husband...

* * *

"May I know where have you been all night?" enquired his father as Prudhvi walked into the hall.

He was a man close to fifty, with a typical Indian brown complexion. He was still physically fit from years of daily drill, and his thick black hair was dyed, oiled and neatly combed back. His face was clean-shaven, and the long moustache was finely trimmed. From a distance, it took some effort to tell if he was Prudhvi's father or brother.

By the time Prudhvi walked in, he was in his all-black-work-suit checking some documents while getting ready for the office. It's already 08:15 am.

"It's you I am talking to, Prudhvi."

"Group studies, dad. Rudhra's home," he lied pulling off his shoes. He could use only his name among other friends as no one ever went to school.

"Then why the hell did your boots had water in them?" he said taking his monocle off and staring at Prudhvi for an answer.

"The roads had water pits. Rains dad."

"It hasn't rained in months."

"Oh, really? I am busy concentrating on studies these days," he said standing with the boots in his hands. "May be it's the broken pipes, then."

"That's not a responsible answer, Prudhvi." Anger filled his voice and nerves.

"Dad, please. Why are you losing your cool now?"

"Because you are supposed to be on a ship to England by now… But you're not. See for yourself," he said pointing the monocle in his hand towards him. "You're wasting your time blabbering about your further studies in India. Seriously? India?"

"Ok dad, listen," he said. "First of all, I love you, and I respect you with all my heart. But as I already told you, I can't leave Sanju. Accept it or not, but she's my wife. That's final dad. Please don't ask me again."

He went ahead to place the shoes in the rack to the door side and walked away towards his room.

His father sighed, raging in anger. He hated the fact that he had a reason to hate his son. 'Sanjuktha' he named it.

It was quite a place where they lived – spacious and rich. His father worked for the government and was in a well-respected cadre. They were not rich when he was born or until he had turned ten. But now they were. All their relatives hated his father for working for the British while they were laying out their lives for freedom. But he loved his father for what he was – his father. His mother died when he was an infant and had never known her. His father never talked about her too. His uncle, Mr. Chakradev, his mother's brother, was the only one to narrate some stories about his mother now and then. He loved his sister a lot and still missed her. It was Sanjuktha's mother who took care of Prudhvi when he was a kid. Back then, they used to live in the same house; Prudhvi, his dad, Chakradev and his wife. Sanjuktha was still not born.

When he was about a year old, he heard her for the first time. He heard her cry from the room where his uncle and aunt stayed. His father told him that his wife was born. And all that he had known about that word – 'Wife,' was someone who marries you, gives birth to your child and dies before he sees her creation. They asked him to come see her, but he never entered that room. He feared something that he could not explain. All that he knew of her was the pain in her cry and the sweetness of her smile.

It was in her third month he saw her for the first time. He never thought that she'll be that small and damn cute.

He gave her the finger, and she grabbed it with all her fist. And the smile that followed reverberated in his ears for days. That was the day he fell for her.

They grew up together getting close to each other for every day that passed. When they were of three and two years old, one day, his father told him that he was going to get married to her the next morning. Prudhvi ran away that night. But hadn't been far enough to avoid their relatives from spotting him. One of his uncles who came to attend their wedding had seen him at the bus depot and dragged the groom back home. Prudhvi cried his eyes out that day.

Throughout the ceremony, he sobbed uncontrollably, while Sanjuktha held on to her smile for the relatives who came to wish them and ate all the sweets they brought. No matter how much he cried, they made him tie those three auspicious knots to the Mangalsutra around her neck. (When translated to English 'Mangal' means 'Holy' and 'Sutra' means 'Thread.' It's a kind of necklace worn by women that symbolize Hindu marriage). Meanwhile, many others asked him why he was crying, but he replied to none. He knew that once they get married, Sanjuktha would die in no time. She might be giving him a son, but he didn't want one. He wanted her. He wanted to live his entire life with her, cry with her, smile with her, grow old with her and one-day die in her hands listening to her sweetest tone – something that he had first known of her.

"Donll you wolly. I will nevel leave you," she said with her cheeks dancing up and down for every word she's spelling. She's hardly forty inches high and the ghagra choli she wore was so big than her that it literally swept the floor when she walked. Her fist, face and half of her neck were covered in the curd. They were eating their first lunch as Mister and Misses while the whole bunch of relatives stood around them and watched the little kids eat.

Prudhvi went into his room pushing the door and banging it back. The minute he saw the bed that was cosily done with soft pillows and smooth mattress, he crashed on to it without a second thought. He knew that he could meet her in the evening when his father left for his meeting in 'The Woods,' the place where the rebels lived. As he slipped slow and soft into his sleep, the sound of her voice started filling his dreams.

* * *

It was 07:10 pm when he reached her house, and it already went dark. Almost the whole village would have slept by now. As he walked in, he saw Rudhra in his balcony stretching his body and yawning. He lived next door to Sanjuktha. Prudhvi waved to his friend and he waved back smiling.

By the time he entered in, the whole house was filled with a mouth-watering aroma. It was an old-fashioned Indian house in the shape of a rectangle, with a huge hole in the center of the roof. The roof was made of wooden logs arranged in triangular symmetry and red clay tiles assembled on top of them. Thoroughly polished huge teak wood pillars supported the entire arrangement.

The house was dimly illuminated with few lanterns hung in a scattered sequence, and the moon light was entering in from the center space. Prudhvi walked the entire length of the house from the center to reach the rare entrance.

Passing which, came this small separate room with red clay tiles on top of it too - the kitchen.

"What's for dinner dear?" enquired Prudhvi excited as he walked in.

Sanjuktha turned to look up at him from the place she was sitting. That was the first time she was seeing him after days, and the first thing she wanted to talk to him was not about the flag, but about his father coming to her with something very disgusting to talk about. But she didn't want to start a discussion now. "He just walked in excited. Let him settle," she thought and turned back to answer him.

"Nothing special. Mango-Dal and potato fry," she said.

There was a lantern hung above the fire on which she was cooking. So the room had sufficient light to stare at her in detail.

"Why do you always cook the same?" he growled.

"Because I can only cook-" she said and stopped at once biting her tongue.

"Ya ya ya…" he said laughing. "Let it come out. Madam, don't stop."

"What?!" she shouted turning back to him in childish anger. "I can cook. Very well."

Her skin complexion level was way fairer than the native Indian averages, and he always loved the way she looked with that kind of anger that turned her cheeks pink.

"Ya… I heard it," he said, decided to turn them red. "May be you should feed it to the Britishers."

"What?"

"Ya… who knows? That might free us. Who wants to rule a country that cooks like… you know…"

"I'll kill you, idiot," she said running on to him at once with the long wooden spoon that she was using to fry the potatoes. He stood up straight ready to face her, and as she neared him, he caught hold of her hand with the spoon and turned around making her turn too, twisting her hand on to her back and dragged her close to him. They always fought like that.

"Aaaaaww…" Sanjuktha screamed in pain. "I am sorry, I am sorry pleaseeee," she turned into a cutie pie in the split second. "Leave me, please. My cute little potato, it hurts." There was butter dripping from every word she spoke.

"Aaaha? You should try politics Sanju," he said with his grip still firm on her twisted hand. "So many variations, just over seconds."

"Please sweeto, let me go…" she said lifting her head back to look at him with puppy eyes. "Don't look at me like that…" he cried inside, before leaving her free.

"I'll tell dad that you tried to kill me," she started complaining all at once walking away from him. Throwing some vegetables that were on the table on to him, she wiggled her hand that he twisted.

"He'll felicitate me for saving the country from your food," he said smiling and trying to duck the approaching flying veggies.

All this was just to see her turn angry. In real, he always loved the way she cooked. Only just Mango-Dal and potato fry, but she did master them.

"Get lost," she said moving away to sit in front of the pit again, "I don't entertain goons who try to kill me."

He smiled seeing her turn all girlish. The stubborn and heroic daughter of Mr Chakradev and the future leader of their group, turning girlish to the peaks.

"So… have you been to the 'Whatever you call it' today?"

"Silent protest," she said in a lame tone immersed in the cooking again.

"Ya, whatever," he said uninterested in knowing what they called it. Prudhvi was never interested in fighting for freedom. The British, for him, was the epitome of goodness, refined culture and success. All that he saw was the good side. Though he had a fine idea of what was happening outside, in the country, he always thought that if this continued for few more years, the British would eventually stop harassing us anyways and after few more, India would be a flourishing arm of an extended British civilization, which will be for our own good.

He also hated the 'Varnasrama Dharma' – dividing humans and their line of work according to their caste. During the reign of Lord Rama, the same system existed, but an individual got to decide his caste according to his interests in different fields of work. But now, one's caste will be decided according to the family he took birth in.

Though he did have some valid points to his argument, he always failed to see what will come next if western culture ever took over India. The very existence of India would be questioned, as India is not just a country. It's a culture.

"No, today I stayed back. Not feeling well," she said as realistically as possible. Sanjuktha didn't want him to know about what happened this morning.

"You stayed back?!" he exclaimed. "You made a bet that might have killed me, and now you stayed back?"

"*I* made a bet?" she said turning back at once. "It's you who said that you'll replace the flag." She felt fortunate that he did switch them.

"Yes, I did. But why? You asked me to prove that I can do anything for you and I chose something that's almost impossible."

"Impossible?" she said throwing some extra wood into the pit and blowing air into it with a wooden pipe. "One among two men in our country can do that."

"You know what?" he said hiding his smile. "It's not switching the flags. It's you that's impossible."

She smiled while she picked up the pan to deep-fry some spices, red chillies and curry leaves; and dropped them hot, along with the oil into the dal she prepared earlier. That made a sizzling sound, and a thick cloud of smoke marked an end to the delicacy she was preparing.

"Hmmmmm…" Prudhvi said filling his lungs with the aroma again. "What a fragrance. I am so lucky to have a wife who cooks like this."

"Aaaha? I too am lucky to have a husband who praises his wife," she said and stood up to walk to the other side of the room to fetch something.

"No, I mean it. I am just trying to tease you earlier. I love the way you cook." He walked to her and reached for the container she was struggling to reach. "Why to place it there when you can't reach it properly?" he said as she took it from him.

"Mom used to keep it there." She tried to open the lid with all her strength. "*Your* mom."

"My mom?" he said. "How can you say that? You don't know her."

"My mom did right. And I too know her. Better than you do."

"You were not even an embryo when she was alive."

"To know someone, it's not mandatory to live in the time of that person."

"What?" he said confused. "You sound like she anticipated your birth and left you some personal notes or something."

All of a sudden, that made her remember a very special letter of his mother that she left with Mr. Chakradev. It was not addressed to her. It was for her son, Prudhvi. And it disclosed a lot about her, just in a width of few simple lines. Her father also had a grey scale photograph of her. A simple and celestial lady she was, with a smile that seemed like it withered in no circumstances. Sanjuktha never felt her anything less than her own mother. She knew her as she lived with her. But this was not the right time to talk about that either. There were topics with higher priority at this point, which were to be broached with no delay.

Prudhvi smiled looking at her sit before the fire again without answering his sarcastic question. "Is uncle home?" he enquired.

"As if you can come in if he is," she said placing a pot containing rice and water on the three sided mud frame that's built around the fire to support vessels. Throwing some extra sticks into the fire, she stood up drying her hands in the pallu and tucking the hair to the back of the ear.

Prudhvi left a sigh seeing her sweat. Her perfect shaped body and the right places that were showing out of the saree made him stare at her with eyes all over. The fire and the lantern faded out before her burning beauty. But the semi-darkness in the room added some mood, though.

From the very day he had stepped into his teenage years, and started having urges, Prudhvi never slept a single night without fantasizing his first kiss with her. The way she dressed when she was home, the way she smiled when she was happy, her cute little expressions, naughty little daunts and on top of everything, her eternally sweet and soft tone; all of them combined made him burn in love and lust at the same time.

"What?" she said as she reached him. "Why do you always stare at me like you'll never see me again?"

"I love you, Sanju," was his immediate response.

She smiled as she always did, looking at him in the eye. "I know that you love me. Tell me something new."

"When I say that I love you, why do you never say that you love me too?" he said following her out of the kitchen.

"Why do you never stop asking that question when you already know the answer?"

"I don't know why you don't love me. We are married," he said with pain filled in his tone and she stopped at once to answer him.

"It's not love when you love someone just because you're married to them. Love is something more than that Prudhvi."

"But at least, you should stay together when you're married to someone right?"

"Oh yes. Let me think what the answer was. May be it is '*Because your father hates me?*' or '*I can't stay with someone who feeds me the British food?*'" she said with anger that one show on their close ones.

Prudhvi was ten years old when his father took him away from that house. The same house he's standing in right now. Until then he never thought, even in his wildest dreams that he would live apart from Sanjuktha. During the early days, they both cried at nights. But the only difference was that Sanju never said that to him. As time burned, Prudhvi got himself accustomed to not seeing her every day and to meet her only after weeks of waiting. And at nights dreaming of her, in her room, dreaming about him. Of course, fantasizing about the kiss too.

"Dad doesn't hate you guys. I know that," he said trying to convince her.

"Even though he hadn't hated me till now, after few days he will."

"How can you be so sure of that?"

"What's there to ask again? It's obvious that you are not leaving India just because of me. Who else will he hate for the ruined career of his son?"

"He can't blame you for my mistakes. And wanting to be with you is not a mistake. You're my wife, Sanju. And I want to be there for you," he said looking straight into her eye. She suddenly lost the words that she prepared to speak out.

"You're saying that I am your wife," she said trying not to sound harsh. But it's time to split out her pain. "But when your dad met me few days back, he said that I am your 'Keep?'"

"What?" he exclaimed with impulsive anger that burned his heart to the core.

Sanju hated her being the reason for Prudhvi not leaving to London.

"Don't get surprised Prudhvi. He's not completely wrong. We are officially married. You love me, and everyone knows that. But we don't stay together. And now you visit me when my dad was not home. Today it's just your dad. Wait for few more days and the whole world would call me your bitch."

"Sanju pleaseeee," he shouted closing his ears and moving back until he hit the wall. Tears rolled out of his eyes unable to cope with the word she lastly spelled. She was not his bitch. She was his angel. His goddess to whom he turned his heart into a temple.

Sanjuktha's heart too sank seeing him cry. But she's left with no other option than to be hard on him.

"You should leave, Prudhvi," she said trying to hold back her tears.

"Why are you doing this, Sanju?"

She said nothing but stared at him in silence. Her throat was swelled with a lump formed inside it and she struggled to turn feelings into words.

"I don't know Prudhvi. If you really love me, and you don't want people to call me," and he turned to her at once, to stop that word from coming out of her mouth again. She did understand that angry stare, "I mean if you don't want people to call me *names*... You should leave. If not for me, leave for the girl you love."

She went silent again, staring at him, praying to make him understand her pain.

No one talked for the next few minutes. They just stood there, in that narrow space between the kitchen and the house.

"I will leave, if you really wanted me to" he finally said. That did start breaking her. "But before that, tell me that you love me. And that you'll wait for me to return."

"What?" she frowned. "How can I do that?"

She said that not because she knew that Prudhvi had a very impulsive anger, and would often take swift decisions if that could be used. Sanjuktha had always liked him more than anyone after her parents. But she never loved him really. She knew that she couldn't live without seeing him or talking to him, but that was not love. She said that to him in all possible ways and many times till now. He never understood. She tried to avoid him too, but her own self hadn't let her do that. She always feared that one day her desire to stick around him might cause him a loss that no one can bring him back from, but can never accept him as her husband or love him. She wanted a man who fought for his country and was willing to die for it. Like any other girl of her kind of mind set, her dream was to fall for a warrior.

"How can I say that I love you?" she said.

"Why can't you?" cried Prudhvi, "Why can't you and why do you never say that out?"

"Because I don't love you at all… And if I say that I do, it will be a lie," she said with her voice shivering with pain that emerged seeing herself hurting him more and more with every passing second.

Because I don't love you at all… – it echoed in his ears and heart like they would haunt him forever. For the first time in his life, when she said that she doesn't love him, it felt like she really meant it. It also felt like he belonged to no one in this world anymore. His heart burned with grief and anger at the same time.

Prudhvi wanted to run away from this, forget that he had a life before this second and just run away to some place where no one knew him; a place where they know no love and thus no pain. He turned back to leave with his eyes raining as he had nothing to do here anymore. But just before he left, he stopped to ask her something.

"Tell me, Sanju," he said turning back to her. She was also crying now and looked up at him with her wet eyes. "If you really never loved me, why do you still have that Mangalsutra around your neck?"

Sanjuktha stood there in shock as he left her with the question she could never answer to.

That night, she too cried like never before.

* * *

The next morning, she had a dream of Canning shooting Prudhvi to death. She woke up with sweat all over her body. She felt very disturbed for the day before and decided to go apologize to him for the way she behaved.

While she bolted the outer gate, Rudhra came to her and handed her a neatly folded letter without anyone watching them. He said that Prudhvi was leaving for London, and he wanted him to give her that letter. Sanjuktha suddenly went weak. To her, it felt like she was still in that dream.

"His bus to the railway station leaves in fifteen minutes," he said talking as fast as he can. "And from there he'll reach Bombay where his ship to London awaits him."

Sanjuktha cried like a kid while she ran on the dusty streets with all her energy. Running in a saree was not that easy, but she stopped nowhere until she reached the bus depot. It was when she was just a few more kilometers away from the depot; she saw Prudhvi standing near a bus that seemed like a tram with rubber wheels. Though she couldn't see him clearly, she could surely say that it was him. He watched his servants lift his luggage on to the bus. He had a blazer that matched his black pants, a light blue colored formal shirt that was tucked in with his usual suspenders and a black ascot cap neatly complementing the look.

Sanjuktha lent out a cry calling him as she ran with all her might. Prudhvi got into the bus, and the engine roared as she almost reached it. She missed him in the last second. No one on the bus noticed her running in the distance, and the driver had no reason to look into the rear view mirror.

She fell on to her knees losing the ultimate energy one can possess – hope. Her eyes started overflowing with tears again, and the dust upraised by the bus blew on to her, making her feel even more deserted. She knew that she would never see him again. His father too would never let him return to India. One stupid mistake and there was no more Prudhvi in her life.

Sitting on a bench in the depot she opened the letter he wrote. What it read made her heart stop at every single word

Dear Sanjuktha,

Don't mind that I am talking about death in my last letter to you. But I must tell you this. I always dreamed of living my entire life with you, Sanju - happily and in prosperity. And it never seemed like a distant dream to me, until our paths started taking different turns. I thought that we may be apart for some time, but will surely be together again. I was ok if my dreams on how we are going to be together flicker with time, but I never wanted to sacrifice my last wish. I always wanted to grow old with you and one fine day, die in your arms, while you sing 'our' song to me. You know that I love your songs like I love you. That's the first thing I had ever known about you, and I wanted it to be the last. But you see what I did now? Anything can happen there in London, and I might die too. Still I am leaving, just because you wanted me to. And also, no one will call you names now. But remember, I sacrificed even my last wish for you, lady. That's how much I love you.

Prudhvi

Sitting on that bench, she cried endlessly, holding the Mangalsutra in her hand.

Chapter 3

"Because I don't love you at all…" she shouted on his face and Prudhvi woke up with a jolt. The minute he sat up straight, he started taking deeper breaths as his suffocating heart demanded extra oxygen. He's on his bed in his hostel room, in the newly built block for the freshman year students, Imperial King's College, London.

It was a more than spacious room with an attached bathroom but was allocated to only two. Prudhvi stashed his luggage, an iron trunk box and a leather suitcase, under his bed. His roommate hadn't shown up yet, and he was alone in the room. There were two iron frame beds with mattresses, two closets and a common bookshelf in there. The plastering all over the walls was so smooth and shiny that one could easily say that it was brand new.

Prudhvi felt weak in the spine. The dizzying spell was pushing him to bed. The traces of sea sickness hadn't left his body, but this time, there was an added emotional pull that made him feel worse, unlike the times when he accompanied his father on government business.

He felt something moving inside his throat and wanted to puke. He closed his eyes tight and opened them back wide, as it took more than the usual time for them to adjust to the dim light in the room. He pushed his hand into his pajama pocket with all the remaining energy to take his pocket watch out. It ticked 06:55 pm.

Noticing the time on the watch, his brain made a quick calculation to inform him that he hadn't eaten in the last twenty-two hours. Pushing all the other feelings aside, he started feeling hungry. It didn't matter how sad, how happy, how broken or how excited you are, your body will always be selfish. It needs what it needs. He gathered some more energy from few other parts of his body to transfer it to his limbs and stood up, to walk towards the bath. The western style bathrooms never bothered him, but it was the unnaturally freezing temperatures that always did. But he never complained, not knowing whom to complain to. And how can one possibly blame almost half of this world for the way it poops?!

With his rectum emptied, his hunger stared taking even bigger hits on his intestine, and the digestive acids started burning. He changed from pajamas to his usual dressing within seconds. He took his black knee-length overcoat that he had flung on to the floor last night and waved it hard to get rid of the dust. Few of his joints made cracking sounds. Slipping it on, he opened the door to enter the empty corridor and closed it behind to leave the building, and the college premises.

London hadn't changed in two years. It was the same old pleasant place with clean roads in every street, cool breeze that sailed westwards, flower shops on the side walk, ancient brick buildings with romantic architectures, designer lamp posts in the junctions and electric tramcars crawling all over the city. The roads appeared freshly washed from the rain as it was the month of November and the wind was frosty. In England, white Christmases were unusual. It only snowed mostly in late January and February.

Darkness had descended, and the streets were filled with people by the time Prudhvi stepped out of the campus. Men were in their suits, overcoats, long hats and some with their walking sticks and spectacles with chains around their necks; while women were in half-sleeved knee size gowns that boasted of fancy embroiders around the neck and tied tight at the hip with a matching ribbon. The older women had their woollen overcoats with bulgy woollen collars and the woollen hats that suited the coats. The younger ones must have worn some skin tight thermals inside their gowns, without which survival in these temperatures was impossible.

Irrespective of the gender, most of them also had leather gloves on their hands and wet umbrellas that are folded in. May be it just stopped raining. The roads are wet too, reflecting the blurred images of any source of light that's on the street.

Prudhvi walked along the side path that was made of symmetrically laid square red concrete bricks, to reach the Central park area that he pointed out on the map he took from the reception. That was the place around which most of the hotels were located. The street had trees on both the sides, which made the air around even more piercing. He walked with the crowd that was headed towards the Central park.

Along with tram trains in the middle of the roads, there were also fine-bred cars like Wolseley 14/60, Series-2 Mercedes W150 and Rolls-Royce Silver Wraith; and horse driven fiacres being used at the same time, representing the age of transformation.

Prudhvi flipped the collar up and thrust his hands into the pockets of the coat while using a portion of his brain to think what he should order first. He hadn't remembered what they ate last time. He never ordered anything. Only his father did. As he started thinking of going for any dish that sounded spicy, someone from behind suddenly said: "Mango-Dal and potato fry." He turned back immediately taking a sudden halt, and the world started going silent at once. Few heads turned to him, and those who are behind him went past making a curve around. He stood there, taking longer breaths as the hot air that left his lungs condensed into mist; leaving out smoulder like he was smoking. Prudhvi hated the way she was haunting him but loved the way she sounded.

"Four years Prudhvi. Just four short years," he said to himself and turned back to walk again, this time trying not to think about her. One part of his brain cried for food, and the other wanted to starve to death. He suddenly lost his appetite but still walked into a hotel as he doesn't want to give up so quickly.

"What would you like to have sir?" asked a fat British lady dressed in white chef's suit and a toque blanche on her head.

"Do you have a menu card?" he said in the most respectful way possible.

He sat near the wooden counter that covered the length of that small hotel, separating the kitchen from the dining area. Through the glass wall that was behind the tables arranged in a single row in front of the counter, the streets were clearly visible; though the label of the hotel, *Eat Inn*, that was printed in curvature over the glass, was obstructing some view.

"Menu, sir," she said pushing a small wooden board towards him making Prudhvi turn his focus back from the streets.

"Thank you," he said as she left him, and started searching for anything that may seem familiar.

As he quickly surfed through the items and their costs, he suddenly remembered that he left his wallet back in the room.

"God..." he almost screamed jumping off the bar stool. He cursed his fate in England on the first day itself.

Having no other options left, he started to search his pockets frantically in the hope of any lucky money. He hated Sanjuktha for taking over the rational part of his brain when he left the room. Hunger started playing its turn again, knowing that he had no money on him to buy dinner.

"Lost your wallet?" someone said in a British accent from behind, and Prudhvi turned to look at her.

Her sparkling eyes were what he saw first. As he tried to come back from the sudden blow of the beautiful aroma that followed her, he realised that actually the whole package was sparkling. She stood there, in front of him, smiling like she had known him for years.

"You lost your wallet?" she repeated.

"Ya... I actually..." stammered Prudhvi for the first few seconds as he never had a conversation with a white girl. "I forgot it in my room." He finally managed.

"Ohhh…" She tilted her eyes down. "Hi, I am Emily," she said, now looking straight at him again, extending her hand.

"I am Prudhvi," he shook her hand.

It felt so soft and tiny in his muscular grip. She kind of liked it.

"Let me buy you dinner then," she said excitedly.

"No no no… I don't want to trouble you…" He tried to be decent, even though he's on the edges of chewing the menu card in his hand.

"It's ok. There's no trouble in it," she said smiling even brighter. "After all, we are eating from your country since centuries."

"You know what country I am from?!"

She started to say something, stopped and smiled looking down to the floor again.

"What?" he smiled, for the first time in days. "Say it… I don't mind."

"There is…" she said making her eyes meet his. "There is India written all over your face."

They sat on the last table in the dim corner. Prudhvi asked her to order something that tasted spicy, and she got busy looking for one in the menu card that he handed her. While she surfed through it, Prudhvi stared at her waiting for her to decide. She was a typical English teenage girl in a cute baby pink lace gown, that was, as usual, tied up at the hip with a fancy blue ribbon. She had no stockings or a hat on but had a portable black leather hand bag that she carried in her hand. The shoes she wore are also pink, with two blue rose figures glued on each, to the opposite sides. May be they came with the dress.

Her face looked like it was flawlessly moulded by whom so ever god that manufactured humans in this country, like Lord Brahma manufactured Indians. The mascara, the eye lining, the thick red lipstick, the perfectly shaped eyebrows, her neither long nor short half up half down vintage style golden hair that's curled at the ends, it all seemed like magic to Prudhvi.

"How cute and classy these English girls look," he wondered.

"Yes…" she finally said, "this is the spiciest thing in the whole country. Let's try this."

"You too will have the same?"

"No way," she said waving her hand in rebuff. "I just joined my college. Let me attend at least one class."

"College? Which one?" he enquired out of surprise.

"The Imperial King's obviously. What else do they have here?"

"Bingo," he said smiling.

"You too?" she squeaked.

"Yup. Communications."

"Get out…" she said even more surprised. But Prudhvi didn't understand why he should get out.

"What?" he said confused.

"Me too… Communications."

"You too get out," he said as the revenge for her get out.

She smiled again. He smiled back.

The dish that she ordered was only a quarter spicy of what Prudhvi ate in India, but he tried to act out as if it was way hotter than he thought it would be. She smiled with pride, and he smiled with hate towards the country which cooked like this. But it can be forgiven there, for the way it designed its women. After few minutes, his body felt relaxed as something or the other went in to generate some energy. As time progressed, he started appreciating the dish, and the one who ordered it.

"You eat with your bear hand?" she said when he first lifted up a piece of veggie from his plate.

"I am sure my hand is clean. Are you sure the cutlery is?" he said pushing that leaf into his mouth and smiling.

Looking at the fish fork in her hand for few doubt-filled seconds, she placed it back on the table and smiled uncomfortably at him trying to pick up the fish. She seldom ate with her bare hand and that too in a public place. He enjoyed her discomfort like he hated her beauty. She lifted the piece above her lip-level and dropped it slowly into her sufficiently wide open mouth, without the texture of the lipstick getting disturbed. Trying to chew it, she looked back at him and smiled hard with her cheeks outlining the stuffed fish that filled her mouth.

"Bravo," said Prudhvi lifting his glass of wine. Her smile turned into a blush.

Seen from the other side of the glass, they talked in inaudible dialogs and smiled during the whole dinner.

* * *

The classroom was decorated with shining ribbons, balloons and welcome posters hanging all around. It was done by the sophomore students as a welcome gesture for the freshman class. The classroom was so different when compared to those that one usually see in India. First to notice, the board was not black but green. Prudhvi wondered if it was the freezing temperatures of this country that changed the color of the board over years. There was also a podium near the board for the teacher to stand on. But the desk that they provided seemed same – a simple brown wooden table with chalk dust all over it. There was also a television set locked inside an iron frame that hung to the left of the podium.

"May be it's for the teacher when no one shows up to attend his class," Prudhvi thought.

Also instead of a single long bench that fits four to five students, there were only single seated wooden benches with attached planks arranged in an organised pattern. There was also a neatly folded woollen rug and a muffler hat on the plank of each bench. Prudhvi felt awkward when he first saw them, but when the introduction class started he felt thankful to the management. The whole class covered themselves in the rug wrapped around them, and the cap tied tight to their heads so that the ears are fully covered. It's freakily freezing. Prudhvi pushed the ear buds they gave him on the ship, into his ears inside the muffler, so that the jabbering of the teacher could be avoided. He hated being here.

As professor Flintoff started explaining to them how important and interesting the concept of Data Interception was, Emily stared at Prudhvi from her seat that was diagonal to his in the next row. Last night's dinner had swept her off her feet, and now she felt enticed by this Indian boy's charm.

"So even Indians can be cute enough to make the British have a crush," she thought, smiling to herself.

She knew that this was not love. Emily never believed in love. For her, love was that one word that she always enjoyed joking on, making fun of as minefield covered with roses. She was a free-range pony that couldn't be tamed. This, the feeling that was overwhelming for her, was just the uncontrollable lust that girls of her age usually had towards the opposite sex.

With freezing temperatures outside and her blazing body covered in wool trapping the heat, her desires had already started to burn like wild fire. She adjusted the rug to fold her legs inside it still staring at him, when suddenly the professor said, pointing his hand towards her:

"So you, the young lady in the third row," and the whole class turned to her, making her go bewildered, coming back to reality from the dreams where she was just about to be kissed by Prudhvi. "Tell me, what's the importance of the kiss that decrypts the message?"

Along with the whole class, Prudhvi too turned back to see it was the same girl he had dinner with last night that the professor was referring to. He also wondered why she was still sitting when the teacher pointed at her. In India, the first thing we do when a teacher points towards us is standing up. Answering the question is secondary.

"Kiss that decodes the message?" Emily thought to herself immersed in a deep muddle. She immediately turned to the board to find what was going on. There were some words like *Signalling*, *Encryption*, *Key* and *Security* written at random places. She stared at them for a while before realising that it's not *Kiss* but *Key*. The key to decrypt the message…

Even now, she had no idea what the professor was talking about. The whole class was still staring at her, and she felt a big embarrassment coming her way. Prudhvi saw fear and doubt in her cute little eyes and wanted to help her, but didn't know how to. He hadn't heard the question at least.

It was then; Luke suddenly entered the class with his fellow mates, breaking the silence at once.

"Hello freshmen…" he shouted running on to the podium making Mr Flintoff step aside.

He was a strong British teenager with a well-built body, formally attired and with a smile on his face.

"Welcome to the Imperial King's. I am Luke Trueman, President of the Imperial Student's Council, and these are my board members – Jane, Harry, Mathew and Louis." He gave a quick introduction by pointing his hand towards the respective person while he spelled their names. They smiled waving their hands.

"Remember our faces, smile at us or don't, but do reach us in the Administration building, cabin T-38, if you have any issues regarding anything in this campus. Food in the canteen to booze in the hostels, academic table to extra-curricular, anything you have a problem with." Saying so, he turned back to look at the professor. "Ohhh Professor Flintoff? So I am not going to hear anything regarding academics from this class then. You're in the best hands," and the professor faked a smile.

Like all the other staff, he too hated Luke for his arrogance.

"Ok then," he said adjusting his coat that had the Imperial King's emblem; two golden rearing horses opposite to each other, in front of a shield that was colored according to the flag of England and two burning swords crossed behind it, "see you when you're in trouble. Have fun until then."

Even without thanking the professor for letting him take his podium, he left as fast as he came in. The professor left a sigh and turned slowly towards the class remembering what they were doing before Luke.

"Oh my god, make him forget…" Emily murmured as Prudhvi turned back to smile at her again. She smiled back, still murmuring. And suddenly the bell rang.

"Thank god…" she said little louder, this time, lifting her head towards the roof. Prudhvi smiled and turned forward as the professor left the class, still thinking.

* * *

The first six months of the new year, 1939, passed like six days to Emily. But to Prudhvi, it felt like six years. During the late weeks of January to mid-March, it snowed and everything around was draped in white, with people roaming in dark clothes. Mostly black. And then the spring prevailed from March to May. In June, the summer raged with highest of 23-degree Celsius. In India, it was still called winter, but being accustomed to the freezing temperatures for almost six months, Prudhvi felt a bit uncomfortable to set back to those temperatures.

During these six months, Emily and Prudhvi became closer than they expected. They spent all most all the time together. Most of the mornings in the classes and the library, and in the evenings it deferred according to their mood and the climate. Sometimes they headed back to their hostels, or sometimes they just strolled in the campus streets chit chatting until it got dark, or sometimes watch a play in the nearby theatres (mostly Shakespeare's political plays), or sometimes even head to a nightclub, which was strictly restricted by the rule book. But Emily never listened to Prudhvi. She always wanted to live on the edge.

In the first month of the summer, they also visited the Lord's stadium continuously for three days, which was just a one-hour bus ride to attend the first test match of the '1939 English Cricket Season.' It lasted for three days, June 24, 26 and 27, in which West Indies lost to England by eight wickets. It was also the one and only season in which English cricket adopted the eight-ball over.

Even though Prudhvi hadn't found any point in the sport during the first day, he too started enjoying it as the test came to an end. Sitting in the stands with bamboo hats and sun glasses on, Emily explained him every rule of the game as they played. She turned into an entirely different person during the game. She wore a simple cotton gown that's just above her knees and full flat sandals other than the hat and the glasses. And the way she behaved; one should see her when her favorite players are batting. She roared like a monster hunting her pray. Prudhvi wondered if Indians can ever play this game and how many more years it will take for Indian girls to shout like this.

On the last day of the test, on their way back home, sitting on the open top level of a double decker bus, 'Love' was discussed for the first time. Prudhvi told her everything about Sanjuktha. Though she controlled her expression not to reveal her grief, she did shed a tear or two inside her heart. She had always known that it was just physical attraction towards him, but these last seven months since she had known him had pushed him close to her heart in one way or the other.

As she heard him narrate the whole story, from how they first met when he was a three-year-old kid to how he left his country just to make her happy; she felt infinitely jealous of the girl back in India. Her heart solicited her for love, for the first time. She loved the idea of a guy who could travel half way around the world, for one simple word of her. She knew that only the blessed ones were offered such love and half of them weren't aware of what they got until it was gone forever.

But Emily too didn't seek for such a love. Prudhvi's love towards Sanjuktha was lukewarm. But Emily wanted something different. She wanted to burn.

"So the final conclusion is that she friend-zoned you, right?" she said to dilute the seriousness created. "Even girls in India do that these days?"

"*Friend-zoned*? What's that?" he enquired, as he heard the word for the first time. But it was definitely not the first new word he heard in London.

"You don't know what a friend-zone is?"

"No. I am hearing it for the first time," he said, and she smiled.

"Let me tell you in a very clear and understandable way, ok," she said turning her body towards him as if she's going to explain something that's not yet derived. "Friend-zone is a Black Hole, where a girl pushes a boy into, and the boy forever hopes that one day he is going to get out of it."

Prudhvi stared at her as he slowly dissected what she meant.

"Who knows, maybe one-day man may break the black hole too," he said smiling with hope.

"May be..." she said as a matter of fact. "But even then, your girl remains the same – unbreakable."

"How come you know that?"

"A girl knows. I am telling you, mister, she's a nightmare dressed like a day dream," she said, and they both smiled.

Chapter 4

"Then indulge yourself into something that keeps you busy," Emily said as they walked on the path that was paved with stones in the middle of the garden. It was 06:00 pm when they started roaming the campus, and now it's 08:00.

It all went dark around, but the electrical lamp posts that were installed recently along the path were emitting light that's well enough to roam around without being lost in the darkness.

"*Indulge into something*...Like what?" he said.

"*Like what?*" she repeated looking towards the dark sky, thinking. She was suggesting him ways on how to spend the four long years without actually counting every other day. They were dressed in the least number of layers possible, as the summer's heat was still on. He in his formals, a blue shirt, tucked into a black trouser, no suspenders; and she in her usual summer gowns – an orange one this time.

"May be a relationship?" she said at once, turning to him excited.

"Relationship? With whom? You?" He smiled.

"Yes," Emily wanted to say. Though she said that just to start a joke, now she loved the thought of it.

"What? I don't suit your standards?" she said taking a halt, resting her hands on her hips. Prudhvi too stopped turning back to her smiling. "From freshman to the senior year, almost all the boys had a crush on me. You know that?"

"Yeah…" He smiled and started walking away with hands in his pockets.

"What?!" she said out of mere shock and ran to him in small steps. "What does that 'Yeah…' mean?" Her eyes glittered with the cutest tinge of anger.

"Nothing," he said continuing to smile and trying to ignore her.

"Hello mister," she yelled stopping Prudhvi, pulling him by his shoulder. He stepped back with a sudden force, almost falling on to her. Emily loved the distance that took a sudden leap down. Prudhvi too wondered how sweet she smelled from this distance. She always did that – being well groomed at any time of the day.

They stood at the iron arch that's made as the entrance into the garden, facing each other in silence. Emily let out a shy smile and tried to say something as he waited to hear what that made her smile.

"Wow wow wow…" screamed Luke, walking through the arch from nowhere. They turned to him in surprise as his mates followed him into the garden. "A British girl, an Indian boy, the King's campus… what a cult combo."

His mates laughed hard as if he made the funniest joke of the year. They had an almost-emptied scotch bottle in each of their hands. The whole batch was in their jeans and leather jackets, including that one girl.

"Prudhvi, let's go," Emily said folding her hand around his shoulder and trying to make him walk. But he hadn't moved.

She knew that Prudhvi always had a furious hatred towards this guy, Luke. He may be the President of the Student's Council, but also was the most criminal-minded person Prudhvi had ever seen. He sold drugs in the campus, harassed girls, disrespected the staff and even beat up anyone who questioned him, while they were in the locker room. That was his ground where he played games like those. But he still won the elections every year, as he had his father who was a trustee of the college and he himself had the guts to kill even a person for what he wished for. The whole college feared him. But Prudhvi Prathap Raju never did.

He already tried to beat the crap out of him once, when he assaulted his roommate for questioning him about the biased results in the inter-college football team selections. Luke broke his leg with a cricket bat in the locker room, and he's still walking with a stick. That day, Prudhvi took the same bat from the sports room, with which he broke his friend's leg and searched for him everywhere in the campus. It was Emily who stopped him making him promise her that he will never try to do such a foolish thing again.

"Prudhvi?" Emily whispered in with fear-filled anger, still trying to pull him. But he stood there as hard as a rock, and staring straight at Luke with all the anger he ever had, accumulating into his eyes.

"Please sir, please don't look at me like that. I am scared to death." Luke said overreacting as if he was really scared, and suddenly stood straight to look directly into his eye. "What Mr Freshman? Don't you respect the senior? Then I think you're looking for some seeeeerious trouble." he said and turned to look at Emily. "Hmmmm… some great architecture was done here." The others laughed. "Leave her to us and fuck the hell out of here," he said returning the stare to Prudhvi.

Prudhvi clenched his fist with violent anger while Emily made her grip on his hand tighter to stop him at any cost.

"What? What are you still staring at ha?" Luke said losing his cool. "WHAT?" he shouted out loud and it echoed in the distance. Emily stepped back to hide behind Prudhvi and tears started filling her eyes. She almost started crying.

"Answer me, mister," Luke said moving even closer to Prudhvi and shacking with anger. "You got her registered in your name? Is she yours?"

"Yes, sir," Prudhvi said penetrating into his eyes. And suddenly pulled Emily forward, caught hold of her by her hip and pulled her close and tight towards him. "She's mine."

Emily being crushed to a side of his muscular body caught hold of him by his shoulder with her hand folded from his back. With his grip tight on her hip, her feet almost left the ground, and she was flying in his arms. She hadn't seen that coming at all.

"And if," Prudhvi continued, "you, sir, ever try to even touch her. Like ever. I promise that you will surely regret having balls."

As they both stared into each other's eyes with burning anger, Emily started seeing Prudhvi in slow motion. Her eye lids went lighter and cheeks heavier. She stared at him mesmerized and prayed for the fight to last forever.

She loved the way her body was resting on to his. She loved the way he looked in his side profile. And above everything, she loved the rising temperatures of his body. She wanted to kiss him on the neck no matter what the people around think of it.

"One day," Luke said as Emily slowly bent close to Prudhvi, and that disturbed her at once, "we will see… who will be the one that regrets."

Saying so, Luke went past them taking a large sip from his bottle. The gang followed him, throwing different kinds of stares each, at Prudhvi and Emily. It's for the first time Luke feared someone in the campus. Prudhvi's wildest anger that was pouring out of his eyes made him step back.

"I am sorry. That's…" Prudhvi stammered as he left her free from his grip.

"Ya, it's… its fine," she too fought a war to talk, as she started setting her hair back with the tips of her fingers.

They both stared at the ground as they walked, looked at each other in frequent intervals, smiling formally and turned back to the ground. Awkwardness occupied the space between them, as they headed towards their hostels.

* * *

"It's in the 1890s, the 'Invisible Light' was first talked about," said professor Heinrich; professor for Electronic Communications – a stout little man in his formals, with a vest coat on and a watch hanging out of its pocket. "This man ignited gunpowder and rang a bell at a distance, using millimeter range wavelength micro waves, during a public demonstration. A 'public demonstration…' No wires at all. And this so-called Invisible Light even passed through walls and buildings, and thus the science of wireless communication took its first greater steps. Can anyone here," he said pointing his hand towards the class, "guess the name of that man?"

"Jagadish Chandra Bose," Prudhvi murmured to himself as he tested his new algorithm to code paragraphs, on his Wireless Communications test book.

"No one?" the professor teased the class for few more minutes before giving away the answer. "You'll know when I tell you. It's Jagadish Chandra Bose. The man who said that plants too have life, they too can feel and understand affection." he said smiling with pride and the class murmured in 'I was about to say that' and 'I knew that already.' "Ok then, going back to where we are…" he said cutting off the students, and the class continued for two more hours.

"Damn…" Prudhvi whimpered, still sitting in his place as the other students started dispersing after the class bell. He was struck at a dead lock in the algorithm.

He thought if Emily can help with it as she always did and turned back to look what she's doing without disturbing him even after thirty seconds from the bell. He found her leaving the class not waiting or, at least, informing him.

"Emily, wait…" he shouted and picked up his books to throw them into his leather bag. Listening Prudhvi call out for her, she started taking faster and bigger steps. She didn't want to be seen by him like this.

'She's running away from me?' Prudhvi wondered as he followed her at double the pace.

"Why are you running from me?" he said pulling her back by her shoulder as he reached her in the hallway. That made her turn back but she lowered her head at once. "Emily?" he said sensing that something had been wrong.

"I'll talk to you later," she said trying to walk away. Her voice felt different.

"Emily stop." He pulled her back again. "What happened?" he said bending down to look at her face. She still tried to hide, but Prudhvi saw it.

"Emily?!" he screamed at once lifting her head up by her chin. It was swollen at the right eye, and the edge of the upper lip was red as blood. "What happened?" Prudhvi felt a sudden pain in his heart seeing her in such condition. His face too started losing color.

"I… I slipped in the bathroom," she said looking at him. Her cheek was swollen too. She seemed like a cute little puppy that was hit by a bus. He wanted to hug her and make her feel calm and better.

But suddenly in between all the chaos, he found an imprint of some symbol above her eyebrow. Small in size, in between the red swollen part, but clearly visible when seen from a closer point. "What's that?" he said trying to touch smoothly. "It looks like an imprint of… a ring?" he said and in the next split second he lost his ability to think. He knew what it was.

"It's nothing," Emily said. "Probably the knob of the tap that I fell on."

"What happened?" he asked looking straight at her.

"What?"

"What happened?" he repeated patiently with his heart making him take deeper breaths.

"I slipped in the-"

"What happened?" he said cutting her off. She stared right into his eyes, as tears started filling into hers.

"Nothing. I just-"

"WHAT – HAPPENED?" he said in the lowest and toughest tone possible and sounded like he's not going to ask again.

"I…," she said looking at the floor and back at him. She's sobbing now. "Last night, they followed me to my hostel."

* * *

Prudhvi stomped in the hallway, folding the sleeves up his elbow. He seemed like a crazy tornado ready to hit the coast, breaking all that it had into pieces, making mass destruction just over seconds, which could not be recovered from, even in years. The visuals of Luke hitting Emily blurred his vision, and he started going even crazier for every second he failed to find him. He was on the third floor of the administration building, the floor above which the freshman students refer to as the lion's cage. Even the sophomore and junior year students feared those floors, but still walked them when they have appointments with the administration staff. It was the place where the seniors ragged the junior classes. To be precise, it's the place where Luke's friends rag the others. But the man, who entered in, was no mouse. He seemed like a hunter.

As he took the stairs to the fourth floor, which he climbed in three fast leaps, he heard Luke's laughter at a distance. He definitely knew that laugh. He almost ran across the hallway that took a sudden left at the end and found Luke in the middle of the corridor. He's hanging out with his friends – laughing out loud, chilling and bullying the ones that passed his way. Prudhvi walked to him with his body moving in a way which told everyone around that something was going to happen.

Luke turned to look at Prudhvi, who stormed on to him, just in the last minute. He tried to counter attack, but by then Prudhvi had gotten hold of him by his collar and kicked him hard in his balls. Luke bent down in pain falling on to his knees. Prudhvi placed his right leg a step behind, lifted his hand into a fist and smashed it into Luke's face using all the momentum his upper body gave him. Luke went flying into the wall with his head leading his body. He hit the wall with a thud and fell back bouncing with double the force. His nose started to bleed, and he screamed in pain.

Few of Luke's friends tried to fight for him. Mathew came running on to Prudhvi, trying to bull him. Prudhvi stepped aside in an impulse and caught hold of his neck in his elbow's clutch and turned back at once throwing him away, making sure that his neck will cramp. He fell on to the floor with a banging thud and started screaming with his hands on his neck. Though Louis thought of fighting too, he gave up the idea after seeing Mathew fly almost to the end of the corridor.

Prudhvi turned back to Luke and kicked him in the face with his shoe. Luke cried again, even louder. Bending down to him, Prudhvi lifted him by his collar and banged his head hard on to the wall again.

The people around started stepping back seeing Prudhvi turn into a monster. Blood splattered on to the wall as he lifted him to stand and punched him continuously on his face. Prudhvi's knuckles too started bleeding. Some students wanted to stop it before he killed him, but no one moved - some out of the happiness to see Luke being beaten to a pulp, and some out of fear to be kicked by Prudhvi.

Panting hard unable to breath normally, Prudhvi stopped hitting him at last and left him loose. Luke fell on to the floor and rolled like a pig that was bleeding like hell from its nose. Prudhvi was still not happy with the damage that occurred to the moron's face. He wanted to peel the skin literally off it.

"You hit a girl Luke?" Prudhvi finally said after minutes, during which the corridor echoed just with the cries of Luke and the heavy breaths of Prudhvi. "A girl? Haaaa? And you guys call yourself gentlemen?" he said looking at the Student's Council. He was still shaking with anger. This time, he converted it into words.

"*Gentleman* doesn't mean opening the door for your lady. Or pulling the chair for her, or giving her the jacket, letting her go first, or leaving her safely to her door. It means being the same, with every other girl Luke," he said looking back at him and Luke stared up at Prudhvi as he took his name. "With 'every' 'other' 'girl.' And yes… what did you say last night? 'Some nice architecture was done here', right? Don't you think that the same architect worked on your mom too? Your sisters, your wife, your daughters…"

Luke bent his head in anger and disgrace, and the people around started feeling bad for whatever that happened to Prudhvi, as he screamed with so much of pain in his tone. "Even *that* architect should be given life by a woman, Luke. Lord Krishna, Rama, Buddha, Jesus; they all walked this earth only because a mother gave them life. And those who bear the pain that's equivalent to death to make *you* breathe life… should be respected. *Prathibadhnati shreya, puujya puuja vyathikrama.* 'To deny respecting what that should be respected, will drag you to the lowest of all virtues.'

"Listen, everyone," he shouted at once, turning to the people who gathered around, "And inform all the others. You have any problem with the senior year guys, 'any'… from biased judgments in the boards to harassments in the parks, drugs in the college premises to assaults in the locker rooms, anything… come to me. A-wing hostel, Silver block, room 206. Let's form our own squad," he said turning to the haters, "The Anti-Ragging Squad."

Prudhvi left the corridor elbowing the people who had gathered, as Luke watched him leave, with blood flowing out of his nose and ego boiling inside his head.

* * *

"Ouch…" Emily cried out in pain as Prudhvi applied antiseptic to the wound over her eyebrow. "It hurts."

"I know," he said taking some more solution on to the cotton. "But this should be done."

"May be we should apply some on your knuckles too," she said trying to smile, but the pain still had its grip.

"What?" He smiled moving back, throwing the cotton into the dustbin behind the bed. "You're trying to avenge me?"

They are in the university's hospital; Emergency and First Aid block. The management here was way more considerate that they allocated a separate room with all the equipment installed, just for a girl who needs some antiseptic to be rubbed on her wounds.

"You are the avenger here. Not me," she said smiling.

He too smiled back pressing the new piece of cotton with the solution on it, on to her lip. It felt hurting, but Emily said nothing. She liked the way he was touching her lips though there was cotton in between. Prudhvi cleaned the wound and bent down to cut a new piece of cotton from the ball he had in the other hand. Emily bent her head a little to the sideways to have a look at him, and it felt so good to her – being so close and lonely in a room with Prudhvi.

"I don't know if I had done the right thing. But some things should be done," he said pressing the fresh piece of gauze on to her lip again, "for good."

"You are crying, Prudhvi?!" she screamed out of mere shock seeing his eyes wet.

"Nope. It's the antiseptic."

"Shut up," she said holding his hand, stopping him from what he's doing and he looked up into her eye. "Oh my god. You're crying."

He took a deep breath placing the cotton down and moving away. She hated herself for making him move back.

"Away from home," he said looking at her again, "you are all that I got, Emily. You're a friend, an enemy, nothing and everything." It fell like a bomb shell on her heart, and it started pumping like a steam engine – fast and hot. She wanted nothing but just to hug him tight right now and kiss him for eternity. "I hate to see you like this," he continued as she heard with half the consciousness. "I never saw a girl bleed."

"And I never saw a boy cry," she said smiling and pampering him by playing with his hair. It made him bend slightly towards her. The next thing she wanted is to pull him close to her and kiss. "You are way softer than you look," she said instead.

"And you, stronger."

She smiled.

"So, they said that you kicked him in the eggs?"

"Eggs?" he smiled. "What? They hatch or something?"

"I can't say balls right? So…"

"You just said."

"What?"

"You just said balls."

"No. I said I can't say balls."

"Again… Ok. I can't argue with you." He gave up.

"Encrypt it then," she said winking.

"What?!"

"Encrypt your argument, and give me the kiss."

"What?!" he cried even louder this time.

"What 'What'? I said *encrypt your argument and give me the key.*"

"Oh… key…" Prudhvi wondered if he was the one who heard it wrong, or she spelled it right only the second time. Emily smiled seeing him speculate.

"Key," she conformed as he lifted his head to look back at her.

"Hmmm… Are you ok now?"

"What! It's just antiseptic that you rubbed. It still hurts." She smiled.

"I…," he said suddenly struggling to say something, "I shouldn't have left you at the building. Why didn't I walk you to your door?"

"It's not your fault," she said placing her arm on his.

Prudhvi went silent for few seconds before saying, "It scared you?"

"No, it hadn't. You know how it felt when he hit me?" Emily started turning sad at once. "He punched me so hard, that it made me wonder how weak he was. It takes weakness to hit someone. And strength not to, even if you have the power and purpose."

"So I am weak too."

"It's ok. I am happy that I am your weakness," she said placing her hand on his cheek. It felt so cold on him. He took her hand that was on his cheek and touched it soft to make her feel better. They looked at each other for the unending amount of time, and their hearts started beating in sync.

It was Emily who leaned towards him first, and that made him come nearer. She leaned a bit closer to him.

He reciprocated again. Their closeness was blurring their vision now. Their lips shivered with anxiety and their bodies started leaving hot air out. They started taking deeper breaths as their lips almost touched. Emily placed her arm around the back of his neck and caught hold of him with all the want she had. When it happened, it felt like a dream for both of them; like it's not really happening. They started kissing… kissing hard, with their bodies jumping on to each other with hunger. Their basic human instincts started taking over their wisdom.

Emily felt the grip of his hands on her hip and neck. He pulled her up tight, and they fell back on to the bed, with Emily on top of him. She folded her leg on to Prudhvi, and he caught hold of it by her thigh that was bearing out from the gown. She pulled him to turn over, and he took the advantage. Her lips tasted like heaven to him, and he started biting its tips. She folded both her legs on to him and felt no pain from the wounds anymore. Prudhvi started feeling all her body with his hands. The thin cotton cloth was no obstacle to the ride. He pulled her head back getting hold of her hair, and she left a sudden moan. He started tasting her neck, filling it with hard kisses. She enjoyed his rule on her, as she never enjoyed anything. They both burned in lust.

Kissing all over her neck, he slowly descended to the smoother and curvier parts. She wanted what that was coming, to last forever. The thin golden chain that she always wore stopped him as a guard that asks for a permit to enter in. He pulled it out of the gown and the movement of the metal on her skin produced ripples of pleasure. He pulled the entire chain out, and it was a Mangalsutra.

Prudhvi stared at it with disbelief as his hand that held it shivered. That was the one he tied to Sanju.

"Prudhvi?" said Emily, little shocked. That made him look up at her. "What?"

He waved his head in a nothing and turned back to the chain in his hand. It was the one that Emily always had. A normal plain gold chain with a heart-shaped pendent.

"I am sorry," he said getting off her.

Prudhvi stepped down from the bed and started walking away.

"Prudhvi…" Emily shouted to make him stop. She adjusted her gown as she ran to him. "What happened? Is it me?"

"No," he said turning back to her. "It's not you. It's me. I am sorry for that. I don't mean it."

"But I do," she said at once. "I mean it. I always wanted you Prudhvi. From the day we first met, I had a crush on you."

"What?!" he said with sudden shock.

"Yes. I wanted you, from a very long time."

"But I can't do this."

"Why?"

"Because I love someone else."

"Ok."

"*Ok*? I *love* someone else," he said confused.

"What did I say now? I am not asking you to love me," she said though her own words made her heart weep.

"Then what do you call this."

"This? This is not love. It's just…"

"It's just?"

"I don't know. I don't know what to call it," she said trying to be normal. "You tell me. You're the guys who wrote Kamasutra right?"

"I don't know what we call it exactly, but this is wrong Emily. We can't… without love."

"Kamasutra said that?" she said being irritated with the discussion.

"No. But I believe that we humans, at several stages of our evolution, had always derived *Sex* from *Love*, but never the way around. Love with lust is not lust. But lust without love is…" he said moving away from her. "I am sorry Emily," and walked out of the room.

Sitting back on to the bed, Emily cried with her head buried in her knees, not because he left her, but because she knew that he will never love her.

Chapter 5

One year later

11:55 pm

24th August 1940

Common study rooms. Imperial King's.

"Sorry for whatever happened," she told him the next day, and he said: "It's ok. Let's forget all that and be friends again."

They both knew that it was not going to happen. The damage was already done, and they could never switch back to normal again. They stopped being them. No chit-chatting after the classes, no silent laughter in the library, no strolling in the garden, no Shakespeare plays, no more nightclubs and no cricket matches in the Lord's. They have been in touch, helped each other with academics, looked after each other and never spent a day without smiling over something. But that 'thing,' was gone. Though it made Emily cry, locked up in her room during the first few days, or weeks, or even months may be, now it's all done. Time, the alleged fourth dimension, helped her adjust to some extent.

During this one year of silence that echoed between them, many other things happened in the outer world. March 1939, the British government pledged to aid Poland in the event that it was attacked by Germany. No other country even batted an eye, considering it as one of the many wars that took place until then. But it was on 1st of

September, the same year; it took its turn at the World-War board when the Germans invaded Poland from the west. The after math of that invasion is something that the world never saw.

In September, Britain declared war on Germany, while the Soviet Union invaded Poland from the east. Germany and the Soviet Union divided Poland. During the first week of October, Fuhrer Adolf Hitler himself offered peace, which was rejected by Britain and France while the United States declared neutrality on the topic; and then started the events that made the world's spine shiver – the ruthless slaughtering of Jews. Over six million Jews died in the holocaust – robbed by the Nazis, used as slaves, brutally slammed to death, shot in the heads, gassed in the bunkers, starved in the sun and boiled in sea waters.

In the same month, October, the first German air raids on the British Isles occurred. The war started burning like wild fire, dragging the world into it, country by country. Germany, Italy and Japan joined hands to form the Axis Powers, which fought the Allied Powers – the other part of the world that's against them. The British-ruled-India also joined the Allied Powers, against Hitler.

In the first half of 1940, the primary thing to happen was rationing system being introduced in Britain due to the shortage of commodities. Holland, Belgium and Norway surrendered to Germany, and the British Prime Minister Neville Chamberlain resigned, which made Winston Churchill take the seat. And then began the Battle of Britain.

Though the war was burning the world, it never reached London, and especially the Imperial Kings.

Not even a single class in the curriculum got postponed. And on top of that, the freshman students had their year-end exams starting 27th of August, i.e. within the next three days. Because of which Prudhvi gathered his mates at this hour in the common study for preparation.

After the huge success of the Anti-Ragging Squad, he had become a leader. Many of them even felt that he taught better than most of the staff.

"Written exams are never going to be a problem for us," Prudhvi said standing near the wall which they use as a board. He was not writing anything, but that was the place where the one who took the class stands. "We can easily sail through the written and with much better grades than we expect. But, the main hurdle is one-to-one assessment sessions that follow. No professor is going to give you grades on the basis of your personal rapport with him, and that's for sure."

Emily sat in the last row listening to him talk about how one could impress the professors. To her, he seemed like a man she could never get, and would never let her stop from wanting him. She also hated him for the way he was – loving a girl who may never love him back and ignore the one who loved him to death.

"In earlier days, even Shorthand was used as a method of decryption, as those who knew Shorthand were limited to tens in number in the entire world," Prudhvi said, and he really seemed like a professor in his twenties. "The most tactical part of encrypting a message is that how you leave a key that can decrypt it. And… the even more tactical part is that the key should lie in the encrypted message itself.

As in the case of Shorthand, knowing Shorthand is the key itself. Sometimes you can also decrypt the message even without extracting the key and using it, but that message will not be the right one. The answer was simple, let the end-party have a system that's highly secure and only which can extract the key word from the encrypted file," he said as if that was not the fun part yet.

"But… if we are not interested in sending the message to the end-party. What if you are interested in the third parties who intercept them in the mid-air?" and the class was filled with some energy from the smile he let out at the end of the sentence. Emily hated that smile as it always made her fall for him all over again.

"Which means – One; you want to let the third party decrypt it so that it can be distracted by false information. And two; if your real interest is the third party itself. Like if you are a spy in the enemy camp?" and the class murmured with smiles on their faces. It interested them a lot now. "Case one was way easier. There will be no fooling of the end-party involved as there will be no end-party at all. And the signal can be encrypted to a level, so that the third party should be able to fetch the key, but only with some effort, which was needed to make it look genuine.

"But case two, where you should fool the real end user. How do you send a signal to *that* third party, which is your country, and which looks like a genuine signal to the end-party?" No one even tried to answer waiting eagerly for the master himself to answer it. "Simple again… Design a key, that gives the message to the end-party when used, and which acts as a hint to another key, which when used by the third party gives them the message that was intended to them," the class smiled again for the simple solution. "But..." he said again, with a smile and the tension returned back, "the utmost important thing is that... the key you provided shouldn't seem like a hint to the end-party, which may lead to the revealing of your identity, and your death follows. Then... what's the best way to design a key that seems like a hint, *only* to the third party?"

The whole class went silent, looking at each other's faces and discussing in groups. But the suspense hadn't lasted longer.

"Keep it personal?" Emily said from the last row, and the whole class turned to her. She was hardly visible in that darkness as the bulb over that portion of the study was not working, but Prudhvi knew who she was. He could recognise her even from her shadow.

"That was the exact answer, Ms Emily," he said smiling with a professional face on. She hated being called 'Miss' by him. "Can you elaborate?"

"You should keep it personal," she said in a lame and uninterested tone. "Like only a person from your country may get a hint of it. Use your local slangs, or street words... whatever. And if only *that* particular person can understand it, it will be unbreakable."

Prudhvi stared at her as a professor stared at his best student. He always admired the talent she got. Not many had that gift.

The whole class clapped at once, and the empty study room echoed. As Prudhvi smiled looking at the class clapping for her, he suddenly heard an echo from the distance, which sounded like a motor boat and lasted just for a second or two.

"She will definitely be a spy someday," some guy pranked, and the class laughed. Emily blushed listening to that comment. "Come to the wall madam spy, the class wants to see you," some other guy shouted and the whole class *Wooohoo*ed her as she stood up and walked, with a dazzling smile on her face.

Prudhvi watched her move towards him and that sound got repeated, but from a closer distance now. No one noticed it, but it disturbed Prudhvi for some reason. He walked to the window just beside him, and that sound suddenly became so loud that everyone around covered their ears at once. Prudhvi opened the window as fast as he could, wondering what that was, that too at 12:20 in the night. He pushed open one wing of the window to stare into the darkness and a sudden blast occurred in the building that was few blocks away from them. The huge concrete building just blew away like cardboard.

Over the burning and blasting concrete, a bomber jet flew past it. Prudhvi stood there unable to process what he just saw, as the other students started gathering at the remaining windows. Another jet followed making high-pitched noise. Some students started shouting and running.

Prudhvi stared into the dark side of the fire on that building as he started hearing another high-pitched humming, other than the echo of the jets. It was reverberating between the buildings and grew louder.

Even before he could figure out what it was, he saw a mighty piece of lead flying towards them, out of the distant darkness.

He turned back to look at Emily. She was standing in the middle of the room turning directions with uncertainty in her eyes. She turned to look at Prudhvi as he stared at her, and saw pain in him.

He took a deep breath and ran towards her knowing that the building will blast away in seconds. He ran to her with all the energy and the porcelain floor gave him no grip. Emily wondered if he was going to hug her and say that he loved her. But the way he was running didn't seem so.

For Prudhvi, it all felt so calm, steady and slow. He heard nothing and saw only Emily. He can run past her before the blast and may be that can save himself. He didn't want to die here, in London. He wanted to die on his land, in the hands of his loved one. His heart cried to see her, Sanjuktha, his first and last love. He closed his eyes for few seconds, as Emily wondered why he did that and saw her smile. His wife, smiling and running in the paddy fields of their village as he chased her. They were very happy, with nothing to worry about. No war, no slavery, no murders and no bombings.

He opened his eyes reaching out to Emily, got hold of her with both his hands around her, lifted her up as he ran towards the exit and all at once the wall blasted off with a huge explosion and threw them like nothing, to the other side of the room. The whole area exploded into pieces.

The bombing continued all night and the Imperial King's burned in that darkness, along with the other great buildings which turned into ashes over seconds.

That was the first time Germany ever bombed London, destroying homes and killing civilians.

* * *

"May be the war broke out just for you," she said trying to smile.

Prudhvi said nothing but stared out from the gap between the two white silk curtains on the window. They were in a private cab his father arranged, to take him to river Thames. He didn't want Emily to come with him, but she insisted.

The marks from the blast that night showed clearly on their faces. Emily still had a neck fixer, and Prudhvi had his left hand in a black support sling that was hanging from his neck. If it was not because of Prudhvi, Emily would have been dead by now. After he had carried her for few seconds, only the waves of the blast hit them, and they missed the roof that collapsed form the blast just in a matter of meters. But unlike them, hundreds of students died that night.

"So you are heading back to your parents?" Prudhvi finally said turning to her. His tone had lost weight in it.

"Yes. Two days from now, my dad will take me home."

"Hmmm…" he left a sigh. "Any address I can write you to?"

"No," she said making their eyes meet. "We will be moving to a new place, somewhere safer. And I still don't know where it is."

"Then you can write to me first."

She just stared into his eyes without an answer. Her neck was still hurting. If there was no way of getting him, she wanted to let go off him completely. She never wanted to see him again or been written from. But before that, she wanted to ask him for one last time, for one last thing. 'Can you ever love me? What if Sanjuktha rejects you for life?'

"What if-" she started saying, and the cab came to a sudden halt making them fall on to the separating wall.

They sat on a bench in the port, while the men loaded the ship with the passenger's luggage. For most of the time, it's just silence that prevailed again.

"Talk something," she said unable to bear his silence anymore.

"You remember?" he said at once as if he's waiting for her to ask. "That day, when Luke stopped us in the garden?"

"Hmmm…" she moved her head but confused.

"Before that, when you asked me if you're not of my standards, I just said 'Yeah…' and walked away?"

"I remember."

"Sir…" said the driver from behind as Prudhvi tried to tell her something, "the captain calls for the passengers."

Emily's heart sank listening to him. 'Can you ever love me?' she still wanted to ask.

"I'll be there. Just few more seconds," he said, and the driver walked away.

'Few more seconds…' she went week in her knees even if she's not standing.

"Yes, I was saying," he said turning to her. His eyes started filling with tears. "Yeah… You asked me what that meant. You want to know?"

She just moved her aching head in a yes, unable to produce the sound.

"It means," he said with his voice turning heavier for every second, "yes, you don't suit my standards. You deserve much better than me, Emily. Way better."

"Deserving is one thing, and want another," she wanted to say. But nothing came out of her mouth again. The ship gave a sudden honk and the chimneys on the top started emitting black smoke out of them. They both turned to look at it.

As Emily turned back to look at him, he's still staring at the chimneys. She wondered what he was thinking.

"I hate you, Emily," he said turning to her at once. His eyes started raining. "You know how happy I should be now. For my dream finally coming true. My father himself wanted me back in India, and I can see Sanju every other day, few days from now, and I am still not happy."

"Why are you not happy?" she said hoping for the answer she wanted. Tears rolled off her eyes too.

"You… I am not happy just because of you," he said pointing his good hand at her. "I hate the way things ended between us. I always wanted to remember you as the Emily who tickles me to shout in the library, the Emily who shares everything with me and listens to every story of mine, the Emily who drags me to night clubs, the Emily who helps me solve algorithms, the Emily who cries on little things, the Emily who loves cricket and Shakespeare, the Emily who eats with her bare hand when she eats with me, the Emily who's stronger than I think she is…"

She started sobbing unable to bear the pain.

"But now?" he continued. "Do you think you're that Emily?"

"Stay back. I can be," she said looking into his wet eyes.

"You can't ask me that."

"You too can't ask me for the time that's lost. And can't blame me for…" she made a sudden halt. 'For loving you,' she wanted to say. "You can't blame me for-"

"Sir… it's time," shouted the guard at the detachable stairs into the ship.

They both turned to him at once. Prudhvi stood up to leave. She too stood, with all her energy. Both their faces turned pale from this drift that was about to become a saddening permanence.

"See you, Emily," he said.

She said nothing but just stared at him, as he started stepping away from her; and turned back at once to leave. Tears rolled uncontrollably out of Prudhvi's eyes as he reached the staircase. He realised that missing your friend, was equally hurting as missing your love.

Emily stood there, with her hands folded close to her chest and her eyes drenching, as she watched the ship sail away, taking her first love with it, to the far away continents. It all happened in a flash, and there was no Prudhvi in her life any more. She fell back on to the bench and sobbed, with tears sliding off her cheeks, soaking her neck band.

As she cried her life out, once and forever Emily learnt that Love was just a word that we joke about, but only until someone comes along and make us realise that it's not.

She hated herself for walking into the hotel that night.

* * *

Prudhvi hugged his father as tight as he could, letting out all the pain that mounted upon his loneliness over days on the ship. He missed the warm hug of his father that never let him realise the absence of his mother.

Mr. Koundinya Prathap hugged back his son who came back from the dead and cried for the first time in decades. On the day he heard the news about the bombing on the King's, he fell unconscious in a meeting. His higher officials ordered for an immediate search for his son and his return.

"You look so tired, dad," Prudhvi said as they walked away from the ship, towards their carriage. He was in his grey suit with a black shirt inside. Smartly dressed, neatly groomed, but his state of being hadn't suited them.

"I am so worried about you, son," he said without turning to Prudhvi. Prudhvi felt his pain much lesser when compared to that of his father. He would have literally been in hell until he saw his son fit and fine.

"Good that I took the bandage off my hand," Prudhvi thought.

"How's Sanju, dad?" he wanted to ask. But left it off that way, as what Sanjuktha always said was true. He hated her in a way. There was no doubt at all that he wouldn't have bothered the least to enquire about their wellbeing.

'What should I talk to her first about?' Prudhvi thought as he walked again on the mud roads after years. He had no feelings about being back to India, or eating the Indian food after so long time, or not even for escaping the sickness this time. Though he felt some comfort having a candid lunch spending the whole afternoon chatting with his father; the excitement to see Sanjuktha finally, after all these years took over everything. Even his hand was not bothering him anymore.

He wondered how she'll react; shout, scream, or may be standing still in shock. He smiled as he started jogging unable to bear the suspense. He knew that she may also say few things to hurt him again, but, this time, none of them were going to work. He just wanted to reach her, hug her, and cry all the pain out.

He heard her shout at her father, as he opened the outer gate without letting it make any noise. Her voice felt so soothing to his ears. But at the same time, it had been so different than when he left her. Whatever, it was his Sanju and her sweet humming tone.

"Surprise," he wanted to shout, but his uncle may not entertain that. So he just stepped in softly and banged the front door which was wide open. He heard the sound of anklets that was approaching from inside. He walked to the center space, as his heart started racing to see her.

A lady in her late thirties walked out.

"Yes?" she said.

"Ahh…it's…" he babbled, wondering if his uncle married again. "Sanjuktha?"

"Sanjuktha?" she said surprised. "There's no one with that name here."

That took him off guard. "What?" he said with impulsive surprise. "This is her home. How can't she be here?"

"See mister, I don't know whom you're talking about," she retorted. "We are living here from the past one year, and I know no one with that name. You can leave now."

He wanted to ask her many questions. 'But I heard her talk!' he wanted to say first. However, the lady seemed offended by his presence in there. So he left the house to step outside.

"They are not here? May be they have shifted. But why will they? This house was their own, and they had been here since generation."

His brain started to shout for answers. He needed someone to answer what's going on with him right now.

"Rudhra…" he thought of once and ran towards the next door.

"Rudhra went to the Force Prudhvi," his mother said in a dull tone. "He's fighting for the British now. Ironic…"

"So he has done it finally," Prudhvi thought and prayed for his friend.

"Ahh, aunty…" he dragged, preparing to start, "do you know where Sanjuktha and her dad went? I mean the family that used to live-"

"Sanjuktha?" she said in a how-can-I-forget-her tone. "She's in the woods now."

"*Woods*?" he sounded more than surprised.

"Yes, 'The Woods'."

"Why is she in the woods," Prudhvi cried out as if to make her tell the real truth.

"Because that's where the rebels live right?" she said.

Chapter 6

"Here. Have some," said Rudhra's mother placing a glass of water near Prudhvi. He was sitting on a wooden chair in the hall, with his mind stretching itself in infinite directions. He was dying to cope with what he just heard.

"Why would she do that?" he said looking at her, who sat on the floor in front of him.

"She was left with no other option. Poor girl," she said with concern, "It's actually the rebels who took her into the woods, after finding her in Canning's farmhouse."

"What? Whose... Whose farmhouse?"

"Canning. That irrigation officer?"

"Why was she in his farmhouse?"

"It was him actually," she said irritating him with her slow and dragging accent. "He killed her father too."

Prudhvi started to fight his breath. "Killed her father?"

"Aunty please," he said getting down on to his knees, making his eye line equal hers, "tell me what happened, clearly. Please don't..." he tried to search for words while his eyes started blurring out from the tears.

"Ok..." she said sitting straight, threatened by the way he was crying. "One day, almost before sixteen months from now, Canning came along with his personal army to arrest Chakradev, as he allegedly had contacts with the rebels. Sanjuktha tried to stop him from taking away her father. And…" she paused. Prudhvi stared at her losing all the salts through his eyes

"And he tried to drag her too into the jeep. Chakradev pushed him away from touching her daughter. Canning shot him there on the road itself." Prudhvi trembled listening to that. "He dragged Sanjuktha into his jeep, took her to his farmhouse and… and raped her for weeks."

His hands shivered with record frequencies, and his senses started dying. He was not crying anymore. He started turning pale, and it seemed like he was going to pass out. *Raped her for weeks* – it felt like a hot melting metal being impaled into his heart.

"His guards shot these kids too, Saleem and Suryam, who tried to stop him from taking her away."

Nothing happened to Prudhvi. He was out of all the limits of pain. He just listened. But she was not talking now. She stared at him not knowing what else to say. Her heart felt so week seeing the kid in this position.

"And?" he said looking at her. His eyes were red as hell. "Then what happened?"

"Then…then one day she killed him. Sanjuktha killed Canning. She… she slit his throat with a letter opener. And the rebels went to save her the same night. They found her sitting in silence, next to Canning's dead body and took her with them, into the woods. They say that now she's leading the group.

"It's because of her, that we had some water to drink today. Even the British fear her existence in there. Such a brave girl she is. People of many villages around are having, at least, some basic needs supplied, just because of the attacks she ordered on their government offices and police stations, demanding to fulfil the public needs."

Saying so, she stopped again and made not another sound. Prudhvi stared at nothing, turning her even more tensed for every passing second.

"Thank you," he finally said. He stood up at once, and she followed. "Thanks for your information," he said before leaving the house.

He walked away as if he had nowhere to go.

"Hmmm… God knows when this country will be free from all this," she talked to herself as she took the glass that Prudhvi left untouched and walked into the kitchen.

* * *

'He raped her…' he repeated it inside his head as he walked, 'He raped my wife, for weeks, and killed my friends.'

Images of Sanju crying out for help as Canning pulled her by her hair, into his bedroom, made his brain wiggle inside his head. Echoes of her loud screams made his ears bleed. Dead bodies of Suryam and Saleem on which their parents were sobbing to death flashed in front of his eyes like it was happening now. His mind went weak, unable to get on with the sudden turn of events. Prudhvi found no one else to blame for all this but his own self. He hated himself. And Sanjuktha too, for killing Canning.

He didn't want him to die in such a painless way. He wanted to torture him to death. Pull his nails out, peel his eye lids off, feed his male organ to wild rats while it was still intact, make him eat his own excreta, repeat it for infinity and then beat him to death with his bare hands.

Shaking with anger, Prudhvi lost his energy to walk and fell on to the ground that was full of high raised grass. He folded himself close, with his knees into his stomach and cried out loud, like after this he can never make a sound again in his entire life. He wanted to see her right now – the girl who's his love, his innocent wife. He wanted to hug her close and tell her that she was still the same old Sanjuktha. Nothing happened to her, and she was still as pure as he believes his mother was. He wanted to marry her again, bring her out from the woods and start a new life.

Almost five hours passed, where he cried uncontrollably, but not even 1% of his grief settled. Wanting to meet her at any cost, he finally stood up to walk again, towards the clump of trees that were visible in the faraway grounds, which were the starting point of the forest. He walked for about fifteen minutes to reach that tall and mighty green wall. He was not worried, or there's no fear at all. All that he knew was not to give up until he saw her.

He walked into the forest for almost six continuous hours, and it went dark by then. There was no moon in the sky too. Or maybe the thickly-formed forest roof was not letting the light in. Prudhvi felt it very hard even to see what was there in front of him. He was just using his hands to make way. The humidity was also not so great making him sweat like a pig. He needed a strategy now as he needed oxygen.

He decided that it was not the best way to travel anymore and should rest until the first light broke in. He somehow found a huge tree that extended its vast branches in directions and decided to make it his bed tonight. The more height he took, the safer he would be. He climbed to the highest point where the stems were strong enough to sleep on, and rested for the day, tying his limbs around the branch with his suspenders, in case he slips aside in sleep.

It's the chirping of the birds that woke him up early in the morning. He descended the tree and started walking again. But to where? God knows... Even before that, he felt the need to hydrate his body. He found some leaves that were convenient enough for the fog to turn into water and settle on, and drank it until he felt like he needed no more. He found some eatable leaves and fruits too. With a satchel made out of banana leaves tied together with a string he pulled down from a tree used as a handle, he filled it with those fruits and leaves that were left and started walking again.

As he walked deep into the forest, he started finding places that were once used as camps. And in there, he found few more things like a long stick that's sharpened at one end, a thick polythene sheet to cover him, some charcoal to apply on his body as a camouflage and a hand knife with which he can cut his way through denser areas.

He started seeing more of such places as he followed the direction in which the footprints left the camp. The rebels never stay at a place for long. They keep shifting base. There were also marks all along the way, like a cut down bush, the imprints where they placed their camp bags, the places where they had rested and few of them had a beedi (Indian cigar) or two, and they helped him to connect from camp to camp.

On his way, he also came across few snakes, some of which are extremely venomous, monkeys that tried to steal his satchel, wild mosquito groups, forest boars, pangolins and also heard dreadful roars from the distance. He observed his surroundings very keenly and carefully as he walked. Whenever he found a living thing, he always took a way around or waited in the bushes until it left the place. Out of luck, he had both his pants and the shirt dark colored and the black colored mixture of coal and mud that he rubbed all over his skin that was visible, helped him to hide better. He folded his sleeves up his elbow, tucked in the shirt and wound the suspenders around his hip to use it as a holder for the knife.

Four of them, Prudhvi, Rudhra, Saleem and Suryam, used to trek in the forest whenever they found time to. And thus, he knew some techniques. He still remembered the time when once Saleem ate a berry, and he almost died. With the memories of his friends refreshing at once, Prudhvi went low and took a halt to sit in the roots of a tree. He was exhausted too.

Staring at the light slowly fading out into darkness, he wondered if god was still a kid who played rough with his own toys. His heart started coming back to normal speeds from the weariness of the trek. Tears started filling his eyes again as the thoughts of Sanju being raped started filling back into his mind again. He cursed fate for being so ruthless.

"Why should this happen to Sanju but no one else? And why should this happen to anyone at all? Why should we life at the mercy of the British? This is our land, and we are the kings," he thought, and reality started sneaking into his head, pushing out the childish thoughts of British ruling us forever. He slowly started realising what Sanju always tried to teach him – rather than to live kneeling, it was better to die standing.

* * *

Darkness had set in by the time Prudhvi opened his eyes. He wondered when in hell he slipped in. He was still in those roots, with his body crying for more sleep. But his mind made him feel an immediate necessity to look for a convenient tree to rest for the night. It was his luck last night that no wild animal passed his way in that darkness. But today it may not happen again. He stood up from the roots and while thinking of having a fruit or some leaves before bed, he suddenly heard a stone roll. He turned back to once picking up the stick. He stared into the trees with his nerves throbbing. He heard some dry stems crack and it was not just a pair of legs that was walking towards him. He moved back in slow and steady steps while his eyes started searching for a tree that he can climb fast. There were none around.

His face was still black from the charcoal, and maybe it could help to hide in the trees. But most of the four-legged animals, first set you as a target, and never take their eyes of you. They may attack from any direction, that too in the most unaccepted speeds. There was no use of trying to hide.

With no other options left, Prudhvi decided to fight it. "I can kill it with the hand knife. Easy," he thought as the bushes in front of him started stirring. He stared at it with his muscles tightened and his grip firm on the knife in one hand and the stick in the other. He waited patiently until it came out of the scrubs.

It was a gun's barrel that he saw first, and a man followed, pointing it towards him. He was in the rebel's uniform – a dark brown shirt and trouser, with a belt of bullets around the hip. He had only one arm, and the sleeve on the other side is rolled up to his shoulder. The shirt did have a full sleeve stitched, meaning that he lost his arm recently.

"I am not the enemy," Prudhvi said leaving both his organic and metallic weapons at once and raising his empty hands into the air.

Few more men emerged out of the bushes, pointing their guns at him. Prudhvi's eyes searched for Sanjuktha, but there was no sign of her.

"Who are you?" shouted the one-armed man, who seemed like the leader of that group.

"My name is Prudhvi, and I am not an enemy," he said with more stress on the line 'Not an enemy.' "I am here to meet Sanjuktha."

"Sanjuktha?" he said in surprise. "What do you want from her?"

"I need to talk to her. Very important."

"*Important?* For whom?"

"For me. For her…"

"I don't believe you," he said moving his head in a 'No.'

"Please. I… I am her husband." If that may make them believe in him.

"You're the son of Koundinya Prathap?" the leader said lowering his gun. The others followed.

"Yes, I am." Prudhvi was excited to see them turn friendly.

The leader just stared at him, as if thinking whether to believe him or not and all at once ordered: "Kill him."

"Wait," shouted someone from behind. It was a lady.

She came out of the bushes with her double barrel riffle in her hand. The same uniform and the same bullet belt.

"What's happening here?" she talked in an authoritative tone and turned to Prudhvi. "Who's this?"

Prudhvi said nothing and did nothing. He just stared at her in disbelief. It was her, Sanju. But it was not her again. Not the way she was dressed, not the way she was talking, not the way she was moving and definitely not the way she was holding the gun like an expert. Prudhvi closed his eyes tight in pain. The images of a three-months-old baby holding his one-year-old finger and smiling brightly started flashing his mind. He saw the cute little bride with curd all over her.

Prudhvi wondered if he should call her 'Sanju' or 'Sanjuktha' now. She seemed so familiar and much strange. But his heart was pumping too fast to talk anyways.

He started walking towards her opening his eyes, leaving a deep sigh.

"Hey, stay back," the leader shouted lifting his gun, and all the other guns rose at him again.

"Stay where you are." It was Sanjuktha. "Or you'll die."

Now she too had her gun pointed at him, but he just walked to her.

"Chief, order…" the leader whisper shouted to her. But she didn't want to kill a man unless she knew that he was worth shooting at. All the others waited with their fingers on the triggers.

As he walked towards her, he closed his hands on to his face and started wiping off the color. He was just a few meters away now, and Sanjuktha started fearing potential risk. He might have an explosive on him. She stared at his hips and legs to see if there were any extra baggage wound around them inside.

"Hey," shouted the leader stepping forward, "stop there. NOW…"

Sanju lifted her head up to look at his face as he almost reached her and the word 'Fire' was on the tips of her lips. And then came a wave of shock.

It was Prudhvi, she saw.

He came walking and stopped just at the point blank range of her gun. The others rounded him off.

Staring into her eyes, he smiled with tears filling into his. Looking into the depths of his stare, Sanjuktha felt like a girl again. Like everything was back to normal. Like he had never been to London, and she had never been to the woods. Like they were kids again.

No one else in this world could ever make her feel as calm and better as he could, and she loved the way it worked every other time. Seeing him like this after years, with the charcoal rubbed over his face and all, she smiled at once, lowering her gun. Tears filled her eyes as she stared at him – the one for whom she prays every night. The rebels around too slowly moved their barrels towards the ground, turning to each other in surprise.

"I almost had my last wish fulfilled," Prudhvi said wiping tears off his cheeks, and she stared in surprise. "*Dying in your hands.* Though I never meant it *this* literally," he said smiling brightly.

"I thought you died in that bombing over London," she said fighting those tears that were trying to overpower her.

"No." Prudhvi moved his head in censure and started to cry. "Not without hugging you, at least once in this life."

Leaving a deep sigh, she dropped the gun in her hand and jumped on to him, hugging him tight. The rebels around moved away at once smiling and some covering their mouths with their hands in disbelief, that their strict and disciplined leader, Madam Sanjuktha was embracing a man.

This was the first time they ever hugged, and the wild air around echoed… as they both sobbed like kids in each other's arms.

* * *

Prudhvi sat on a wooden box in front of a tent and sipped tea from a steel mug. It felt so refreshing, not because he was starving almost from a day, but because it's Sanju-Made.

He was in the rebel's camp – tents, guns, fire, guards and food.

As he sipped his tea, he stared at Sanju on the other side of the camp fire, who was cooking on a fire pit. There were few other guys helping her with the vegetables. She turned to look at him from that distance as if his stare called her name out. Prudhvi lifted his mug in cheers to her. She smiled with all the happiness and turned back to cook, still smiling.

Prudhvi wondered how she used to look in a saree, as all his images of her in that attire got evaporated seeing her like this. To his surprise, the rebel's uniform suited her very well. She seemed tall and elegant in those full and full dark brown clothes that hugged her as they love her. The shirt was a full-sleeved one out of which her little white hands emerged, and the trouser was tucked into her long ankle combat boots. The leather belt which was making the lower part of her shirt bulge a little, had bullets arranged all around it, and there's also a leather knife holder attached on its right side. Her thick black hair was French-Flattened with the braid tied across the back of her head to fall forward from a side, and few free strands of hair are trying to kiss her cheeks from both the sides. And among all these, her face was glowing like a wild forest flower that had tiny fog precipitations all over it.

"Such a detailed artist you are," Prudhvi praised Lord Brahma for his master piece.

He slowly started believing the fact that he was finally with her again.

"I am sorry," someone said from behind and Prudhvi turned back. It was the man who tried to shoot him. He came with a mug in his hand too and sat on the wooden box on the other side of the tent placing the mug beside him.

"It's ok," Prudhvi tried to smile, taking a look at his hanging sleeve and back at his face.

"I am Bilva."

"Prudhvi," he said, and they shook hands.

"So, does she cook every day?" Prudhvi said trying to start a conversation.

"*Cook*?" Bilva exclaimed, picking his mug back. "This is the first time I ever saw her on that side of the camp fire."

"Why is there a roof over the camp fire?" he enquired with the mention of it.

"So that the fire can't be seen from the skies."

"Oh... Cautious..." Prudhvi felt inferior to ask him something he didn't know. "So who are the real cooks then?" he said diverting the topic.

"You see those two guys? Handing her things?" Bilva pointed with the mug.

"Ya."

"They are the cooks."

"Ok..." Prudhvi said smiling in surprise.

"You know what? Today, it's so calm. Like... real calm."

"I didn't get you."

"Every day, by now, Madam Sanjuktha would be drawing a sketch here," he said pointing at the ground between them. "What to do next, which government buildings are to be attacked, how to get hold of more arms and ammunition etc. etc," he said leaving a sigh. "But you came, and things flipped. She's *cooking*..."

"To Indian wives," Prudhvi said raising his mug.

"To Indian wives," he repeated hitting the mug with his, and they both laughed.

"But I should say," Bilva said after few minutes of casual talk, "how sorry I am for your loss. I mean for your friends, your uncle and… Madam Sanjuktha."

Prudhvi moved his head in a dull nod.

"She's such a brave girl," Bilva said.

"Yes. But I never thought that she's *this* brave."

"You should see her when they killed our leader, Major Dandapaani," he said making his eyes bigger. "She turned into Kalika that day."

Kalika – one of the avatars of Parvathi, wife of Lord Shiva, in which she turns into a dangerous monster that tears evil apart.

"She ordered for an immediate strike back with all that we had. No one turned back that day while she led us. We walked straight into a British assembly building and shot twenty-six officers who were attending a meeting. None survived.

"She took a bullet too that day. On her left shoulder. After that, she stopped nowhere. You know what they say?" he said with pride in his eyes and words. "Even Bose praises her now."

"Who?" Prudhvi exclaimed.

"Bose. Subhash Chandra Bose."

"Why would he know her?"

"Because he's the one to whom we report."

"Bose... is your leader?" Prudhvi said in astonishment.

"Ya, he's the one. And all that we believe is this: There's nothing that can be done with non-violence," he said starting to turn furious. "The British had treated us cheaper than slaves for centuries, and now our government is supplying them with men to fight the war? How immoral and shameless that was. And sending men to war is not an act of encouraging violence? Enemy to enemy is a friend. That's the law of war. We shouldn't fight for British. We should fight British."

"Seriously? Bose?" Prudhvi was still in shock.

"Yes, sir..." Bilva smiled. "It's Bose."

"So you're against our leaders then?" Prudhvi said, trying to digest the fact.

"Yes. Even your uncle never wanted this to happen. He always tried to preach us non-violence."

"Wait a second," he said with sudden doubt. "Mr. Chakradev was not with you guys?"

"Against us."

"Then why had they tried to arrest him? Misunderstanding?"

"No," Bilva said smiling. "Your father."

"My father?"

"Yes. He's the one who wanted Chakradev to be arrested."

"But why?" Prudhvi asked in that-can-not-be-true tone.

"At first, even we thought that it's really a misunderstanding. But," Bilva said looking deep in his eye, "when your father approached Major Dandapaani with a deal, few days before we were attacked, we came to know what the real deal was."

"Which is?"

"He wanted Sanjuktha to be dead."

"What?" Prudhvi exclaimed, and it literally echoed.

"Don't get shocked. That's true," Bilva said smiling again. "He wanted Sanjuktha to be out of your life. Out of the world that is, as he knows how much you love her. He went to Mr Canning for that, alleged her father as a part of our group and promised that he would give him Sanjuktha for few days before he can kill her too. But as no one had expected, *she* killed him and joined us.

"Your father came running to us as Sanjuktha started growing here. He feared that one day she may outgrow his power and stature. He offered Major Dandapaani a pact – give me Sanjuktha; I'll give you whatever you want. Dandapaani rejected his offer, and in the next few days, we were attacked."

Prudhvi felt shame rubbed all over his skin. He hated his own existence as his son and raged with anger towards a man who ruined his life. He was the reason for all this.

"My father?" he cried inside his heart.

It was not difficult for him to believe it. His father had always done such acts, but never with his own family. Prudhvi could not ever imagine that he could do that. He killed his uncle, his friends and traded his wife for a British dog. Prudhvi clasped the mug in his hand, and it started bending in.

"If Sanjuktha should start killing," Bilva said, and Prudhvi turned to him with his eyes burning with anger and grief, "she should start with your father. But you know what she always said? 'I got no one left in this world to call a family. I know how it feels to lose a father, and I don't want Prudhvi to feel the same.' That's Madam Sanjuktha."

Saying so, he stood up and walked into the forest, to light the spy-fire; leaving Prudhvi to burn in resentment. Trying not to cry, Prudhvi turned his head to look at Sanju, who was looking at him by then.

"What happened?" she mouthed from the distance and moved her hand in an invitation.

He tried to suppress his anger as he walked towards her. She seemed so innocent to him with that smile on her face, and all the furious stories Bilva just narrated about her turned into fairy tales.

His father had shattered her life into pieces, and she was still not angry on him. He wanted him to live just because he was his father. Prudhvi felt pride filling his heart that had love towards a girl of such character.

"It's my privilege to love you, Sanju," he thought as he reached her.

"Dinner?" she said smiling.

He thought that one can do anything to take away that smile from her, but no one can ever succeed. He wanted to ask her about his father but found no point in discussing it.

"Hello? Why do you always stare at me like that?" she said still smiling and waving her hand in front of his eyes. "Do you want to eat or not?"

"Ya, I should," he said taking her hand into his and pulling her close. "What do we have?"

Staring cutely into his eyes, she smiled before she answered. "Mango-Dal and potato fry," she said blushing.

Chapter 7

It was the best dinner he ever had. Not because they were his favorite dishes, but because he enjoyed them with even more tenderness, as the forest, camp fire, the darkness and her smile added more ambience to the evening. He treasured the thought of being in her company and filled every second into his heart that already had limitless happiness in it.

Sanjuktha ate less than half of what she usually eat. Not because she saw him after years and that filled her heart, but because she was busy staring at him who still felt like a dream to her. She acted as if she chewed a chilli when few uncontrollable tears rolled out at a point.

It was 9 pm now and the whole camp settled down after dinner. The guards were changing shifts and the ones who stood guard until then headed for their tents with dinner plates in their hands. Leaving the bigger tent in the center empty, they were occupying the remaining ones. It was to divert the enemy, in the case of attack. The British always attacked the leader first. Prudhvi walked past the big tent in search of Sanjuktha. After dinner, she suddenly disappeared into the darkness of the woods and had been there for a considerably long time.

"She might be somewhere nearby, cleaning her gun or something," Prudhvi thought as he strolled away from the camp, into the distantly grown but thick trees. He started hearing something that sounded like the humming of a motor car as he progressed. He wondered what it was. It started getting darker every few meters, and he blamed himself for not carrying a torch. After few more meters of rambling, he finally crossed the last line of trees, and it suddenly felt as if he accidentally stepped into a dream.

There was a deep valley just after the forest that made the land he stood on look like it's the edge of the world. The land ended abruptly, and the surroundings went so open and spacious all at once. Leaving few meters of land after them, the tall and elegant trees stood in a perfectly straight line as if someone planted them to be so. To his right, on a faraway land, there was a huge water fall that seemed so quiet from this distance. The valley beneath was bleeding greenish black, and there was a furiously flowing river that was almost invisible, making its way through the forest. The night sky extended its curvature over the entire landscape and was shining with the lights from the already dead and still living stars. Bright and luminous was its texture. There was no moon, and its absence too was not felt anyway.

Prudhvi stood there in astonishment with the sudden change in his mind's aesthetic levels. He loved the way it all seemed – like a heaven on earth. The cool breeze of the night, a humid touch of the forest, sweet sound of the river and the shining sky that's reflecting the entire universe. He turned his head in a slow and heavy progress, powerless to take a look at the beauty all at once. As he finally turned to his extreme left, in the distant darkness he saw someone at the edge of the cliff.

It was Sanjuktha on her knees, and her hands were folded in prayer. She seemed so pure and pious in that posture. It felt like she was just physically present there.

Prudhvi smiled and started jumping over the rocks towards her, thinking 'How much more beautiful this night can get?'

"...and I will be fast every Wednesday as promised," she talked in a low tone and her eyes were tightly shut. "Thank you for listening. Thank you for bringing him back... Please don't let him leave me, Krishna. Never in this life again and for the next six lives too. Thanks for saving him from all the dangers that came by his way. Thanks for-"

"Talking to your Krishna?" Prudhvi shouted from a distance, and that gave her a mild jolt. She opened back her eyes and they were wet with tears; the tears which are the only physical proofs for years of her pain. "Say 'Hi' from my side."

"Ya, even he wants to talk to you," she said standing without turning back and rubbing the tears off as if she was just cleaning her face with her palms. "He says that you need to stop following me everywhere."

"You have the same habit madam," he said climbing the rock on which she stood. "You too follow me everywhere."

That really struck her. She said nothing in reply, but just turned back looking into his eye and walked past him smiling. She blushed descending the rock.

"See? You're blushing. Which means I am right," he said turning back to her.

"Aaaha? Then why did you come here in the first place? It's you who always follow. Not me," she said raising her head, not to look straight at him but in pride.

"Who said I followed you?" said Prudhvi climbing down to her. "I am in search of a place where I can puke. You see… the dinner you cooked-"

"Idiottttt… I hate you," Sanju shouted at once, trying to punch him as hard as she can. "You know I hate it when you tease me on how I cook." Her face started turning red. Her eyes went smaller, and her lower lip extended itself out making her look like an angry baby.

She was still in her wild trails to hurt him. But for Prudhvi, it all felt so calm and quite. He was happy to have her again, to see her alive, to able to touch her and all these were not just in a mere dream. He loved that they are fighting again and the way she turned into a kid over seconds.

He caught hold of both her hands at once, dragged her close and hugged her.

That came like more than a shock to her, but she immediately realised his intensions in doing so. He hugged her tighter than she had fantasized; meaning he missed her way more than she imagined. She hugged him back to tell him that she too felt the same way.

In front of the mighty forest and on the edges of the deepest valley, in the company of their silence echoing from the infinity, they hugged each other until the sky turned even darker.

* * *

"I am sorry for what happened to you," he wanted to say.

"It's ok. I don't regret anything now," she would have replied.

"I can't say how fortunate I am, that you are still alive," may be his next line.

"I am… just to see you return to me one day," might be hers.

But no one spoke. They just slept in the roots of a tree on the cliff and were staring at the stars. Sanjuktha slept on his left arm; with her head on his chest and hugging him close. He rolled his hand around her and held her tight. They were not lovers in lust. They were not a couple by marriage. They were just partners in fate.

"Sanju?" he said finally.

"Hmm?"

"Can I ask you something?"

"Hmm…"

"You must not say 'No'."

"Hmm…"

"Stop that," he said looking down to her.

"Hmmm…" She repeated controlling her giggle.

"Stop Hmming me, idiot," he cried out loud pinching her cheek.

"Awww…" she too cried, but in pain. "It hurts…" she complained rubbing her cheek. It stated turning reddish pink, and Prudhvi loved it.

"Why do you always want to kill me?" she screamed egging him with her puppy eyes.

"Awww… so sweet," he said rubbing the cheek he just pinched. It felt so soft and smooth on his rough palm. "Sing for me," he said at once.

"What?! No way..." she slept back adjusting herself.

"Please, Sanju..." Prudhvi started begging as his desperation took its turn.

"No," she smiled.

"Please please please... Ok, not even a complete song. Just a few lines."

Sanju loved the way he tried to please her. She always found it so calming, to sing to him. But never let him read her thoughts. "Which song?" she said.

"Our song?"

"Hmmm... You shouldn't laugh ok?"

"Did I ever do that?"

For the first time, she felt it little hard to start singing. 'Why am I feeling so shy to sing to whom I spent all my childhood singing to?' she wondered. He never made, at least, the silliest joke on how she sang. She too never thought what if he did. But this time, it was completely different. This time, she wanted to impress him.

She adjusted her throat and took in some extra reserve of oxygen into her lungs, as Prudhvi waited with butterflies in his stomach. The very thought of her singing made him go weak. And when she finally did, he felt heaven.

One morning, one morning, one morning in-

She ended it abruptly. 'What happened?' he thought of asking, but she took off again.

One morning, one morning, one morning in May,
I spied a young couple, just making their way.

Now, one was a soldier, and a brave one was he,
and the other was a lady, and a fine one was she.

And it's "Where are you going?" said the soldier, so free.
'I'm going to yon river; it's flowing for me.
Going down to yon river, and sit by that spring,
and watch the water gliding, hear the-"

And she smiled at once closing her face with her palm.

"What?" wondered Prudhvi trying to pull the hand off her face.

"Nothing," she blushed again. "That's it. You said *few lines* right?"

He fell back to his place smiling with pride. Those *few lines* were still reverberating in his ears.

'How could someone sing so sweet that only a few lines can make you feel an entire song?' He dragged her close and closed his eyes.

"I love you Sanju," he wanted to say. But ever other time he did that, they either ended up arguing, crying or getting separated for years. He wanted none of it to repeat now.

"Never sing to the British," he said instead.

She smiled knowing how big a compliment it was.

"I better cook for them. Right?"

"Right..." he smiled.

Slowly and warmly... silence intruded again. They hadn't uttered a word or left a sound except their pulsating breaths. They both took their time in adjusting their feelings.

It was Sanjuktha who spoke again.

"What if I had shot you?" she said at once.

"I know you wouldn't have."

"I would have… I can."

"You believe that you can, and I believed that you don't. Our actions depend on our beliefs."

"Like you don't believe in freedom?"

"And beliefs, too, change."

"It's opinions that change, not beliefs."

"Sometimes we believe that they are our beliefs. But they actually might be our opinions. Or might be our opinion on beliefs."

"So it's your opinion or…" she said smiling out of perplexity.

"Freedom?"

"Yeah."

"Once it was an opinion. Now I believe it, as I believe in you. You are freedom."

"Then the entire country wants me," she said smiling again.

"You're *my* freedom. But it's ok; I'll try to give you up then."

"What if something happens to me?"

"You tell me."

"Nothing may be. This world will just lose a crazy girl."

"And someone even crazier, will lose his world," he added, and that made her go calm for a second.

"You know something?" she said, still staring at the stars.

"Hmm…"

"The love that you have on me, *your* freedom… Standing point blank in front of a loaded gun… I wonder how it looks like if you have the same love towards the real freedom. What if my freedom, becomes yours?"

"What changes?"

"Me?" she said at once as if it's an involuntary dialog. "I may change. I may start looking at you in a different way. May be when you're willing to die for this country, I may be looking at you even more differently. May be with love?" Prudhvi looked down at her with surprise, but she hadn't moved. "But that's not right," she said immediately as if taking her words back. "I can't ask you to change. That won't be called love if I love you when you change for my love."

He thought of calming her down but failed to find ways. Sanju took her hand, the one with which she's hugging him, to wipe a tear from the corner of her eye and hugged him back. She wanted to love him, but she couldn't. She hated herself but loved the girl he loved.

Prudhvi started breathing heavy unable to bear her pain. 'Why do girls turn sentimental all the time?' he cursed. But rather than wondering about things that we can never change, it was better to act on it in one or the other way. So he finally did.

"I kissed a girl in London," he said at once.

"What?" Sanjuktha sprang out of shock raising her upper body to look back at him.

"Yup… I did," he smiled. "But she's just a friend, and that was just a moment."

"*Moment?*" she said in shock. "Oh my god. This is why you left me for London?"

"Who knows…" he tried to tease her.

"Get lost," she shrugged away from him. "Don't touch me with those hands."

"Sanju…" he shouted, pulling her back on to him. She fell back with a thud, and her face slammed on to his chest. "Listen to me. Really it was just a moment."

"Leave me, idiot," she said trying to get free of his hold. "I hate you."

"You won't stop without a fight ha?" He pulled her back even harder, getting hold of her tight by both her hands twisted back and restricting her from any movement. They were facing each other with just inches left between then and she still tried to wiggle. Her smooth curves were pressing over his masculine edges. With the sky full of stars in the background and her eyes shining equally bright, she seemed like a painting to him. Little droplets of sweat precipitated on to her skin, and few strands of hair fell on to her face making her look sexily angry.

"Now listen," he said trying to blow her hair back from her face. "And then tell me if you still hate me."

He struggled to start narrating. Sanju being so close to him and that too in a steaming hot avatar, with her babyish skin crying for him to kiss… but he did start.

For the next few minutes, Prudhvi narrated the whole story of his London trip. How he first met Emily, how they became friends, how he hated Luke, how he assaulted her, how they kissed out of innocence, why he left her then, how they survived the bombing that night and how he returned back to India to find her in the forest. Every detail that needed a mention was mentioned.

As he progressed in the story, Sanju slowly went loose from his grip and adjusted to her comfort. Now she was sleeping on her tummy, looking straight at him, with her chin on both her hands that are laid on his chest. Her feet were facing the sky and were moving like they are dancing. She still had her combat boots on.

"You know what?" Sanju said as he finally gave an end. This time, she had surprise written all over her face. "This girl, Emily… I think she loves you."

"What?" Prudhvi said in shock. "Nothing like that. That's not love."

"No, Prudhvi. I can say. A girl can say. She loves you."

"Seriously?"

"Yeah…"

"Should I go back then?" he asked acting grave. And that suddenly made her repent her own words.

"If you really wanted to," she said lowering her voice and sleeping on him, resting her cheek on his chest.

She hugged him again, but this time, to show that she may love him too.

"I won't," he said leaving a smiling sigh and grabbing her close. "She's my friend. Nothing more than that." And she smiled.

'Such tricky creation a girl was!' thought the night. 'She won't accept the love of this boy, and also feels jealous of who may.'

"I never thought you would choose this path," said Prudhvi with a sketch to drive away from this dangerous topic. He was happy that he survived this time and made a mental note of not to bring it up again.

"Which path?" She had no clue what he was talking about.

"Violence," he said as a matter of fact. "I always thought that you wanted to be a nurse."

"I did. But this is what we call destiny."

"Oh, I hate that word."

"Why? You don't want to see me like this?"

"No. You look great like a rebel too," he said patting her shoulder in support.

"Rebel is the not the way we look, Prudhvi. It's the way we react," she said smiling and Prudhvi suddenly felt a bump on her shoulder, under her shirt. He knows what exactly it was. It was the wound from the bullet she took that day. Prudhvi hated the thought of her flesh being cut and her body bleeding out.

"Who made you choose this?" he said, controlling his imaginations from wandering. "The path of violence."

"No one made me choose," she replied, wondering what's with the shift in his tone. "I chose this myself."

"Then what about non-violence that Gandhi was preaching?" He wanted to ask her this from the minute he saw her with a gun in her hand. "Your father always thought you to follow him."

"*Ahimsa paramo dharma*?" she said, after searching deep inside herself. "You know what? That's not the complete truth."

"What do you mean? Gandhi was lying?"

"No," she said in repulse. "Gandhi was not lying. But he's preaching only half-truth. '*Ahimsa paramo dharma. Dharma himsa tathaivu chu*'. That's the full verse. 'Non-violence is the ultimate dharma. So too is violence, in service of dharma.'"

"Who said so?" he enquired vaguely, staring at a star that's slowly making its way through the large group of other stagnant stars.

"Mahabharata," she said smiling, which made him wonder 'Why did she smile?' "Now don't search for your *science* in it darling. Sanskrit is the world's most scientific language."

"But don't you think our government now is on the quite opposite side?" he said watching the star pick up some pace.

"Rama killed Ravana to relieve Sita. Krishna killed Kansa to end his wickedness. And even Chhatrapati Sivaji overpowered and killed Afzal Khan, failing which he might have lost his own life, and many more lives of his people," she said at once. "We can't ignore the basic springs of human actions Prudhvi. Violence is nature's basic instinct."

"But it's not right to condemn the ways of a great leader like Gandhi," Prudhvi said. He felt strange listening to himself talk on such topic. That too with Sanju.

"The ways of *whom*?" she said turning back to him. He looked down from the star, and saw sudden anger creeping into her eyes. "Gandhi? If Gandhi was a leader more than a politician he is, why did he suspend the Non-Cooperation Movement when it was on the edges of pushing these dogs out of our country? Just over a single violent act in a small village when the whole country was still on his tracks? I don't think so. C R Das was dumbfounded with sorrow and resentment, Motilal Nehru also protested, and Lala Lajpat Rai wrote a 70-page letter to him. But nothing could compel him to reject his determined and futile decision. It was a national disaster, Prudhvi."

"If not that, why did he let Bhagat Singh die in the hands of British?" she said sleeping back on him, trying to sound normal. "He could have made it a mandatory clause before he signed the Gandhi-Irwin pact, that they should release Bhagat, Rajguru and Sukhdev. But what did he do? Call them terrorists? Trying to divert the aggression by stating that the Bhagat Singh worship is doing incalculable harm to the country? Don't you remember the outburst of the youth brigade when he reached Karachi to inaugurate the Indian Congress there?"

"Gandhi loves his idealisms more than his motherland, whereas Bose loves his motherland above all ideologies.

There might be other faces to this argument. And I am sure that there are many. But what we believe is in the words that Bose said. 'Remember that the greatest crime is to compromise with injustice and wrong'. It's not just our opinion, but we believe in it. And we follow what we believe. Simple…"

Prudhvi said nothing but just gave her some space to settle her emotions. But that was not what was happening on her side. She was still burning in anger. She wanted to tell him in a way he understood.

Prudhvi never understood freedom. Being liberated even in a cage was freedom. Being controlled out of it was not.

"What would you do if Canning was still alive?" she said at once.

Prudhvi raged with impulsive anger. He clenched his teeth at the very sound of that word 'Canning'.

"You would have killed him for sure," she said. "Because he raped your love, right?"

Prudhvi kept his silence. He didn't want to listen to her and looked up to concentrate on the star again. But it went missing.

"Right?" Sanjuktha said raising her voice as if to tell him that she needed an answer.

"Right," he said trying to pull himself together.

"That's what was happening to our country, Prudhvi. The British are raping our mother. The land we are living on is bleeding. Should we flaunt our second cheek to them? Or should we fight back?"

He went silent again, but this time she was in need of no response.

"I don't know if I can tell you this," she said. "But I think I should. My uncle, your father… Mr. Koundinya Prathap Raju. He raped me, Prudhvi."

"What?" Prudhvi cried out trying to sit up.

"Please… I don't want to look at you," she said pushing him back hugging him tight. He felt tears raging inside her.

"That day, almost after one-week, Canning took me…" she stopped. Her voice was trembling. Prudhvi felt his senses leave his body. He started sliding into trauma. "That day, uncle came to visit me. He asked me to promise that I'll leave you forever. He wanted to bring you back from London once you're done with your studies and join you in the British intelligence. He thought that I'll make you join the freedom fighters.

"I begged him to make me free from all that. I cried my eyes out to get me out of there. I know he treats me as his daughter, but it's just because of you, he hates me. But that's not true… He warned me to stay away from you. I agreed. He wanted me never to see you again in this life. I agreed for that too. But…" she went silent again. It all felt like a dream to Prudhvi and he somehow knew that there was more to come. He was crying his life out, but without making a sound. "He warned me never to tell you what your mother always wanted you to know… And I couldn't promise him that. Your mom took a word from my father to pass you her message, and I promised my father that I would help him keep it. So I said that I can't. He tried to shout it into me. I refused. He slapped me, called me names, pulled my Mangalsutra and threw it away, slammed me into walls… and finally, he did what a man can lastly do to hurt a girl."

"He raped you," Prudhvi said while his tears burned his eyes.

"I thought of killing him. We went to kill him in fact," she said. "But I realised that I still see him as my father. He's no different to me. I failed to kill him, Prudhvi. The man who raised me in his arms once. He might be a monster now. But I still see a father."

Saying so, she went silent again, and no one talked for a while. It's just the wind and the river that made the air tremble into another deep trench of silence.

"Who gave him that power Prudhvi?" she finally said, and her voice was heavier that his heart. She was sobbing now, and he felt her tears burning their way through his chest. "Who filled him with the poison of power? Why did he ever change? Why did he want a child not to know her mother's last words to him? Who on this earth should he-"

"What is it?" Prudhvi said cutting her off, and she turned to look at him, moved by the way he sounded. His eyes were red as blood, and he was dying not to cry. "What's that my mom wanted me to know?" he said, now looking straight at her and that made her realise that the time had come.

"It's a simple message Prudhvi," she said sounding as normal as possible and not caring to move away before she uttered those words. "*I may be dead, even before you know me, son. And that's ok. You can forget someone who carried you until you are born. But please don't forget the one who carries you until you die. The land you stand on… Remember to fight for it, and so I name you Prudhvi – The Earth.*"

"My mom said this?" he said shivering and trying to cope.

"She wrote a letter," she said smiling with pain. "I used to have it all the time. But I never told you. I don't know why I …" She lost words and moved her eyes away in vain. "You know what?" she said looking back at him as if she remembered something. "Your longhand resembles your mom's."

He said nothing but just stared into her eyes wondering how much more pain they can accumulate and how many more secrets they withheld.

They slept under that tree for the night. Actually, it was only Sanjuktha who fell asleep. Prudhvi was up all night touching her shoulder, to feel the wound from the bullet she took. He watched her sleep for, like, hours. Just breathing in, and breathing out. And he knew that she was dreaming, from her eyes rolling under her eyelids. The sky started turning its colors as Prudhvi started sorting all the chaos, turning it into a verdict. He had never been good at swift decisions. But this time, it felt right. With all the pain that left through his eyes, he filled the gap with a strength that the same pain gave him.

* * *

It was the babbling of the river that woke her up. The birds were singing the early-morning rhymes, and the sun was still hiding behind the horizon sending rays that diffracted through the forest fog. She was still in the roots of the tree they slept under last night, but there's no sign of Prudhvi nearby. Sanjuktha got up clearing the dust off her clothes and started walking into the forest. She had never known that the valley seemed this beautiful early in the morning. But she had no time to waste on nature. She wanted to be with him for every second she could, walk the entire forest, making camps, attacking the British and one-day witness freedom together.

She smiled as she walked. Might be some crazy memory from last night. She seemed as a newly-wed teenage girl walking out of her honeymoon room. As she neared the tents, she tried to throw away that face and started acting strict and stiff again. The last few meters asked her to smile for one last time; the girlish smile she always wanted to smile. Hiding behind a tree, she smiled, jumped, blushed and celebrated all her extremeness out; and then walked back as Madam Sanjuktha into the camp. No one can imagine what she's inside right now.

Though she thought of having her first words of the day with Prudhvi, Bilva reached her before she found him.

"Chief, a letter for you," he said handing her a rolled cloth.

"Letter?" she said in surprise. "This is not the time for our spies to reach us. Why did they-"

"It's from your husband, Chief," Bilva said.

Sanjuktha suddenly saw something in his eyes. Bilva had never been this strong while talking to her. He meant something more than she could comprehend.

"Where is he?" she said almost on the edge of breaking.

"He's finally on the right path, Chief. He had-"

"I said WHERE-IS-HE?" she shouted, and the whole camp echoed. She knew that something went terribly wrong. "Bring him back, now. Or you're all going to die in my bloody hands."

No one moved from their places, and even Bilva feared to talk now.

"It's you I am talking to, fool," she went on to him as if to smash his face. He fell back a few steps. "Where the hell is my husband?"

"He…" Bilva tried to tell her the truth but also feared she might really shoot him. "He went on to join Bose," he finally said.

"What?! What did you say?"

"He wanted to join Bose," Bilva said gathering all this courage. "He wanted to fight for freedom. He said he had skills, which may get wasted here, and can help you in your fight only if he walks away for now."

Sanjuktha said nothing. She found no reason to. 'He left to join Bose?' she taught trying to take it in as calmly as possible. Few edgy minutes passed by in silence, and no one moved.

*Prudhvi wanted to fight for freedom…*she still wondered. It felt like her aunt, and her father was smiling somewhere. 'Prudhvi wanted to fight for freedom?' she thought to herself again. 'My husband is a freedom fighter?' she smiled on it. It felt like he was still with her. It felt like one can call them *Made for each other* now.

But the girl inside was still crying unable to bear the distance, and Sanjuktha was dying to stop her from proving her existence. Half the amount of tears that was leaving her eyes was out of pride, and the other half, with pain. Her heart started extending itself in opposite directions, and it felt like it was going to break into halves.

'How can someone love as he does?' Sanju wondered. She realised what she failed to see all this time. Not all great things in life come at a price. Some are given for free. It's we who ignore their value as we kept no efforts in getting them.

"He can always stay here with you Chief," Bilva said breaking the silence. But she was still staring at the grass at her feet. "That's what he always wanted right? He could have easily done that. But now he loves freedom more than he loves you, just because you love it more than you love him. Husbands of that kind are rare Chief," he said and moved away, turning back to leave. But something stopped him. He had few last words to tell her.

"Chief," he said, and Sanjuktha looked up at him. "Happy married life."

* * *

Dear Sanjuktha,

Remember these as my words: 'What that asks you to change for good… is definitely Love.' And you had done me the greatest favor of my life. You gave me a chance to make you love me. I'll see you Sanju when you see freedom. Meanwhile, keep singing whenever you get a chance to. And you'll see me whenever you sing. I'll touch you like the wind, feel you like the rain and reach you as a dream. But will definitely miss your Mango-Dal and potato fry.

Love,
Prudhvi.

P.S: Last night was the best night of my life.

This was the hundredth time she was reading his letter, but still crying as the first. She wanted that one day, the day on which they are together again to repeat forever. If not, she wanted to stay here, in her tent and cry all day long and this day to repeat forever. But none was possible. They should move, and she must lead. She was the Chief now, and there was no place for grief or sorrow in her schedule. There were lives of her men depending on her decisions.

Knowing that there was no more chance to; she wanted to hug him really bad. She wanted to cry in his hands, get teased by him and fight with him for one last time. But what she did was to stand up, pushing all other thoughts to the darkest corners of her heart, to walk out of her tent and ordered her men to evacuate the area.

No one talked while cleaning or a word uttered.

It was when she reached the center space to pick up her bags she left near the camp fire last night; Bilva came running with a transceiver kit hanging by his good side and the headset around his neck. He seemed as if he heard something.

"What happened?" she said in shock.

What Bilva said in reply, made her go numb and fall back on to a camp chair behind her.

"Someone killed your uncle and threw him into the river," he said panting.

Chapter 8

Four months later

03:35 am

25th December 1940

Dum Dum Airfield. Calcutta.

Dressed in his brown business suit Prudhvi waited for someone in the dark. His hair was thoroughly oiled, combed and face was neatly shaved. The semi-formal shoes were the best he could manage, but they were not the main concern now. It felt like the light sky blue colored tie that was trying it's best to choke him to death hadn't suited the attire. 'But it won't look good without a tie,' he thought being on the edges of not knowing whether to pull it off.

This meeting was very important to him. He was going to meet a man who could help him meet Bose. Drutha was his name, and he was the quality inspector on the construction site at the airport. It had been already late, and no one knew when the British will arrest Bose again. Even though he was at his home in Calcutta now, he had been surrounded by the British force all the time. It was only because of the hunger strike Bose went on during the last week of November, they released him, pretending as if a neutral situation was created. The British knew that a dead Bose could turn more dangerous than a living one.

A sudden chill passed down his spine, and his body left an impulsive shiver. The temperatures of December, that too on an early hour like this, are unbearable. Prudhvi was standing near a small and thin blue iron gate; that was part of the right wing of a much bigger, thick and tall gate made of the same metal and of the same color. It seemed like it may take more than a group of people to open them wide. Both sides of the higher gates had unending concrete walls of an equal height extending into the night. It was still very dark, and there was no source of light anywhere near him. Even if there was one, it might not have helped much due to the heavy fog that was restricting his visibility to just a few meters. He tried to create some frictional heat with his palms but that hadn't helped much.

"Hello," said someone from his right and Prudhvi turned at once. A blurred-out figure walked towards him through the fog. The light from the infinity gave some visibility. Prudhvi made his eyes smaller to have a keen look at it, to see a man in the same attire as his, walk towards him. But his suit was black in color, and he had a hat on. He was little chubby when compared to Prudhvi with a typical north Indian fair complexion. There was no tie around his neck, and it seemed like it was not being missed. He carried a brown leather suitcase too.

"Merry Christmas," he said extending his hand to Prudhvi and blinking his eyes.

"Merry Christmas…" Prudhvi shook his hand trying hard to remember his name. The way the man is behaving; it's diverting his focus to even wider extents. It's weird that he flapped his eyelids for more than thirty times by now.

Drutha wrote in his letter that he will meet a Bearded-Indo-Christian man in a black suit at exact 03:30 in the morning and his name followed. Beard, Black suit, Indo-Christian… everything matched and he even seemed like a man too. But what was his name?

"It was Christmas for us. I mean 'Us'." The man said pointing his figure towards himself, and smiling like a fool. "But for the Jews, it's the Hanukkah. You know what Hanukkah is?"

"No…" Prudhvi said still trying to the name.

"It's the," and he smiled again. The same smile. "It's the Jewish festival of lights. Like Diwali for us. I mean 'Us'," he said pointing his figure towards Prudhvi now and smiled again. For every smile, he's bending a little and closing his eyes tight.

Prudhvi felt the brilliance of Drutha – using a mentally unstable man to smuggle him inside.

"My name is Prudhvi," he said, hoping for him to reply with his.

"But Christmas had also been celebrated by the early Church on January 6th," he said looking away from Prudhvi and wanting to spit out all the information he knew about the occasion. "On the same day, they also celebrated the Epiphany. And… And it is…" he struggled to remember as Prudhvi stared at him in silence, to let him speak. He felt so bad to use someone like him to get his work done. "It means the revelation that Jesus was God's son; and the Baptism of Jesus… Epiphany mainly celebrates the visit of the 'Wise Men' to the baby Jesus." Finishing off the last lines even quickly, he turned back to Prudhvi.

"I am Richards," he said extending his hand again and panting.

"Richards ya ya right," Prudhvi said shaking his hand and finally out of the doubt.

Richards took his hand back, stared at the passage door and back at Prudhvi, done some heavy math in his suffocating brain and finally looked up at him, blinking eyes.

"Let's get...... inside," he said opening the door. The door made a loud squeak and he gave a sudden halt turning back to Prudhvi with doubt pouring out of his eyes. Prudhvi felt that something was very wrong. Richards may not be as foolish as Prudhvi thought he was. He was staring at him like a professional detective, and all the foolishness was gone now. Prudhvi was on his edge and no immediate plan of action crossed his mind.

He walked back to Prudhvi swiftly, gazed at him in some anger-type-of expression and said in breaking sentences, "I hate... hate the color. Your tie... throw it off."

Prudhvi's jaw dropped at once.

"Throw it off... and follow me," he said walking past the gate in quick movements.

Prudhvi smiled as he finally pulled the tie off his neck and took some extra oxygen in, in celebration.

* * *

As they walked across the vast empty concrete land, towards the hangar that stood alone hiding in the darkness; Richards spoke nothing. Not even a single word, but just turned back to Prudhvi in frequent intervals as if to check if he was following or not. Every time Richards turned back, Prudhvi smiled at him. A very friendly smile, to let him know that he was no different than him. But it seemed that the message was not properly received.

For the first few meters, it felt like they were in a concrete desert. What Prudhvi saw was fog, darkness and Richards's back. But after a walk of approximately 800 meters, during which Prudhvi jogged at intervals to keep in pace with the fast walker Mr Richards, he started seeing lights, but blurry as it appeared beyond the fog.

When they finally did reach the hangar; unexpectedly the fog started clearing off, and the wind started blowing heavy, as if it was going to rain. The sudden change in the climate surprised Prudhvi. Normally wind didn't mix up with fog. But Richards was as calm as he already had this weird weather report. They walked with their hands above their eye levels to avoid the strong wind from pushing the lids down and tilted their bodies a little in the opposite direction of the blow. Richards held his suitcase with one hand while the other stopped his hat from flying away. The wind turned even stronger as they progressed and all of a sudden, it stopped. The fog ended and Prudhvi's jaw dropped again, this time to much deeper depths.

He was on the premises of a construction site where they were laying a runway alongside the hangar. A very large section of the land is being used, and there were large electronic blades all over the place that are rotating at high speeds, clearing the fog off the land. Prudhvi turned back to see that they had just crossed one of them. He stepped away from it fearing that it may drag him into it.

There were large wooden towers standing in a circle around the site, from which the brightest of lights are being focused on to the center area, making the surroundings turn much darker. Each of the towers also had a British guard on it, holding a Double Rifle hunting gun. In the circle, there were manually operated mixers, bullock carts bringing bags of concrete, women carrying water pots to fill the tankers on the other side, imported tractors, some tents in between the towers, asphalt boiling in drums and huge iron rollers being pulled by Indian workmen.

Few British soldiers were roaming around in the site, inspecting the work. There is also a crew of well-educated people near the tents, who were in their work formals, inspecting a blueprint that was spread wide on the table between them. All of them seemed Indian, and Prudhvi knew that one of them was Drutha.

"The tent… the backside of the light," Richards said, and Prudhvi turned to him from the shock. "See?" he said pointing his hand with the suitcase to their left.

Prudhvi turned to look at what he was trying to show him. It took few seconds to the tent that was behind the light towers to fall into his visible bandwidths.

"See it?" Richards said starting to get irritated.

"Ya ya… I see it. I see it."

"Wait there. Sir Drutha will see… try to see you," he said stepping away and stopped to turn back. "He will see you," he repeated as if correcting a mistake, and left him alone, walking towards the tent on the site, blinking his eyes.

'What in hell did he do here?' thought Prudhvi, as he walked towards the tent taking a stroll around the hangar to avoid attention.

* * *

"So you are the one?" said Drutha walking into the tent, after making him wait for almost 40 minutes.

"Sir." Prudhvi stood up at once.

He was a man in his late thirties and the bald spot looked like it was older than him. Side effects of being a genius. He wore a light brown colored cotton shirt that he tucked into his black pleated silk pants. His leather suspenders made Prudhvi remember his. The black and thick safety shoes, sleeves that are folded tight up to the elbow level and the dust all over him completed the quality inspector look.

"Drutha," he said extending his hand.

"Prudhvi, sir." They shook hands.

"Why there is a shock in your eyes?" said Drutha moving to the other side of the tent.

"Nothing, sir," he said trying to duck. Prudhvi wanted no unnecessary topics to be discussed. He waited for months to meet this guy, and there was no more time to waste.

"That's a new runway being built," he said pouring some tea from a kettle into two porcelain cups and it seemed as if the tea was as cold as ice. Prudhvi hated it that way. "19R-01L; it's going to be about 8000 ft. and will be extensively used to launch B17 bombers to the Japan occupied Burma front. May turnout to be one of the fastest laid runways in history."

"War can make us push any limit, sir."

"Ya, right," he said with a small and heavy curve on his lips. "You're in the Indian army?"

"Yes sir, the fake one."

That made Drutha turn to Prudhvi at once. He stared at him for a second or two and broke out laughing.

"Nice to hear that young man," he said laughing out loud.

Prudhvi stood in silence as Drutha dropped two cubes of sugar in each cup. He smiled again as he carried the cups to Prudhvi. Prudhvi took his cup trying to hide his own smile. It felt good, making the first impression.

"So you want to work for the real army?" he said resting on the iron bed. "Sit down."

Prudhvi sat on the camp chair. "Yes, sir. I want to free this country at any cost. I want to work for the real leader, Mr Bose."

"Owwowww… Easy young man. Relax," said Drutha turning directions to look at any moving shadows near the tent.

"Sorry sir," he said lowering his voice.

"I know what you meant Prudhvi. And you even sounded like Mr Bose himself for a second," he said moving close to Prudhvi. "But the situations are not so well now. Bose can't stay here in the country for long. He's planning to leave."

"Leave?" Prudhvi shouted in a whisper out of shock. "Leave where?"

"Russia."

"What's there in Russia, sir?"

"Support," he said with more stress on that word. "That had gone extinct for rebels in our country."

"But how can-" he stopped not knowing how to react and what to ask.

"See Prudhvi," said Drutha as if to calm him down, "there are not just white dogs in our country now. There are brown ones too. And most of them had power in their hands. It's impossible to fight back with what we have."

"We had Bose."

"Not for a long time if he stays here," he said moving his head in support of his sentence.

Prudhvi left a sigh trying to exhale his disappointment out.

"We can't smuggle people from here to join us," he said. "But you can maintain in the Indian army and form a group of your own. Instil them with ideas as yours, and when we return with the army formed by means of Indian prisoners in Africa, Germany and many other lands, you can join us with your group and fight for freedom."

That hadn't calmed Prudhvi down. Not even to the minimal extent. He wanted to join them right away. He can't wait for someone to return. He wanted to walk with them when they do.

"Sorry Prudhvi," Drutha said.

"You agreed to meet me to tell *this*?" he wanted to ask. But instead, he said: "I don't want to leave empty-handed, sir. But if you are to send me so, I had my strings in your Intelligence. I can follow you guys and meet you up where you land."

Drutha was dumbfounded by his comment, and the look on his face made Prudhvi wonder if the arrow in the dark struck the target.

"I know you're just trying to break me," Drutha said as confident as he literally knew the truth. "But how do you know that we had our Intelligence?"

"India is a very vast land, sir. And you connect to rebels far away from here, somewhere in the thickest of the forests."

Drutha smiled. "Ya, that's easy to guess. Have you worked for any kind of intelligence, ever?"

"No, sir. But I have passed all the rounds to call myself qualified to work in the SIGNIT wing. I can, at least, help you with it until-"

"Signal Intelligence?!" said Drutha as if he heard the whole sentence wrong.

"Yes sir, Signal Intelligence."

"Oh my god," he said standing up, and Prudhvi followed. "You know this stuff about encryptions and decryptions?"

"Yes, sir."

"Not many Indians do these days," he thought to himself and turned to him again. "How good are you?"

"High level cryptography, sir. Topper for three consecutive semesters. Imperial King's, London."

Now it was Drutha's turn to have a shock in his eyes. "And then?"

"And then, sir…the Germans bombed our college," he said smiling.

"Oh my god," Drutha too smiled. "You may perfectly suit the role we are searching for."

Each of the words felt like honey to his ears. He said 'You *may*…' but Prudhvi knew that 'He *can*…' by hook or crook. Actually 'He *should*…' It was the only shot he got now.

"I *will be* sir," he said trying to cope up with the excitement of the elderly man. "I can suit any job you wish me to take up. All that I want is to meet Mr Bose once and-"

"But there might be few constraints," said Drutha talking to himself again, uninterested in Prudhvi's words anymore. "You should get to know this guy. But there's no time to if you are to be hired for the job."

"Know whom sir?" Prudhvi said trying his best to hide his impatience.

"The one for whom you need to work. Have you heard of the recent breakthrough in tracking the German signals?"

"No, sir."

"It's the brilliancy of this guy who's saving the British, I mean Indians who fight for British in the battle field. He works for the government. The fake one, as you may say. And also for us. He's our best guy inside the system. Sit down," he said calming down and trying to keep up his cool again.

They sat back in their places and Drutha started explaining him the excellence of Indians in helping the enemy.

"Every day, at 04:46 am our time, the Germans transmit a signal. It travels all its way to Imperial Japan; counting its major air time on Russia and touching the lands of Poland, Belarus, Kazakhstan and China. The transmission only lasts for one and a half minute and every day, on the same time, in the given interval, an Indian from his office in Kashmir, tracks it.

"Not just tracking, but he retrieves the key, and decode the message. It mostly contains information of the very next attack that they plan. The Axis Powers never trusted each other as the Allied forces did and they exchange information only in the last minute.

"They transmit horizontally polarized waves which extends one of its two main lobes towards Indian subcontinent. They can opt for vertical polarization to avoid that, and even it's the recommended option for ground-wave transmission. But they can't, as the Japanese use only horizontally polarized receivers. So the Germans transmit highly powerful signals to avoid the decaying that occur in horizontal polarization. And that had been an added advantage to us."

"But suddenly one day, when the Germans came to know that most of their surprise attacks are getting countered and are being handled with unexpected preparations, they changed their Omni-directional transmitters to Directional. The power of two lobes is packed into one, and it is pointed away from the British-India. They also built a middle office on the lands between Kara and Laptev Sea. It's the farthest part of Russian land from India. Thus, the distance got even farther, and the power from even the back lobe is not enough to reach us. We can't ask the Soviet Union for help, as Stalin was still ignoring the reports of the German invasion. He's on their side after the ten years Non-Aggression pact.

"So we lost it… May be we can come up with a new technique to tap the back lobe though it's full of noise, but it will be of no use. The signal they transmit is a Symmetric-Chained-Key signal. One of the key from the last four days will help you decode today. You lose the signal continuously for four days, and you're gone. We also had no time to consult the American government and ask them for help as they are still neutral. Everyone thought that it's impossible to break them now. But on the third day… this guy started sending codes to Delhi again."

"What?" exclaimed Prudhvi. "How did he do that?"

"Simple. The strength of the signal is higher than normal even from the start, because of the polarization issue. And now two such lobes are merged into one. Imagine how far it can reach. He travelled from Kashmir to the southernmost point in the Nicobar Islands and tracked it all the way around the globe."

"Damn," Prudhvi laughed tapping his thigh. "Such a simple thing? Wow…"

"All simple things are once very difficult," he said taking a sip of his tea. "Have it."

Prudhvi too sipped his tea smiling. It felt good with the excitement now. "He started sending the codes on the third day... Which meant, he decided to travel just in a span of few hours after he came to know the situation? And how could he reach there in two days?"

"That day the government provided him with a personal helicopter that takes him to any place he wanted in India, just in the count of hours."

"Great. I would love to work for a guy like him, sir." Prudhvi said, really excited.

"Rudhra. Now I remember," Drutha said. "Rudhra was his name."

"Rudhra?" Prudhvi said smiling. "There used to be a guy with that name, sir. My best friend. Now he's in the-", and he stopped at once. His mind started to bark at him like a crazy dog. "Sir, do this Rudhra belong to somewhere near Narsipatnam?" he said with shock that made Drutha look up from his cup.

"Yes," he said in a slow and dragging tone. "Why did you ask?"

"Rudhrama Naidu, is that his full name?!"

"Yes. I think that's it," Drutha said with doubt in his eyes. Not because of the name, but because of the question 'How did this guy know that?' "Do you know him?" he said placing his cup aside and turning eager for his answer.

'Rudhra?!' Prudhvi thought to himself and the image of a sixteen-year-old boy holding his friend in his arms grip trying to tease him, on the bank of a lake, in the middle of the night; flashed before his eyes. He couldn't believe what he just heard. The same guy, who once said that he could even go on a real suicide mission if he got to kill at least a British soldier; was now really on the other side, risking his life. And Prudhvi was going to join him in it.

'I will die either for freedom or in freedom,' Rudhra once told Prudhvi, and he never understood his friend. Prudhvi argued with him that day and left them in anger as Suryam and Saleem stood in support for Rudhra. 'You're not sick Prudhvi. You're mad. Sick makes it sound like there's a cure,' Rudhra shouted at him as he left. He hated his friends when it was about freedom. And he was regretting it now. He wanted to be with them for one last time. Tell them that he failed to see what they always tried to teach him. Ask them for an apology. And he suddenly realised that Saleem and Suryam were no more…

All at once, his heart started crying for the companionship of his friends. 'It's not the dead who die… It's the living' he realised.

"You ok?" Drutha said placing his hand in support on his shoulder. Prudhvi is in tears. He hated himself for years of his innocence and a life time of arrogance.

"I am sorry, sir." Prudhvi sniffed and rubbed his face in fast movements of his hands. "Some old memories of my friends who were heroes.

"I have treated them in a very wrong way, sir," he said turning to look at Drutha.

"It's ok," Drutha said. "At one or the other time, we all might have done some dreadful things in our lives. Or have felt the urge to. What that counts is, we shouldn't die with them."

They sat in silence for the next few minutes.

Drutha smiled remembering some old memories. He too was missing his good old days with his friends. "Where did your friends come from all of a sudden?" he finally said trying to smile, so that Prudhvi may smile back.

"Rudhra is one among them, sir."

"What?!" he yelled at once.

"Yes, sir. We were friends," he said with pride, and it felt great to call himself his friend.

"Close?" Drutha enquired with his growing interest in finding the perfect pair of spies Mr Bose was in search of.

Prudhvi had thought for a second before he answered. "I don't know if you can believe this, sir," he said looking deep into his eye. "We used to play cryptography as kids."

* * *

"I can't believe that all this is happening," Drutha said as they walked into the darkness, towards the hangar. "You fell out of nowhere, turned out to be a SIGNIT expert and a very good friend of Rudhra. This seems like even the gods want our country to be free at last."

Prudhvi smiled at his words. "Where are we headed, sir?" he said trying not to fall forward from the push of the wind. The men on the site were still deeply immersed in their work.

In no time, there are in the fog and darkness again.

"To see Mr Bose," Drutha replied after a long pause.

"What?!" Prudhvi made a sudden halt.

Drutha too stopped to turn to him. "Don't get shocked. We *are* going to meet him."

"But he's surrounded by the British right now."

"Remember this for future reference kid," he said walking back to Prudhvi. "No army in this world is big enough to contain Bose. He *is*, and he *will be* as free as the wind."

"But…" Prudhvi tried to spit out few of his unstoppable doubts. However, he decided better not to.

"I know. I know," smiled Drutha as they walked again. "You had your doubts. But still… are you excited to meet him?"

"Yes, sir," he said involuntarily, still involved in his own doubts.

"But actually," Drutha said turning back to Prudhvi and making a halt again. They are near the side wall of the hangar. "You already met him," he said smiling.

"What?!" he looked up to Drutha at once.

"You already met him Prudhvi."

"I met who, sir?"

"What 'who'? Mr Bose. You already met him." Drutha enjoyed the change of colors on Prudhvi's face.

"I didn't get you, sir. Is this a joke or-" and it struck him with a jolt. Prudhvi stared at Drutha with his mouth wide open as he smiled at him. "Richards?" he said.

Drutha smiled brighter, in a 'Yes.'

* * *

Prudhvi was still in shock. He was dying to cope up with the fact that Richards was Bose himself. He had seen him many times in many newspapers, but no features of Richards matched them. He might be acting like a mentally unstable man, but even the physical sorts were not in sync. What was with the heavy beard? Where were the typical Bose-type round framed spectacles? And how did he elude the British guards all around his house?"

"Don't think of it too much," Drutha told him when they walked past the small iron gates that lead them into the hangar. "It's not your fault. He's the master of disguise, deception and competence."

Now they were in the small thin and long office room that was built with temporary cardboard walls. To reach here, they walked all the length of the huge and hollow hangar, passing many fighter aircrafts. The royal and beastly beauty of the single-engine monoplane fighters, and few heavy bomber aircrafts that were parked inside the hangar turned Prudhvi speechless. Most of them had propeller blades in front of them with round beaks, three fixed wheels and very curvy edges that made them look more like stuffed toys than bomber planes. 'In a way, they are just toys really. It's us, who use them for a different purpose,' Prudhvi thought making his palm feel the smooth mightiness of a bomber prototype's belly.

Witnessing mass-scale potential death in a single place made Prudhvi realise that over the past few centuries, the human race has developed into a very sophisticated and technologically advanced group of mammals which can get itself extinct just over a silly conflict. There was even a highly believed rumor that the Americans now had the plan of a fission bomb that broke very large atoms like Uranium or Plutonium in a super-critical chain reaction, causing damage that can swipe countries off the face of the earth. It's being alleged that they already had few working prototypes too.

"Here he comes," said Drutha making Prudhvi jump up from his bottomless thoughts.

Prudhvi was standing against the rusty iron table in one corner of the room, which had loads of files dumped on it; while Drutha stood at the other end, near the rectangular hole cut in the cardboard wall that's used as an entrance into the room. Prudhvi was staring at Drutha who's gazing out of the door, and the distance between his eye balls decreased gradually as if his eyes are on someone who's walking towards him. It's his shadow that strolled through the entrance first and Drutha's lips curved into a friendly smile. And then he walked in. Richards.

They shook hands and slid into a quick conversation. They were talking something that was inaudible to Prudhvi. Drutha was so excited to be where he was, and Richards too smiled like he was being entertained. While they conversed inaudibly, every now and then Drutha was turning to look at Prudhvi, who was gawking at the man in front of him.

After a few more minutes of chat, which turned into a more professional and serious one towards the end, Drutha pointed his figure towards Prudhvi and Richards turned to look at him in surprise. That made Prudhvi go weak in his stomach, and it felt like Richards could tear his skin apart any second from now, turning into Mr Bose.

And it did happen, in a way. They both started walking towards Prudhvi, as Richards took off his hat, revealing a clean bald spot that is almost to the back of his head. The hair that remained was black and shiny. He was still blinking his eyes as he tried to take a good look at Prudhvi.

"It's very difficult without the glasses," he said in a steady tone, glancing at Drutha and smiling. Drutha too smiled. Turning back to Prudhvi, he took a pair of lenses out of his coat's inner pocket, which were fitted inside a round metal frame. The split second he wore the magic glasses on, they turned Richards into a completely different man. A man the whole country is looking for and looking up to – Mr Subhash Chandra Bose.

"Hello Mr. Prudhvi," said Bose, extending his hand and smiling. "Nice to meet you, again."

Prudhvi extended his hand in slow and heavy motion, with his mouth still wide open and his eyes glued to the face of the man who's smiling like a legend. 'Am I going to shake hands with Subhash Chandra Bose?' he wondered. The touch of his hand made Prudhvi shiver with bewilderedness. He's breathing heavy now, and the pores on his skin started pouring.

"I think you need a doctor," Bose smiled again. This time, Prudhvi too smiled back along with Drutha. "You seem like someone who easily gives away in an enemy troop."

"No, sir," Prudhvi said in an immediate response as Drutha tried to jump for his rescue. He stopped in half a step and went back to his place turning to Prudhvi.

"Nothing of that kind," he said looking straight into Bose's eye. He knows he should make the first impression here too. "My own people always make me wonder. The enemy is easier to deal with."

Bose broke into an impulsive smile. That made Prudhvi's heart stop racing, and it started coming back to normal.

"It seems like your sprit is unbreakable. Is it?" Bose said.

Prudhvi wanted to make a second impression too. The stronger, the better.

"No, sir. Actually, it's very easily breakable," he said. "But the thing is that I always build it back, immediately."

There was a smile again, brighter than before. Bose turned to Drutha as he smiled and then back at Prudhvi.

"Sit down, young man," he said dragging an old wooden chair for him and patting on his shoulder, making him sit. Drutha sat on a drum that was stacked near the wall, as Bose adjusted another chair to face Prudhvi. "Tell me, how far you can go to make your country free. How deep is your belief in freedom through aggression?"

Prudhvi said nothing but lowered his eyes from him. He's in the presence of a person he never thought he would meet in this life. A great rebel he is and a soft man from inside, as the nation called him. Prudhvi wanted to tell him the truth. The truth that he never believed in freedom. But that may lead to misunderstandings. It's a very thin thread that hangs between reality and certainty. But whatever the case was, Prudhvi hated the thought of bluffing with a man, who was a legitimate leader.

"What difference will it make, sir?" Prudhvi said turning back to Bose, to warm it up before the actual truth was spelled. "What is that with our beliefs?"

Bose smiled combing his thick beard with his hand. 'Why in the hell did he grow a beard? Is it too a part of the plan?' Prudhvi thought.

"A man is made by his beliefs. As he believes, so he is – Bhagavad Gita," said Bose in an intensive tone. He sounded like Sanjuktha for a second. "You need to believe in what you wish for. Don't you believe in freedom through-"

"I don't believe in freedom at all, sir," Prudhvi said at once.

"What?" exclaimed Drutha from behind and they both turned to him.

"You don't believe in freedom?" Bose asked in a calm and steady tone, turning to Prudhvi.

He looked back at Bose but took his time before he opened his mouth to prepare the exact words that should be uttered. "No, sir. I never believed in freedom. I regret it now, but… I don't know if I still believe."

Bose said nothing but stared at Drutha. Prudhvi wanted to turn back, to see what he was talking with his eyes. But he didn't. He was left with things to say.

"A man is made by his beliefs, sir," he said, making Bose turn back to him. "So does he, by his choices. I choose to fight for freedom. In any way, you want me to."

"Why do you choose something in which you don't believe?"

"They say that we are the choices we make, sir," he said moving his head in a 'No.' "Not always. Sometimes we are the choices others make too."

Bose said nothing but just stared at him for seconds. Prudhvi too held his strength. He stared back to tell him that he meant it, and could fight for what he chose.

"If I am not wrong," Bose said smiling at last in doubt. "Is all this for a girl?"

That took Prudhvi by shock. He hadn't expected that the least. How could he do that? And that too, just over a smile. An uncontrollable sparkle left his eyes.

"How did you do that, sir?" he said smiling. Bose too smiled like he was really enjoying the chat.

"Is she that special?" he said.

"Yes, sir. She is."

"You may be sent to a war gentleman. You may die… She worth it?"

"In a given life, you will meet a maximum of one person, who are worth dying for, sir. You should live for them."

"You know what?" smiled Bose. "You sound exceptionally serious, in an extremely silly way."

"I think that's how it works, sir," Prudhvi said looking deep at him feeling a raging pain in his teenage eyes. He knew that the kid meant every single word he spelled. And there was something really stirring about him. "That's how it may have worked from the day humans evolved. When you witness situations, you never imagined you would see…

You will turn into a person you never thought you would be."

Those last two lines… They made Bose remember someone very close to him.

"You know what?" he said trying to smile. "You sound like Bapu."

Prudhvi stared at him in mere surprise. Bapu meant Gandhi. And that word made him remember many of his doubts that he always fantasized to ask Bose. But this was no dream anymore. He was with the born-rebel himself.

"Sir, why did you leave Congress?" he said at once. "You were the president by then. Did someone force you to leave?"

"What?" Bose said leaving a spontaneous smile. "No one forced me. And I know who you are referring to Prudhvi. Gandhi is a good man. He's the one who made me the President of Congress when I was in exile. He's not against me. He's against my ideologies. Gandhi still treats me as his child."

"But a spoilt one it is," Prudhvi said with anger brewing in his nerves.

"I don't know. I don't want to judge it. The nation will," he said. "The thing is that I too consider Gandhi as my father, but an irresponsible one."

Prudhvi and Drutha felt the pain that was beaming through his eyes.

"*To kick the enemy when he's down is wrong*, Gandhi said. He asked me to wait until the war was over, and then we can fight for freedom. That's a real great notion. But we did the same in World War I right? What was the outcome? Jallianwala Bagh?"

They said nothing in answer but just waited for him to talk more. It was making sense for them like never before.

"I always wondered why I opened my eyes to darkness every day," he said as if his heart was crying and burning at the same time. "It is Gandhi ji, who told me this – *For light, it's your heart that you should open.* Freedom is not what that keeps your outer world happy. But it's something that keeps your inside peaceful. Before fighting for freedom around, we should search it within."

"I did. And I opened my heart. You know what I realised?" he said turning his eyes to Prudhvi and Drutha alternately. "We are not in need of just freedom now. We need liberation. We should bring back our culture. The British are not just ruling our land, but they are ruining our systems too. Freedom is just the half success I tell you. Even when we get it and we won't concentrate on being real Indians again, getting back to what we were before British; one day we will turn into British anyway. We will no more be Indians.

"The British know that it's our culture that makes us much stronger than what they are. They are making us loose tracks of it. They are turning us into them, and they are trying to turn into us. They had plans to abduct our Vedas when they did leave us. Why do you think that it's that important? Because that's the very ground on which a great empire like India was built. '*I do not think we would ever conquer this country unless we break the very backbone of this nation, which is her spiritual and cultural heritage,*' said Lord McCaulay, in one of his British Parliament speeches in 1935. That's their key motto, and we should stop them, as early as possible. Or else, even the freedom can't help us."

"Sounds terrifying," murmured Drutha.

"I need you to listen to me Prudhvi, very carefully," said Bose, and that made him more alert than he was. "It's really a blessing of Kaalimaa that you know Rudhra. Let me explain you the plan in as many details as I can for now. We won't get a chance to meet again. I am leaving for Russia, any day now."

"How can we fight without you, sir?" said Prudhvi in hasty helplessness.

"What?"

"Don't you think you should stay here in India? You are supposed to stand in front of us, lead us…"

"Young man," he said smiling. "Remember my words when you tell your grandchildren about this day – *If your only aim is to lead, you can be anywhere in the group.*"

Prudhvi said nothing in reply, as he was left with no words to talk. Such a visionary he should be, to say something like that. Prudhvi felt the aura of a great leader, a great human and a great soldier. No politician in our country could ever match any of his standards as no one was even worth being compared to.

"Our politics are not in *that* good shape to see the real truth," continued Bose. "You know what's happening in our country right now? Those who work are having respect.

Those who teach are being followed. Those who entertain are highly praised. Those who question are getting killed.

"And to be a rebel, you should still have the strength to question, the notoriousness to spy and the courage to kill."

"Had you ever killed anyone?" said Drutha smiling from behind.

Bose too smiled. "He's just trying to rag you," he said. "Don't tell me you killed at an age like this."

"No, sir... I..." Prudhvi tried to split it out, but something invisible is trying to stop him. "I did make a kill," he said at last.

"Really?" Drutha smiled again, but Prudhvi hadn't turned back. "Is it a human?"

"Drutha stop," smiled Bose.

"No, sir. He's no human," he said, and his eyes started to fill. Bose's smile disappeared at once, so did Drutha's. "He was no human by the time I stabbed him in the heart, sir. The heart in which there's just malice and nothing else. Once it used to have warmth and love in it."

"So you really made a kill. Whom did you kill?" said Drutha walking up to them, to see tears rolling out of Prudhvi's eyes.

He turned to look at Drutha to answer. "My father, sir," he said.

That took Bose and Drutha with more than shock. They turned to each other with the bolt from the blue.

"He works for the British, and is so sincere in his job. He got his reward finally," he said trying to stop any more tears from leaving his eyes. "My mom would have wanted the same, sir."

Bose felt a thumping urge to hug the kid at once. Such a brave soldier he had become. Who thought him this? Whoever it might be, they created a weapon that's sharp in every direction.

"Son," said Bose, making Prudhvi look in his eye. He touched his arm, not in support, but to tell him that something that was vital is going to leave his lips. "Before I talk real business, let me tell you something much more important than that."

Prudhvi felt the air around slow down with the whipping and intense look of Bose.

"Remember this very carefully," he said. "It's *me*, who killed your father."

Chapter 9

Four years later.

1945

The world had burned down to ashes in these four years. World War had achieved its meaning in making them call it the 'World'-War. Nations raged, armies battled, civilians died, and the leaders still fought for their egos. For the first time in the history of evolution, a race feared its own kind like it never did. But none understood that war is a beast which feasts on not blood and flesh, but on more war. Every country fed it with its affordable amount of violence.

During 1941, the Germans made the world realise that there could be no other group as brutal as theirs. Germany invaded and occupied Greece, Yugoslavia, Belgrade and many other lands. But specific to mention, it attacked the Soviet Union too. The nation with which they signed a Non-Aggression Pact that was supposed to last for ten years. Over 62,000 Jews were murdered in Western Russia proving the ruthlessness of Hitler, yet another time.

Joseph Stalin too fell powerless in shades of the rising German clouds. Hitler started metamorphosing into the next Alexander and it seemed like humanity was left with no other option but to live under a cold-blooded dictator like him.

However, as they say, history repeated itself. There will always be a Porus for every Alexander. It happened on

7th December, 1941. The Japanese bombed the United Sates fleet at Pearl Harbour, on the coast of Hawaii. A whole fleet of Yankee ships was blown up like Christmas crackers, and Franklin Roosevelt declared that America is at war. Winston Churchill supported them with an immediate declaration of the battle between Britain and Japan. Germany and Italy announced war on America in support of Japan. And thus started the real fight.

August 1942 saw the dawn of the battle of Guadalcanal. The first major offensive and a decisive victory for the Allies in the Pacific Theatre. With Japanese troops stationed in a section of the Solomon Islands, American marines launched a surprise attack and took control of an air base under construction. Both sides endured heavy losses, but the Japanese suffered a far greater toll of casualties, forcing their withdrawal from Guadalcanal by February 1943.

For the next two years, Britain and America together slaughtered every chance of victory for the Axis Powers. Blood soaked the land; wind carried gun shots and smoke covered the skies. From Axis Powers vs. Allies Forces, today it had changed to Hitler vs. Stalin, Roosevelt and Churchill.

But that was not the major concern for the Indian-British now - that affected India the least regarding its freedom fight. The real problem that spawned the destiny of Indian independence to newer directions was, Subhash Chandra Bose escaping from his house arrest on 23rd January, 1941. That was the issue which was shaking up the British right now. After his escape, they realised that how vast and deep his network was inside their own system, as its way farther than impossible for a man with no spies, to escape the British C.I.D.

It took the entire nation by storm and even some great men like Rabindranath Tagore, and Gandhi wrote telegrams to Bose's family in support.

In the early days, it was believed that Bose had renounced the world and gone to Bangkok to become a Buddhist monk. Later they searched every bearded man in every religious place in India; including Pondicherry and Varanasi. Then they issued a shoot-at-sight order on him. Many public and private sectors stirred their pool of spies in search of Bose. The hunt went on to extents that no human had ever faced, but there was still no trace of him. Not even a clue.

Like every great story that decays with time, by the end of almost a year, Bose's disappearance too lost its strength in the mouth of public, though the government was still on to him with all they had.

But just until that day – the day on which India received an open radio transmission from Berlin. And it was Bose himself who spoke.

The so-called mass-leaders shuddered to his words. The desperate son of Bengal living in the camps of Adolf Hitler made them sweat with the thoughts of its consequences. The transmissions continued for months, on the Azad Hind Radio where Bose referred the British Broadcasting Corporation as the Bluff and Bluster Corporation and the All India Radio as the Anti-Indian Radio. The British government tried all the ways it had, legal and illegal, to make him come back to India. But they had never known that one day, he definitely will. And that day, he won't be alone.

At first, when he escaped the British, Bose planned to travel to Soviet Russia via Kabul. But the Russian embassy in Kabul had no time to talk to him. Even his connections inside failed. And that made him walk into the German embassy, where he was received with a warm welcome, which eventually made him leave for Berlin on 18th March 1941, in expectation of help from Hitler. Germany offered him its extended support, and they called him 'Netaji' there, meaning 'Respected Leader.' Bose wanted to form an army with the Indian war prisoners in Germany and few other parts of the western Asia and Africa, and rally into India through the Soviet Russia.

When almost everything fell into its place, Hitler attacked the Soviet Union, making the plan of Bose to march through their lands fall into the gutter. Bose hadn't met Hitler until then, and he was even warned that Hitler may imprison him if his proposal to form a government proved to have no strength. The Germans were completely unaware of this man's potential.

A meeting was scheduled by Hitler's men, where Bose got to talk in person with Hitler himself. But even before that, Bose went on to meet someone else – Japan's representative in the Japanese embassy, Berlin. He got the friendly word of Japan with him that he can reach them for help.

Bose finally met him, Fuhrer Adolf Hitler, on 27th May 1942 and shook hands with the devil. Hitler was highly impressed to meet a man who travelled the world, against his government, against their rules and against all the odds, to make his country free from the British. However, he refused to help Bose more in his struggle but offered him his help in the way of safely transporting him to the land of his choice. Even Hitler suggested him Japan, the nearest piece of land to India when compared to Germany. Bose wanted to fly to Japan, but Hitler felt it impossible and quite foolish. He offered Bose an alternative passage. Through a submarine it was.

Kiel Harbour, 8th February 1943. Bose got on to a German submarine, U-180, in which he travelled for weeks until he switched into a Japanese submarine, I-29, near Madagascar, Indian Ocean. It was recorded as the first-ever switch, from one submarine to another. On 6th May 1943, Bose reached Sabang, Indonesia. It could be considered forever as one of the greatest adventures of a freedom fighter to save his motherland.

On 4th of July the same year, he attended a meeting in Cathay cinema hall, Singapore, where he took the leadership of Indian Independence league and Indian National Army from Rasbihari Bose – the man who kept the spirit of India alive for 30 years in Japan and Southeast Asia.

Bose also met the man who was responsible for the attack on Pearl Harbour – Prime Minister Hideki Tojo. They met in Tojo's office in Tokyo and Bose thanked him for helping him raise the Indian National Army on their lands. Tojo assured him unconditional support of Japan, and thus, Indian National Army (INA) was formed on 9th July, 1943. It received its official recognition on 31st October the same year. INA had a wing that consisted of only women soldiers. 'Rani of Jhansi Brigade' was its name. Bose also named his brigades by the name of Gandhi and Nehru.

Bose addressed Gandhi as 'Father of the nation' and asked for his support for the struggles of INA. But Gandhi at once realised that cooperation with Bose meant to get freedom within the next five to six months. And if that happened, Bose was going to be the next Prime minister of free India - which was unthinkable and beyond acceptance to him and his followers. So Gandhi denied Bose and declared INA as the Japanese Invader. INA hadn't got any support from India. Bose was described as an enemy of the country, and the Communist party called him as the pet dog of Tojo. Indian hadn't behaved honorably with him.

But breaking every hurdle that came by its way, today INA had already made its mark on the face of the British army. Troops of Indian soldiers marched into India with the motto 'Chalo Delhi' (On to Delhi). British forces started losing their strength both in numbers and in a number of victories. Chindwin river crossing, Kohima pass, Moirang, Pallel airfield Manipur; many border places were attacked. In few of the attacks, the Indian soldiers who were on the British side started running on to the other side or shooting back at the British in their own groups; and that news fell like a bomb shell on Delhi. The walls of Viceroy's House trembled with echoes of his slogans – *Give me blood, and I will give you freedom.*

They knew that if this is continued for few more months, Indians will be independent in no time, and Bose had to be stopped immediately at any cost. An emergency protocol was called on 6th March, 1944. It's the only aim was to find and kill Netaji Subhash Chandra Bose. A full-fledged team was built up with London as its head office. World's best spies were employed for the on field intelligence, extremely secured lines were being maintained for any level of communications and highly developed warfare machinery was ready to be used at any point in time, just over a simple 'Go Ahead' message.

On 19th November 1944, this nameless secret agency made its first attack on Bose, when he was attending a meeting in Sadhugon village, Burma. Sudden and violent it turned out to be, but Bose managed to escape with minor injuries. They had never known the real hands behind that attack, but Bose went underground after that day. All his actions and activities got confined to the knowledge of only few of his generals.

But nothing changed regarding the attacks of Indians, on India.

* * *

08:50 am

31st March, 1945

Administrative Building, Signal Intelligence Bureau, Delhi.

"Excuse me, sir" he said stopping someone who was already in a hurry of his own.

"Yes?" the man in his mid-fifties who looked like a asylum-run-away halted, with one of his legs still in the direction he should head to.

"Administrative office?"

"You are in it," he said moving his head in a quick nod and walked away in swift movement.

"Sir, Mr Rudhra's offi-" he tried to stop him again, but the man was too fast for his age. "Damn," cursed Eshwar. It felt like the building went vacant with the only man he saw in the last few minutes gone.

He walked past a huge full-steel statue of some unknown British general, which was located in the center space of the main lobby. His face seemed like he was in pain from years of standing. There was a name plate in front of it, but Eshwar was reluctant to read. There was no reception found in any corner of the corridor and he was running out of time.

He had an appointment with a man who he always considered his role model. Other than attending few of his Signals and Systems lectures, he had never met him in person. But if nothing went wrong today, he might get a chance to work for him. Except that, even the first impression was going to be bad for sure. Who wants to hire someone who's late on the very first day of his internship?

Eshwar ran helter-skelter unable to process his next plan of action. 'Please meet Mr Rudhrama Naidu in the Administrative Building, by 9 o'clock tomorrow morning' they wrote to his hostel address. But where the hell is his office in this chaotic empire?

The walls around were filled with large wooden charts of rules and regulations, Dos and Don'ts, list of achievements of the bureau (the non-confidential ones for sure) etc. that were hanging just below the roof. The boards were as clean and shining as the wall they hung to. Their upper edges were leaning a bit more away from the surface, that it seemed like the least of an earthquake could make them fall on to someone staring at them, crushing them beneath their weight. How did they lift them up in the first place?

But amid of all these mighty wood work, there was not even a single signboard that showed way to the staff offices.

"Where the hell did all the employees go?" he wondered as he ran towards a rotatable door at the rare end of a long and narrow hallway to the right of the lobby. There was another hallway same as this to the left too, but right was his favorite direction. So he took it first. The neatly polished white pentagonal tiles were so slippery that they restricted his pace and he almost fell forward few times. His formal shoes were of no help here.

Meanwhile, the heat of the Indian summer started making him sweat like he had just soaked his 6 feet 2 inch, well-built body from head to toe. The executive suit on top of it is making things worse. Black is its color – the color that was most likely to absorb heat. At least his military style hair cut was making him feel relatively free from the layers of clothing all over his body. Eshwar always hated the idea of English dressing on Indian land.

He made a halt when he was almost few more meters from the door, to breath in some extra oxygen and pulled up his suit's sleeve to take a look at the watch his principal gifted him when he cleared the final round into the British Institute of Technological Sciences. The clock ticked 09:04.

"Thank god." He left a sigh unbuttoning the coat, revealing his cream-colored cotton shirt and started running again. Eshwar had a habit of setting his watch ten minutes faster than the actual time. "Six more minutes.

Plenty enough to head back to the other lobby," he thought as he ran towards the door.

Eshwar had always dreamed of working as a SIGNIT engineer. Data encryptions and decryptions, high level signal tapings, spyware detections; they all make him weak in his knees. They kept him up all night in his hostel room, dragging him into their unending loops and deceptive iterations, asking him to make them yield the intended messages. He found solitude in zeros and ones like he never did in any of his other subjects.

He had constantly been the toper of his class and would have even been selected for the British government's scholarship program last year, where they sent few selected students to study in London colleges. But only if he had picked just another topic in the Annual-Day essay writing competitions. Not just the academics but every other curricular and extra-curricular activity was taken into consideration in preparing the final list of the students. It was his strong respect that always burned in his heart towards his mother land and the selfless heroes who were fighting for its independence that made him pick up the topic – 'My take on Subhash Chandra Bose's ways.' He supported him in a very detailed and elaborated manner, that no one could add any contradiction to his argument. He explained how great Bose was a spy and why British could never stop him from getting what he wanted.

It won all their hearts, the lecturers who taught him and even the visiting professors talked about him in the staff rooms. But they never let the essay reach the final round, fearing that it may get him killed. And thus Eshwar, the top-ranked student, remained in the same college struggling for a scholarship.

"Stop where you are." A sudden shout form nowhere made him jump. The door he was running to, rotated at once and an armed British soldier ran out of it, pointing his gun towards him. "Stay low. Hands on your head. Now…"

He knew the drill. He had been trained in it. But to be on the other side.

Eshwar went down on to his knees at once and lifted his hands onto the back of his head.

"Who the hell are you, dickhead?" the soldier said placing the edge of the machine's long tunnel on Eshwar's head. "This is a restricted military zone. Do you know that?" he shouted to the heights of his tone.

"No, sir. I really don't," he said panting with sudden shock. "I am so… I am sorry, sir. I am here to meet Mr Rudhrama Naidu. I am an intern."

Two more soldiers emerged out. They all seem like there was a war going on the other side of the door. Heavily equipped with grenades, hand knives and pistols stuffed into uncountable number of pockets of their thick brown military uniforms.

"What's wrong?" said the heavy guy in a more stressed British accent.

"This dog tried to intrude and was trying to turn into an intern now," he said pushing Eshwar with the gun.

"Sir, can I see your ID?" the heavy guy said walking towards him.

"I don't have one," replied Eshwar lifting his face up to look into his eye.

There was no one to be seen in the building until now and all of a sudden he got British soldiers holding guns to his head. 'This was definitely not the Administrative Building' he realised.

"You said you're an intern."

"I am here to join as one. This is my first day."

"Whom should you report to, sir?"

"Mr Rudhrama Naidu."

He said nothing in reply, but just stared at Eshwar with his whitish skin turning red. "Call for Mr Rudhra," he said looking back at the third guy who ran inside at once.

"We'll see what happens to you when he says that you're not here to join." It was the one who was aiming at him. 'What's with this guy?' Eshwar wondered. He sounded like he had a personal grudge on him. "I know very well about pigs like you. You bloody filthy Indian," he said as if he's going to spit on him next.

It happened again. All of a sudden, the 'Thing' that Eshwar always feared of had happened. That corner of his heart got poked, where he hid all his short temper, ego and pride. He hated it to core when someone talked bad about him being an Indian, or any Indian for that matter.

Eshwar's eyes widened at once. He moved his head to feel the gun, spiralled back without leaving touch of his head to the barrel and pushing it away from him, stood up while doing so, turned around in a split second, got hold of the gun with one hand, lifting the soldier hard on to the wall behind with another.

"No no no… Don't," Eshwar warned, aiming at the heavy guy, for whom it took few seconds to react. By then, he had a gun pointed at him. "I am not here to hurt you, sir." Eshwar said as calm as possible. "I swear. I am just an intern but… I will keep my respect."

"Say sorry," he said turning to the one who was struggling to get the muscular hand off his breaking neck. The heavy guy wanted to do something, but Eshwar's grip on the weapon felt dangerously professional.

"Say sorry," he repeated again, much harsher now, pushing him even harder on to the wall, making his legs leave the ground. "Don't tempt me to blow your brains off," he shouted turning the gun on to his head. His eyes were raging, with anger thumping out of them, like lava from a volcano.

"Horhy…" the guard left a sound unable to cope up with the pain and his legs wiggled to touch the ground.

"What? I don't hear you." He left him free to stand again and loosened the grip on his neck. "Say it again. Clearly…"

"I am sorry," he said breathing heavy, but maintaining the clarity the guy with the gun wanted.

"That's good. Never dare to look down on any Indian again… sir."

Moving the gun in sign of warning, he stepped away to throw it back at him and kneeled down again, raising his hands to the back of his head.

Leaving the soldiers with no other options, but to look at each other in bewilderment.

* * *

They made him sit in a room that seemed like more of an interrogation cell than a waiting hall. It was a small rectangle block with three sides of it covered with low lying wooden benches attached to the walls, which will make your thighs go parallel to the ground when sat straight. Eshwar was seated in the top right corner, and hadn't moved till now. It's been 09:20, the actual time, but no one opened the door that the heavy guy closed behind him a while ago.

As he waited restlessly, Eshwar heard commotion outside the room. People walking by, chatting with their colleagues, discussing everyday topics like Bose's agenda for his next attack, Americans support to Quit India Movement and the war that was raging like wild fire. Some were making enquiries at the reception that he passed to reach this room and even few pair of legs ran across the hall from time to time.

As minutes flew by, Eshwar began feeling claustrophobic. But he was half conscious that it was not just fear but his grief of losing the job he hoped for so much. He finally looked up from the floor, unable to bear the pain anymore.

It suddenly caught his attention, that the wooden walls around, except the one with the door, had tampered glass from half of their height. It struck him, if there were people behind them, watching his left alone behavior. He knew that such rooms existed.

Eshwar stood up at once to see his reflection, up to the chest level, on the black glass around. "God, they are watching me," he thought. "Am I in deeper trouble than I think I was?"

There was nothing that could be done now. Assaulting a British soldier while he was on duty was way more than a crime. Not even a soldier, hitting a British civilian could kill you. But there would always be a way out. He could do something to save his skin. May be a simple sorry? But what had he done wrong to say sorry? And what hadn't he done again?

"Ok I need to do something," he decided. "They are watching me and may be hearing too."

"See," he started talking to his reflection on the glass. "I know that I have… Wait… What side they are watching me from?" he wondered turning to all the three sides and waving hands.

Nothing happened. May be they were set only to watch. But he still waved hands in fool's hope.

"What are you doing?" someone said and he turned back at once.

It was him. The man who was his inspiration – Mr Rudhrama Naidu, the chief of SIGNIT wing, standing near the door. He had the impression of a man still in his late teens. Dressed in black pleated silk formal pants into which a white full sleeves shirt was tucked in; he seemed like an engineer who walked off on a break from his hectic work. His rectangle framed spectacles, folded up sleeves and the loosened brown tie with white dots all over it; perfected the look.

"Sir," Eshwar walked towards him buttoning his coat and extending his hand to him. "Eshwar. I got a letter yester-"

"I said, what the hell do you think you are doing?" Rudhra said irritated and walking on to him. "Do you know why I wrote that letter to you? Just you?"

"Yes, sir," he said drawing back his hand and wondering: 'He wrote the letter himself?' "I am the topper in every single test I-"

"Hell with the marks mister."

Eshwar stood there stunned by his actions. 'Hell with the marks? I am the topper in every single test I took for every single-'

"You are not here because of your bloody marks," said Rudhra, cutting his thoughts too. He walked in at once closing the door behind him and it clicked. Rudhra waited, as if to hear the click. "The sixteen-page essay you wrote in support of Bose last year. Remember?"

"Yes, sir. I do."

"You lost the competition *and* the scholarship. But you did have your prize Eshwar." Rudhra said making him sit and sat by his side pulling up his trousers a bit for comfort. His moods seemed to swing violently. He turned friendly, all at once. "I see that you understood the concepts of spying very well. And you have the technical skills too. Would you like to join us?" Rudhra said staring deep into his eye. To Eshwar, he seemed like a man who was toughened by fate.

"*Us*?" Eshwar said making his eyes bigger.

"You know what it means."

"It means..." he wanted a safety check.

"It means what it means," Rudhra said. "Don't worry. Things like this always happen when you least expect them. We don't choose you if we think you won't blend in or accept the offer. I know you're fit to be one."

"One?"

"*One* among *us*."

"You're asking me to be a..." He wanted the word.

"Don't you know what it is?"

"Yes, sir," Eshwar said moving his head in disbelief. "Yes I do. But... But I never thought that you would be one among them."

"There are hundreds of us. And we need more," he said staring at him in trust. "You have already been selected as an intern Eshwar. I have been observing you very closely from almost a year now. You cannot imagine. But I want you to be more."

'I have been observing you...' that sounded more exciting than Rudhra asking him to be a spy.

"What's your age, Eshwar?"

"Nineteen, sir."

"You're willing to die for your country?"

"I would like to make few kills first." And that made Rudhra smile, for the first time today.

"You're not excited?"

"I am still in the process of digesting it, sir."

"Good," Rudhra said smiling again. "Your work starts today."

"Field work?" he enquired with excitement.

"This is your first day kid. And I see you still in the digesting-phase," Rudhra countered. "You should survive a lot to get some action."

"I will, sir."

"Then this was not surely the way to behave, sir. An ideal spy should maintain low grounds," he said standing up and taking few steps away from him. "He should maintain good rapport, even with the guards. Actually, it's mainly with the guards.

"Why did you hit him in the first place?" Rudhra asked turning back to him, to find him staring into the glasses again. "Don't worry," he said and that made Eshwar turn to him. "There are not one-way glasses. And this room is sound proof with the door closed."

"Great," he smiled. So that's the reason for his mood swings. He wanted people outside to hear him shout.

"And…?"

"Ya… I…" Eshwar found it extremely uncomfortable to explain, as if he was the one with the wrongs on his side. "He called me 'Bloody' 'Filthy' Indian, sir."

"What?" Rudhra yelled in surprise. "Just over a 'Bloody' and a 'Filthy'? God…You're a Punjabi right?"

"Yes, sir"

"Right. Bhuvaneshwar Singh," he said as if he was thinking of something deep inside his head. "So," he looked up to him at once, "you're willing to join us?"

"With all that I had, sir," said Eshwar, walking to him. Even if it really seemed like a sudden dream to him, he felt fortunate that it was happening.

"Good," Rudhra said patting his shoulder. "Welcome to SIGNIT."

"But sir," Eshwar said trying to hide his smile, as they walked towards the door. "Down the line, in few years from now, when they start searching for spies; I think maybe it's you who will cross their minds before me."

"What?!" Rudhra left a sudden cry turning to him, with his grip still on the door knob.

"Yes, sir," he said trying hard to maintain the eye contact. "'An ideal spy maintains low grounds' as you said. And the one who's looking for a spy too knows that right? So…"

Rudhra stared at him with intentional anger in his eyes, which made Eshwar look down. Rudhra smiled the very next second and thought: 'Such a brave and gutsy kid.' He developed a liking towards this him just over minutes. He seemed like someone who could really make a change.

"Follow me," said Rudhra, still smiling and walking past the door. Eshwar jumped with happiness to join a man of his potential and that too as a spy.

"What else can sound any more exciting than this?" he thought as he followed Rudhra out of the Chief Security office, and back to the Administrative Building.

* * *

"My ID, sir," said Eshwar even before they asked him. The soldier with a bandage around his neck stared at him as if he wanted to pluck his teeth off his gums with a wire cutter.

Eshwar exhibited his ID to all the four guards on the other side of the door, including the one who sat in the security booth.

"Enough, stop it," Rudhra smiled as he warned him. Even Rudhra always wanted to punch at least one of them in their faces from a very long time.

Past the mystery rotating door, there was nothing but just an even longer hallway, that was perpendicular to the outer one, and was extended to the left. The hallway from the left side of the main lobby was also connected to this one from the other end. No matter what side you take from the main lobby, you'd end up in the same passage. There was nothing else in this tunnel like hallway but two security booths at both ends. No doors, no windows nothing. Just clean and smooth white walls on three sides, with the same pentagonal tiles on the floor.

"Should we pass that security booth too, sir? And then out of the building again?" Eshwar enquired in mystification as they walked towards the other end and suddenly another turn to the right came into picture in the midway.

"Believe me. Even I hadn't seen it until this point on my first day," said Rudhra, smiling. "Get ready to be surprised."

Eshwar wondered: 'Why did he say that?'

But when he did make a turn, it really took him by surprise.

That turn, led to another short hallway that immediately opened into a huge circular hall that covered almost as equal area as a mini indoor hockey stadium.

"Wait… Had I just switched worlds, sir?" he said making Rudhra smile again.

The room contained the paradox of appearing spacious and cluttered at a glance. There was no other entrance to it than the one they just used. The top point of the hemisphere roof was so far from the floor – the floor that was cut down into circular steps like it's going deep into the earth. Each step had a green floor mat on it and there were closely spaced wooden desks all over its circumference with an employee for every desk. But no one seemed like they had at least a second to turn to the new guy from their papers. May be they had never turned to the next desk as well if there wasn't a purpose. Other than desks and people, there were bunches of thin oak papers, white desk lights with green glass over-shades and modern electric typewriters that were prominently visible on every desk. Few desks had two typewriters.

In the very center of all the circles, on the deepest level, a small podium with a mike attached to it could be seen. Eshwar turned to look up at the dome as they descended the steps. There were huge speakers attached at equal distances all around it.

"To announce emergencies," Rudhra said.

"What are all these people doing here?" Eshwar asked staring directions.

"Decoding a message."

"'A' message?" he said turning to him at once, pushing his eyes out of his skull.

"'A' message," smiled Rudhra.

"All of them?"

"Combined."

Rudhra realised Eshwar's anxiety to know more. "You see the guy over there?" he said pointing his figure to the upper most circle on the exact opposite side of the opening from which they walked in. The desks in between them were placed at little farther distance than normal, making some space to walk, which seemed like a diameter to the outer most circle. The guy at whom Rudhra pointed was at the end of the diameter.

"The blue shirt?" Eshwar enquired.

"Yes. The one who sat in front of the receiver."

"That's a receiver?" he said turning to Rudhra and back again. "I thought it's a part of the wall, sir."

"It's huge right? That's the one which receives the main signal – 'The message.' And that blue shirt, feeds it his circular code. A sequence of letters only and only he knew."

"Then he prints the obtained message and today's key on a paper and passes it to the guy to his right. That guy feeds the next sequence that only and only he knew. And that travels all around this room," he said making a full turn. "And then, another round." And he made another turn as if he was ballet dancing.

"Two thousand?"

"There were only five hundred in this room." He smiled.

"Oh. And then?"

"Then, it reaches the guy who's to the right of that blue shirt. He hands it over to the blue shirt, who hands it to the chief, who, in turn, feeds it with *his* personal sequence, to obtain the fully decrypted message. But all the others should leave the room, before he does that, and only the blue shirt is allowed to talk to the chief."

"And who's that?"

"Me..." Rudhra cried at once.

"Oh I am... I am sorry, sir," Eshwar shrugged trying not to smile.

"And in case if I should take a leave, *that* blue shirt, whose name is Akbar, will be my substitute for the day. And it will be followed by a lot of my explanation to the board."

Eshwar still tried to stop his lips from taking a curve as they descended to the center podium and then walked up towards the blue shirt. The mightiness of the room made Eshwar's masculine body feel tiny as he walked forward. Such a vast and heavily constructed room it was. 500 people all around him, but still one could hear the shuffle of a paper. No one had even kept their pens down for at least a second. There were even women to been seen here and there.

"Sir, I have a doubt," Eshwar said as if something struck him from nowhere. "If the message stays at only one desk at a time, what are all these guys are busy with?"

"In developing their local sequence that should be fed in the second cycle. That need to be worked out combining their personal sequence and today's key sequence. It usually takes more time than the message to reach them again. So they better hurry up."

"Oh my god." Eshwar felt so much of pressure on his little brain. "Do they encrypt it the same way?" he said looking back at Rudhra as they climbed another step. Each level was at the height of two normal stairs combined.

"They say that there was a way similar room back in London. Where there will be 500 counter parts to these 500 guys here, with the same personal sequences and seated in the same order. But the blue shirt there passes his paper to the left side first, after feeding his code to the already scrambled message he receives from his chief. They work in the early hours, like from 12:00–04:00 in the morning, their time. But the duration it takes was the same – three and half hours.

"Even if someone had to break the code, they should get hold of these 500 people and me, make them sit in the required order and then should make them work without any mistakes. Even if it goes wrong finally, they can never know who did it."

"Getting hold of the 500 is impossible in itself," reminded Eshwar.

"So is to break the code."

"Who designed it, sir?"

"For this time, we should praise the British brain. The name is unknown, but he's *my* counterpart in London."

"Making it depend on 500 people… Brilliant," he said, as they finally reached the blue shirt.

"Akbar, do I have a minute?" said Rudhra making him look up from his sheet.

"Sir, always," Akbar said smiling.

Eshwar saw butterfly structures on his sheet. "Fourier Transforms," he thought.

"Akbar this is Eshwar. Eshwar… Akbar," he said tilting his head in a deep nod.

Akbar looked back at Eshwar in surprise. "Welcome soldier," he said smiling. And that made him realise that Akbar too was one among them.

"Ok then, continue with your work," Rudhra said immediately. "I am here just for an extra copy of the message."

"Sir, just a reminder, we are fifteen minutes ahead on schedule," he said loading the type writer with a new paper and started typing carefully.

"What's the time?" Rudhra enquired Eshwar.

"10:55, sir."

"Your watch says 11:05…"

"I set it faster by ten minutes, sir."

Rudhra said nothing, but threw a weird glance before turning back to Akbar. "So today we are not going to repeat the mistake again?"

"No, sir," assured Akbar, dragging a desk out of his table and searching the upper wall with his fingers. Even before Eshwar wondered to the full extent of what he was doing, he took a hidden envelop from inside. Folding the sheet into it, he handed it to Rudhra.

"What was the mistake you're talking about, sir?" enquired Eshwar as they left Akbar.

"We should decode the message by 01:00 pm. Or wait until the next day," Rudhra answered.

* * *

SAU NSW JUT HJU LAU NHI AHG JUO SHJ OKA AJW EHW SJU – SA-JU-TA

"What in hell is this?" smiled Eshwar confused, but excited at the same time.

"That's 'The Message' kiddo. And that's the key sequence," Rudhra said. "Don't flaunt it too much. As per the rules book, no paper should leave that hall."

"Then how come you brought this out, sir?"

"There is a word for it – Smuggling."

Eshwar smiled with his eyes wide open, making Rudhra smile back.

They smiled in intervals for the next few meters.

"So, sir… In the first cycle," Eshwar said after a long smiling silence, "their own personal sequences were fed. Right?"

"Right."

"And then in the second, the combination of their personal and today's key was fed. Right again?"

"As right as the first time."

"And then... the one thousand and oneth time, you feed your personal sequence or the combined?"

"Combined."

"Then don't you need to work on yours, sir?"

"I already did."

"You did?"

"While we were walking out of the building."

"But you saw the key hardly for-"

"I had my ways kid," he said with a cunning smile on and walking past him.

"That's the reason they call you a genius," Eshwar thought standing there, staring at him in surprise.

"So, sir," he said running back to him. "Even *we* can't decode it now?"

"We can," he answered as a matter of fact. "We had all the sequences of those 500 in there. But...it will take days literally."

"Wow..." it amazed him. "And sir, why should we decode it by 01:00 pm?"

"It's a rule."

"Rule? But it sounds weird."

"It's discipline..." Rudhra said. "With 500 people working under your hand, you can't control them without such strict rules. Even I am not allowed inside after 01:00."

"Great..." he smiled. "So... What's there for us to spy on, sir?" Eshwar talked in low tone; even they were walking in an open lawn, heading towards the staff cafeteria.

"Simple," he said. "We are here, listening to the British, talk to the British. And what do they usually talk?"

"Their attacks on the Axis Powers?"

"Most of the times. But sometimes, they talk about attacks on the supporters of Bose too. Most of the times these days."

"Supports of Bose?"

"The rebels," he said making a halt.

"The rebels?"

"Yes. Mr Bose had a parallel government of rebels here in India. Spreading as calm as water under a mat. Not just in the woods... They can be anywhere and they can be anyone. From a potter to a politician."

"From a student to a professor."

"Clever," Rudhra said smiling. "We warn them through our message carriers. Every troop of rebels will have their hand full of spies who keep on travelling. Not just randomly but according to a pattern."

"But the British can easily identify that they had been prepared for them."

"Not always. It did happen once though. When we used to track the German signals to Japan, the Germans did identify. But this time, we had our ways. Either to prepare for few sacrifices for letting them believe that we were not prepared, or sometimes to just move away from the current camp, making it seem like a normal shift."

"But we still lose men," he said finding no point in it.

"They are heroes." Rudhra sounded as if he had seen them die for their group. "One rebel dies in the place of three. They die, but for the lives of the other two. We never lose them. They live in our pain, in our strength, in our smiles. They live forever. That's the sprit Bose wanted, Eshwar. Give me blood-"

"I will give you freedom," he said raging with anger.

"That's it," Rudhra shouted with twice the spirit. And suddenly they both realised they were in the middle of a British empire.

"Let's walk," said Rudhra and they started walking. But occupied with their own thoughts again.

"Why are there hyphens in the key, but not in the message?" Eshwar asked staring at the piece of paper in his hand, as they almost reached the canteen.

"That might be a glitch," said Rudhra, still in pain.

"What type of glitch?" Eshwar wanted to divert him from that.

"You see the long dash that's separating the message and the key?"

"Yes."

"That might have replicated. The key is always a six-letter word in sets of three two-letter words. There should be spaces in between them actually. Or hyphens today, just for you."

Eshwar smiled seeing him smile again. He felt so relieved interning for a friendly guide. He made him feel like he's not with a senior at work but with one of his best friends.

As Eshwar walked forward smiling to himself, Rudhra took a sudden halt. Eshwar turned back to see him staring at the grass, immersed in unexpected deep thoughts.

"Sir?" he said walking back to him.

"There can be glitches in the message. There had been few now and then." He sounded like he was talking to himself. "But the key?" He extended his hand, and Eshwar placed that paper in it immediately.

Rudhra stared at it, squinting his eyes further. "They seem like... like blanks," he said at last.

"Blanks? Like fill in the blanks?" enquired Eshwar and that made Rudhra look up at him in shock. He turned back to the paper, pulling a fountain pen out of his trouser pocket and sat down on the grass. Eshwar too sat on one knee.

"SA space JU space TA," he read it aloud. It seemed like he knew that flow of letters very well. He opened the screw-type cap, pushed his spectacles tight and started writing. It's just two simple letters that had flown down from the streams of his subconscious – A and K.

"S-A-N-J-U-K-T-A," spelled Eshwar peeking into the paper.

"Sanjuktha," said Rudhra as his eyes started blurring out. "Oh my god...Prudhvi?"

Chapter 10

“Sir, who’s Prudhvi? Eshwar enquired for the nth time, but raising his tone for the first; and that worked.

“My friend,” Rudhra said turning back at once, making a sudden halt amid his fierce walk towards the office. “My friend who always hated freedom…”

“Hated freedom? Why would someone do that?” wondered Eshwar.

“What makes you so sure, sir? That it’s him who-”

“What makes me sure? You want to know what makes me *so* sure?” Rudhra tried to shout out his pain, anger or shock; whatever it was. “One year… One year of everyday transmission. Every single day… “A message,’ ‘A long dash’ and ‘The key.’ Not a thing more, not a thing less. I tell you… These hyphens here are not just glitches. Not at all… What made me think they are in the first go?” he scolded himself and started walking again. “It’s him for sure. He created this entire structure with such complexity only because he knew that I will be at the other end. He wanted no one else to break it.”

“All this time, two years, he had stayed low. And now why did he come up suddenly? This is going to be way more serious than we think it is.”

“Do you think a simple hyphen can make that change, sir?” Eshwar tried to debate dying to keep up with his pace. “Is it that important?’

"See? You don't think that it's important. That's why it is… 'This sentence has mistake in it' and 'This sentence has no mistake in it.' Consider these two statements. The 'no' in the second statement makes no difference. Anyways, they both lead to a paradox. Right?"

"Right."

"And that 'no,' which makes no difference, is the place where the play lies. When you receive a transmission – 'This sentence has no mistake in it,' why would the one who transmitted it use an extra word with no added value?"

"Why?"

"To tell you to look close."

Eshwar tried to break some complex algorithms inside his head before saying: "So you did look close. And derived something from it – Samyuktha."

"Sanjuktha," he corrected, as they stepped into the Silver Jubilee building, where the staff offices are located.

"Sorry, 'Sanjuktha'. What now, sir?"

"Use the hint. Find the key."

"This is not the key?"

"No," he said, trying to unlock the door to the office with his trembling hands. "This is just a hint to the key that was intended to us." The door got unlocked and they stepped in. "This is too much of a lesson for you on the first day itself, but I am sure you can take it. It's called the 'Acquaintance Key'."

"What key?"

"'Acquaintance Key. You send a message along with a key, which looks as nothing but just a combination of few random words for the people who don't know you. They can hardly break it down up to the 'Sanjuktha' level. But they'll just smile to themselves thinking that it seems like an Indian name. But the one for whom it was intended to, will surely see it with a sufficient hint. Using that key, we derive from the hint, instead of my personal sequence will fetch us an entirely different message."

"What are the odds that they are not aware of this kind of key?"

"Almost zero," he said, as he stuffed his brown leather travel bag with random things. "May be not more than a handful of people in this entire world knew that such key existed."

"How come!" That really intrigued Eshwar.

"Because it's the man who's using it now is the one who created it when we were still in our half pants. I think we are fishing that day."

"Fishing?" He sounded like he can never believe it.

"Best time to talk technology."

"So… should you guess the key now?"

"No," Rudhra said as if he knew it without a streak of doubt. "I don't think Prudhvi leaves it to probabilities. He knows the time it will consume. May be he wants me to meet her. And if I am not wrong, he surely might have left something with her. Something that she will never throw away."

"Like?"

"Like a letter? A letter that was written in a specific structure or pattern... It takes something as simple as me feeding the exact key what Prudhvi fed there. But we should get hold of the right one." Done with his packing, Rudhra zipped the bag and slid it under his table. "Go get your things for a day's travel. The decryption should have reached the end by now. I'll send the message to Viceroy's House and we shall meet in the parking lot 06."

"Where are we headed, sir?"

"To a forest..."

"A forest?"

"Yeah... In Narsipatnam, Madras."

"We are going to leave now?" he enquired in a deep doubt. "Like *now*?"

"Eshwar," Rudhra said in a calm and steady tone, as if to teach him. "This is war. And in war, 'Now' is all you get."

* * *

Eshwar walked past the uneven part of land in front of the iron gate at the rare side entrance that opened to a stretched and vast parking space located back of the Silver Jubilee building, with empty barren lands extending their plains after the concrete flooring. It was an open parking and there were not more than ten cars that stood as leftovers after a sale. Most of them were older models except the grape red Cadillac custom convertible. He wondered if it belonged to Mr Rudhra, but trashed his assumption in the very next second; as such a cool car could never be his selection.

'Chief seems a bit old-fashioned than his age,' Eshwar thought and smiled over it.

He met Rudhra near the separating section of lot 05 and 06. He was in the same attire but with a black knee-length overcoat and a matching derby hat. His leather bag was hanging from his shoulder reinstating his old-fashioned ways.

"Let's go," said Rudhra walking away even before he reached him. Eshwar ran to him, taking longer steps.

"So, sir," he said, jogging, to equal the speed of his walk. "How could we return in a day? Madras is so far from here."

"Don't worry. I can pilot well."

"Pilot?" he exclaimed. "What pilot?"

"Don't you know what 'Pilot' means?" Rudhra said taking a turn at the edge of the wall and took an immediate halt.

"Ya I do, sir. But… But what-" Eshwar heard a sudden sound of air being beaten into submission and they were standing just few meters from a helipad. He raised his head at once towards the sky, to see a Bell 47 chopper descending towards them.

It was a two-bladed, single-engine, light helicopter that was recently brought into market by Bell Helicopters. The acting president of SIGNIT group presented it to Rudhra on the anniversary of their branch. It could carry two passengers including the pilot, and the huge spherical glass surface that covered the major part of its body helping its passengers savor a great aerial view. All the weight of the engine and the machinery lay below the blades, while the long metal frame tail containing not much weight maintained its balance. The tail had a pair of vertically rotating blades at its end, to counter the torque created by the main blades. It also had two long iron skids beneath it and a pair of tyres too, to provide comfort in landing on any terrain.

But to Eshwar, no specifications or special features of the newly-sketched model made a difference. This was the first time in his entire life he was witnessing something that could fly in real. To him it seemed like a huge metal dragon fly.

The chopper landed blowing off all the dust from the helipad. Their clothes and hair went irreversibly disturbed. Eshwar tried to take a look at the landing even if it was difficult to keep his eyes open.

The pilot jumped out of the chopper to shake hands with Rudhra. They seemed like friends from the way they smiled at each other. For Eshwar, the mighty and long blades that were passing over his head in intervals, with their speed slowing down, seemed like a dream.

"What an astonishing creature man was. Who thought him to dig the earth, extract metals and make them fly?" he thought.

"What should I enter in the records regarding this trip, sir?" he heard the other man ask Rudhra, as he neared them.

"Trip? What trip?" Rudhra said in reply.

"Yes, sir. Have a good day," he said and smiled at Eshwar as he left. Eshwar smiled back.

"So… All set?" enquired Rudhra, adjusting his headphones. They were ready to fly and that made things stir inside Eshwar's stomach. But he was still in the hold of surprise and excitement.

"Yes, sir. All set," he replied in the slowest formation of words.

"What's the time now?"

"12:53, sir." He was still staring at his watch as if making some calculations. Rudhra caught hold of him by his hand and pulled the watch closer, to see on his own. It's 01:03.

"Why do you set it faster?"

"It makes me feel like I am living in the future, sir." He blushed. "I always wanted to travel in time."

Rudhra smiled on the thought of a teenaged Indian kid nurturing fantasies of time travel.

"Finally, you're going to get the action you wanted," he said switching on the engine which made the vehicle tremble and the blades started moving, gaining speed over seconds, making Eshwar to turn more nervous than before. "I am jealous of you… For me, it took years to get on to the field for the first time."

Eshwar left an uninterested smile, still immersed in the trance of being in a chopper.

"How's my ride by the way?" enquired Rudhra, adjusting some knobs on the control panel.

"Coolest vehicle I had ever seen in a parking lot." Rudhra turned to him from the board, as he sounded like a kid who was about to take a ride on the elephant. "You are a rock star, sir," he said in the most genuine tone, making Rudhra smile even brighter.

* * *

It took them nearly nine hours to reach there.

During the first few hours, Eshwar enjoyed every second of the flight. He shivered whenever the vehicle lost some altitude, jumped up from his seat to stare at birds that they overtook and asked infinite number of questions making Rudhra go mad. In the next few, he watched the landscapes, flowing rivers and villages that seemed like miniature maps in silence. Flying at that altitude, that little curvature in the horizon made him realise that they were actually living on a ball that rotates in space, creating and consuming time. As lands of such bigger dimensions seemed so small, he also wondered why man fought for such worthless trivia though he could never get it all.

"May be the greed to have more, will only lead to a much stronger greed of the same kind but nothing else," he contemplated. And after few more hours, it all felt really tiresome. The monotony of the flight started to bore him.

The globe had slowly shifted into the space between the helicopter and the sun now and there was nothing to be seen on the land but just darkness. The half-moon was giving some visibility though. Other than few lights from the British buildings and administrative quarters, the remaining land was brewing black. The clock ticked 10:00, the actual time, as they flew past the village and towards the mighty thick forest.

"You look so disturbed, sir," Eshwar said. If not with the headphones that were connecting them internally, they should have been literally shouting, as the whirring of the blades above their heads would make it hard, even to hear their own voices. Rudhra still tried hard to concentrate on their flight towards the woods. He seemed like he wanted to go back somewhere else. "Are you ok, sir? You're the only one who can drive this thing here."

Rudhra let out a smile. "I am totally fine," he answered looking in his eye for assurance.

"If I can help you with it, I would be very happy, sir."

"No. I am absolutely fine. It's just-" Rudhra wanted to say it out, but was not completely sure how it may have sounded.

"But I am not, sir. With you sitting by my side, having that look on your face. At least share it. I may not help you at all, but it can help *me*."

Rudhra knew how it feels to have someone with an expression as lifeless as his now by their side on a journey like this. "We just flew past my home," he said after a prolonged silence.

"This is your place, sir?" exclaimed Eshwar. "Your home?"

"Yeah. All that I am now is just because I was born here."

"May be we can stop by then."

"That's way riskier. We can't take any chances of the British spotting me here."

"Or just fly at lesser altitudes may be? Your parents may come out of the house to a sound like one this creature makes."

"For now kiddo, this is an antique piece we have here," he tried to smile. The thought of seeing his mother after years, made him weep inside knowing the fact that he can't, even though they were just few nautical miles apart. "They can report the spotting of a Bell 47 and get back to the missing records and then back to me. Not more than five people in the country own something like this."

"That's why I call you a rock star, sir," said Eshwar lifting his hand head-high. Rudhra slapped a high five, really smiling this time. He loved the way this kid could smile in any situation, and make others follow him. One could turn so positive only with great parenting. 'What do your parents do?' he wanted to ask, but something he saw deep down in the forest made him jump out of all those emotions at once.

"That's it," Rudhra said, making the chopper take an abrupt diving turn.

Eshwar suddenly felt his organs moving against his body-sync. He caught hold of the hand support to maintain his balance. His head turned heavy at once and he felt like vomiting.

"What's that, sir?" he enquired looking at a small dot of fire burning in the woods. "Their camp fire?"

"No. Camp fire of the rebels can't be seen from the skies. It's the spy-fire," replied Rudhra. "800 meters 30 degrees North East, 600 meters 310 degrees North West and two kilometers 270 degrees i.e. exact West… you'll be in the Rebels camp."

"Wow…" wondered Eshwar. "Who lights it?"

"Someone in the troop. Mostly the one who's good with directions," he said bending the chopper in sudden movements, searching for a place to land. To Eshwar it seemed like they were the ones who was stagnant and it was the globe that was shaking and moving close to them.

From a distance, the chopper really seemed like a dragon fly, flying over the grass on a dark summer night, searching for a place to rest.

"Every group of Rebels will have their own spy-fire," continued Rudhra. "The British may spot it too, but one should know the readings to reach the camp."

"Who thought you all these tricks, sir?" he enquired in pride.

"Actually," Rudhra said lowering the chopper to land in a gap he found between the trees near the spy-fire. "It's me who thought them."

* * *

"You can't meet her," the one-armed man said, dismissing his question again, for yet another time.

"What do you mean by I can't meet her?" Rudhra was on the edges of thrashing his face. They were trying to break him from the last five minutes, but all that he yielded was the information of Sanjuktha being underground. "I don't care if she's underground, or something even more secured than that. When I say I want to meet her, I mean it in every possible way. Do you understand?"

"Yes, sir. I do… But I can't take you to her. Please try to understand the situation. It's more complicated than you think it is. Please leave."

Rudhra turned away in anger, trying to control himself from losing his cool. They hadn't risked their lives and flew for hours, to listen to a denial. But Bilva too had his constraints, and he seemed like he was trying to hide something on which his life depended.

"I don't know if I can tell you this," Eshwar said inching towards Bilva and Rudhra turned back from his restless state. "Even we don't have an idea of how important it is for us to meet her. But do believe me, it's going to cost more than what our brains can possibly assess and imagine, if you don't allow us to meet her now."

To Rudhra it seemed like that broke him a little.

"Please, sir," Eshwar pleaded. "Someone out there in London wanted us to do this. He's a spy, who risked everything including his life to transmit this message. You can deny us. But you can't deny him."

And that made him break at once. "No matter how important it is right now, you can never meet her, because she's not here," he said in a helpless tone.

"What!" Rudhra walked back to him. "She's not here?"

"No, sir. She went away."

Rudhra turned to Eshwar in incomprehension and back to Bilva. "Where did she go?"

"We don't know, sir. The day when Mr Prudhvi came to visit her and left to work for Bose the very next day… she too left us the day after."

'Prudhvi came here to meet her?' Rudhra wondered.

"But where did she head to? She should be somewhere on this earth right?"

"Right, sir. But I never got a chance to ask," Bilva said irritated. "That day the camp woke up early in the morning to make a move and she was gone by then."

"Just like that?"

"Just like that… It's been four years; we were running this group in the shade that she had been in the underground, operating all the attacks. The British only fear her. Please don't let anyone out there know anything about this. We can't handle it if-"

"Did she leave anything behind?" Rudhra said cutting him.

"Yes. Did she leave anything?" Eshwar repeated.

"Yeah," Bilva answered in doubt. "Actually, she left everything."

* * *

They sat in a tent with all her belongings scattered all over on the ground. Their search had ended now, and it seemed like Mr Rudhra got what he wanted. In the golden brown light from the lantern hanging to the center pole of the tent, Eshwar could see tears that rolled down the cheeks of the tech-genius. He had few letters in his hand which he was reading for the second or third time.

"Is there a message for us, sir?" he wanted to ask, but it felt better to keep quiet and give him some more time. He wondered who this Sanjuktha was. What was her relation with this spy in London? And why was Mr Rudhra crying reading their personal letters?

"I am sorry," Rudhra finally said, taking his glasses off to wipe his face. "I couldn't help myself."

"It's… It's ok, sir." He's still in a doubt whether to ask that question – the newly aroused one. But he did try his turn. "Who are these people, sir?" he said making Rudhra to look in his eye. "Who is Sanjuktha? Who is Prudhvi? Why is all this happening?"

"I can tell you Eshwar," said Rudhra, and his voice felt heavier. "But I am sure that you will regret asking me."

"Never mind, sir. I only regret not asking things." However, his real intension was to calm him down. Grief shared was grief diminished.

But by the time Rudhra completed narrating, he did felt anguished.

Rudhra witnessed the boy trying hard to control his tears.

"How can love be so ruthless, sir?" he said at last.

"It's not love that's ruthless Eshwar. It's fate which always wanted to test it. Love is fearless. That's the reason why it never escapes a test."

"You know what, sir? Now I really wanted to see her – Misses Sanjuktha Prathap."

"Don't you want to see Prudhvi Prathap?" smiled Rudhra.

"No, sir. But I wonder if I can ever love someone like he does."

"Don't even think of," said Rudhra smiling again, as his eyes tried to dry the tears off. "They are the real antiques. Can never be replaced or repeated."

Eshwar too smiled. "So, do we have any lead, sir?"

"No," he said raising the letters. "They are just letters. No clues at all."

After searching the whole tent for one last time, they decided to rest for the day. Rudhra rolled the letters in a letter that was written on cloth and placed them safely in his bag, hoping them to still yield a code.

They fell asleep on the old camp mattresses near the fire, making their over coats as pillows. They placed the riffles that Bilva provided them to protect themselves in case of a surprise attack, in the grass beside the bed with in a hand's reach.

Eshwar slept like he was dead and Rudhra stirred in his sleep like he was going to die. He dreamed of his childhood, where he always watched Prudhvi and Sanjuktha chat for hours sitting in the last bench of the class. They were just kids then, in their white and brown, cute and short school uniforms. Rudhra saw flashes of Prudhvi and Sanjuktha happy in each other's company. That day he prayed to god to keep them as such in every stage of their life. But now they are continents apart, dreaming of getting back together one day and striving to fulfil each other's dreams.

But where had Sanjuktha gone? Why did she leave in the first place? Had she too left for London? How in hell could she do that?

Rudhra woke up with a sudden jolt and sat, breathing heavy. He hadn't remembered what woke him but he never felt this agitated in his entire life. He wanted to meet Sanjuktha at any cost and see if she was fit and fine. Staring at the shining sky through the distantly formed trees, he realised that Sanjuktha too had always been as much as a friend to him as Prudhvi was. She used to take care of his mother when she fell sick now and then. She had smiled and enquired his wellbeing every time they met in the streets. She used to share sweets and special dishes on every festive day.

But now, he didn't even completely remember her face. No information of her was known. Not at least if she was alive somewhere.

"Why did all this ever happen to us?" he whimpered inside his head. "Why can't we have a happy life with all our friends and family around? Why should a nation ever wanted to rule on another? Why can't our lives be just normal?"

Rudhra literally cried, as he sat with his hands around his legs that were folded close to his stomach, and watched the fire burn inside the coal. The company of Eshwar, though he was out of this world now, had felt a bit soothing to him. Such an energetic and jovial kid he was. Some could turn into your best of friends just over hours. Rudhra hoped if he could wake up and talk to him now.

In between all this chaos, it struck him like a flash from the infinity. The way she used to smile at Prudhvi… The spark that glittered in his eyes when she did that… The image of both the lovers smiling in each other's arms… Uncontrollable flow of flashes and uncountable number of dialogs from the past started filling his racing brain. His consciousness wiggled to prove itself.

It's something he heard as an echo from the forest that made all this happen. Had he heard it now? Or that too was from the past? Whatever it might be, it made him remember something which he had never realised until this second that he actually remembered.

"ESHWAR…" Rudhra shouted, shaking him vigorously by his shoulder.

"Sir, yes, sir…" It was Eshwar's turn to shout. He jumped up on his bed and in the next split second his hand was on his riffle. He unlocked it aiming towards the forest. "Let's get those bastards, sir. Let's shoot the life out of those bloody British dogs."

"Eshwar…" Rudhra tried to calm him, realising that he had shaken him up too much. "Eshwar slow down."

"Sir?" he said lowering the weapon. "What happened? We are not under attack?"

"*You* are… In your dreams," he said picking up his coat and went away into the tent, where they left their bags. By the time Eshwar got completely transformed into this world again, he came running with their luggage and two sticks that were burning by their heads.

"Let's go," he said throwing his cloth satchel on to him and handing him one of the torches. "We are running out of time."

"He walks like he runs. And now it looks like he's going to run. God, save me," Eshwar prayed.

"Come on, quick," warned Rudhra running into the forest as the fire in his hand chased away the darkness of the woods.

“We should have started earlier, sir,” he said catching up with him and changing the torch into another hand to have a look at his watch. It was 03:46, his time. “Will it be a major problem if you don’t decode today’s message?”

“Hell with today. I want the code sequence of last-but-one iteration from yesterday.”

“It’s not with you, sir?”

“I should destroy it. But as instructed, Akbar should have left an extra copy on the podium desk. Hope he did it…” he said jumping over a root. Eshwar followed. “We should get in before 01:00 or the doors will be locked, until tomorrow. Something from somewhere was strongly suggesting me that we have no time to waste.”

“But what will we do without the main key?”

“That’s the reason why we are running now,” he said turning to him as they still ran. “I got the key.”

“What!”

* * *

They were on the edges of losing the race with time.

Rudhra hadn’t spoken much during the entire flight, and even if he did, it was only to ask him the time. They flew in the capital’s airspace now and it was a minimum of eight more minutes to reach the helipad.

“Time?” enquired Rudhra, talking after hours.

“12:46, sir.”

“Your time?” he said with little hope.

“Actual time,” replied Eshwar, with his tone lacking life.

Rudhra hadn't spared time to leave a sigh even if he wanted to. He knew that they were going to lose. Even if it took not more than eight minutes to land, the clock ticks 12:54 pm by then. It was a five-minute run all the way into the Administrative Building. Though they reached the hall by 12:59 pm, may be they couldn't reach for the podium and return back with the sheet in one minute. Also on late hours like this, the security checked the chief too. And it was a strict protocol that if someone remained inside the room past 01:00, they should be locked inside till the doors opened again the next day.

They jumped off the chopper the next split second it touched the ground.

"It should be 12:55 in any worst case," thought Rudhra, but felt reluctant to check it with his intern. He feared what he might say. By the time they jumped off it, the chopper was still in control of the inertia of its blades and it slid few meters away as they ran from it.

When they neared the rear side entrance, they saw a 'Work in Progress' board that popped up from nowhere. The iron gate was closed and there were people spreading mixed concrete under it.

"Can you please make an opening? The narrowest one you can make will do," Rudhra pleaded in the fastest formation of words.

"Sorry, sir," one of the worker replied as Eshwar just reached them panting. "There's deep wet cement all over the other side."

It was Rudhra himself who had raised a complaint to fill the uneven land there.

"Damn," he cursed running towards the main gate, which made their journey longer by five more minutes.

Eshwar ran at a distance to Rudhra who was running with all his will, even if it was way more than clear that it will tick 01:00 by the time he reached the main gate itself.

Rudhra sat on one knee holding the gate for support and tried to catch his breath. It felt like all their efforts had gone into vain. But they still got some chance that only depended on their luck. They could wait until the next morning and decode the message, the first thing tomorrow. Rudhra hated himself for not guessing such an obvious key until he travelled half way across the country.

"I am so sorry, sir." He suddenly heard Eshwar shout at him and turned back to take a look. He ran past the gate in a jiffy, making Rudhra turn his head in a flash. "I lied to you in the last go. It's not the actual time. It's my time."

Rudhra sat there with his mouth wide open as Eshwar ran away from him. After taking a lead he wanted to equal him by the time they reach the Administrative Building, Eshwar took a halt to turn back and smiled at his chief.

"How could someone possibly smile in a situation like this?" Rudhra wondered past all his wondering limits.

"You're so dead in my hands," he shouted running on to him who took an immediate flight.

Both the gentlemen adjusted their coats and settled their hair with fingers as they walked past the full-steel statue. Now there was even no need of worrying on how to smuggle the sheet out of the hall. They had enough time to decode it there itself and walk out with the message. But even now, they had to hurry up.

As they neared the hallway that led to the security door, Rudhra's hands impulsively searched for his ID, from years of everyday practice. But today, they found none.

All at once, Rudhra realised that he left his ID back in his bag that was still in the chopper.

"Eshwar," he said taking a sudden halt.

"Sir?" Eshwar walked back to him.

"I forgot the ID in my bag."

Eshwar stared at him in disbelief. "But you're the chief, sir," he said as if suggesting a way out.

"It doesn't matter. No one is allowed inside without an ID."

Eshwar wanted it to happen at any cost. Not just to Rudhra, but even for him someone from somewhere was sending signals of urgency on war foot basis.

'In war, 'Now' is all you get,' echoed in his ears.

"Sir, I have an idea," he said making Rudhra go anxious at once. "But this time, you need to run slow."

The heavy guy opened his desk in the security booth and signalled his friend on the other side waving his hand. He moved his head in an 'Ok' and walked into the booth on his side. They both needed to lock the door at once using both their keys. It had been just 12:54 pm now, but the heavy guy was not so tolerant to hunger.

As he picked up his key from the drawer, he suddenly started hearing footsteps that were approaching them fast. He ran to the door to take a look along with his partner and the hallway was literally echoing now. It was the same kid again. But this time Mr. Rudhra is chasing him.

"Don't stop him," he was shouting.

Even without Rudhra shouting it out, they were still in doubt whether to stop him again or not. But they should perform their duties. They stepped out of the door as Eshwar ran close to them and he was not stopping even with their guns pointed at him.

"Stop where you are," one of them shouted.

They felt their fingers shivering on the triggers. The chief was shouting not to stop the boy and the boy himself seemed like he was not going to stop. They were not quite sure if they could shoot at a person running towards the hall with an ID hanging around his neck and it was still not past 01:00.

He ran past the soldiers elbowing them and wiggling out of their grip as they tried to take hold of him. He jumped into the door and fell on to the other side.

"Are you out of your mind?" shouted Rudhra pushing them again to run into the door. "I said stop him."

The soldiers turned to look at each other.

The guards at the other end saw a kid running towards the hall. But they thought it was just a last-minute worker who's running in, to get out before 01:00, until they saw the chief and the guards of the other side chase him. He ran into the hall by the time they got hold of their guns and aimed at him.

"Don't shoot…" Rudhra shouted again. "I repeat, *don't* shoot. He's just a lunatic intern." And he took off with a pace as if he turned into a human missile. Eshwar ran towards the podium as Rudhra entered the hall with the soldiers behind him with a longer gap between them.

Rudhra stopped nowhere until he reached Eshwar right at the center. He caught hold of him by his collar as he ran past the podium and threw him back on to it. Eshwar went flying and fell on to the wood with a banging thud.

"Do you think this is a joke?" he shouted as Eshwar turned back immediately and opened the cabin in the stand. The width of the podium helped him to hide from the soldiers running from the other side.

Rudhra's heart raced with prayers to let the sheet be there, but they failed.

The cabin was empty. There's nothing but neatly polished wood that formed the interiors. No sign of at least a piece of paper.

Eshwar turned to Rudhra in helplessness, who was still maintaining anger for sake of the guards. He felt so bad for Rudhra for being in a place where he was now.

"I am sorry, sir," Eshwar whispered.

"Not your fault," he whispered back losing faith all over again.

"Wait…" Eshwar said at once, realising something. "Akbar."

He turned and started searching the upper wall of the cabin touching all over the surface with his palm. Like a shooting star that granted wishes, an envelope fell from it, making Rudhra's heart skip a beat.

"Waheguru..." Eshwar left a sigh taking it out and tried to hide it inside his coat's pocket.

"I tell you, you're going to pay for it," Rudhra continued acting like he was raging with anger and bent down as if to hit him, but actually to grab the letter and push it into his pocket. "They may search you." He whispered only half the sentence and the soldiers rounded them by then.

"Don't even think of stepping in SIGNIT again," Rudhra switched his dialog looking deep in his eye as if threatening him.

Eshwar's heart felt a minor tremor. Though Mr Rudhra was just acting, those words – 'Don't even think of stepping in SIGNIT again,' made him weep inside. It seemed like he really lost his chance for life.

"Let us take care of him, sir," the heavy guy said, with his teeth clenched.

"It's ok gentlemen. I'll take care of this."

"No, sir. It's the rule that-"

Eshwar sensed that it was getting off hand and used the exit act they prepared for. "Stop blabbering you punk," he said standing up and acting like he didn't give a damn. "You can never hold me from disrespecting you whenever I wanted to."

The heavy guy burned with rage and wanted to show him what he got. But suddenly in middle of all the edginess, Rudhra turned back to Eshwar drawing a fist and hitting him hard on the face. Eshwar went flying away from the circle formed by the soldiers, who fell into shock to see the chief turn into a maniac.

"You bloody filthy teenagers are the ones that spoil our culture," he said walking to him in heavy steps and caught hold of him by his collar. Eshwar was bleeding from his nose that stirred Rudhra's heart. But he couldn't stop. He started beating him to a pulp. "What is it with you and them? Hah? This is not just enough for you damn it," he said lifting him up by his collar and dragging him out of the hall. "I'll teach you a lesson myself."

The soldiers stood there in shock, and the heavy guy said after few moments: "The chief seems more British than us."

As they all laughed moving out of the hall, locking it off for the day, the sheet in their chief's pocket left the premises, unnoticed.

* * *

Eshwar adjusted the rear view mirror to apply some antiseptic on the heavy cut over his nose. His shirt inside the blazer was stained with the blood that was by now spread into its threads. His blazer too took some, but they were not clearly visible. They were in the Cadillac custom convertible that was parked at the side wall of a Church. The tinted windows were closed and the top was covered.

"Damn," cursed Eshwar as the solution burned his flesh, without unsettling Mr Rudhra's concentration.

"Why do you think it may be the right key, sir?" he said with half doubt whether to disturb him or not.

"Not 'May be' Eshwar," Rudhra spoke, still immersed in his transforms. "It's for sure. There can be no other key as exact as this."

"But it's not a six-letter word."

"It can be any number of letters. You feed what he fed there."

"What do you think the message is going to be, sir?"

"Why to ask the taste, when you're going to have a piece?" he said. But Rudhra too had the same doubt racing in his mind that was dancing on needles.

"Hmmm…" He turned back to look into the mirror and pressed the cotton on his nose again. "Damn…"

"Hurts?" Rudhra said turning his eyes to him.

"No, sir. Feels good."

"I think this generation gap always had a habit of inducing more sarcasm into the younger ones."

"Not at all, sir," he smiled turning back to him. "I mean it. Really… I am even happy that I did it. This is my first official blood for my mother land. But the only thing is that…"

"What?"

"Nothing, sir."

"Eshwar… It's ok. Spit it out."

"Am I ever going to get into SIGNIT again?" he said losing the entire color off his face. "Like ever?"

"Why do you think you won't?"

"With today's incident."

"If I had to do it," Rudhra said with trust in his words, "I'll state that it never happened. It was just the earlier clash between you and the guards that was making them, blame you."

"You can do that, sir?"

"I shouldn't. But I will," he winked.

"I already told you, sir-"

"That I am a rock star?"

"Yes, sir," he smiled scratching his head.

"Same to you, kid. You're a rock star too."

"Me?"

"Yeah... You saved the day, twice. So you're twice a rock star than me."

They both smiled; one out of pride and the other of glee.

"So, how the key, sir?" Eshwar said to neutralise the emotions and also remembering his curiosity to know the trick.

"The forest told me," he said smiling. "And I immediately realised that he chose me not because I know *him*, but because I know *them*."

"Sir, I too heard the forest sing," he said. "I mean how it relates."

"He used to call her this all the time."

"Nightingale?"

"My Nightingale..."

Chapter 11

Same day
09:35 am (03:05 pm, Indian time)
B16 Secret Quarters, London

He was not the blunt and arrogant boy anymore that he once used to be…

Or a fearless freedom fighter that someone always wanted him to be…

He was just the same old admirer, the same old crazy lover and a secret agent. All these years behind the enemy lines, had transformed him into as much a spy as he never thought he would turn into. He mastered the art of floating like butterfly in a second and stinging like a bee in the other.

He may not have looked like, with the British uniform and the officer looks on, but he was Mr. Prudhvi Prathap Raju himself, with a 'Commander in Chief' prefixed to his name.

It had been four years since Prudhvi had joined the SIGNIT group, London and from the last one year, he was also being closely associated with the members of B16 – the secret agency that was set up to take out Bose. It was the support of the officials from India who knew what blood he was and how his father served the British, which were followed by the records of his own services to the British Intelligence, made him one of the most trusted members inside the house today.

It was Prudhvi himself who took an initiative in developing a highly secured mode of communication between London and Delhi. He wanted every message from B16 to pass through his system so that they could guarantee 100% non-transparency. They say that, his highness King George VI himself called him to praise for the exceptional service.

Prudhvi knew that his friend Rudhra, on the other end, would take the required care when he first made the announcement to the heads in India. He was very sure that Rudhra would never afford to let someone else take the chair of chief when there was going to be hell lot of information to spy on and it did happen.

Prudhvi had leaked the most safeguarded transmissions through the world's most secured passage and saved many lives of his fellow rebels till date; even though his friend was completely unaware of his existence on the other end. He never left a chance that would save a soldier's life.

But today, it was completely different. Today, B16 withheld a piece of information with them, that they were not willing to transmit anywhere. Even Prudhvi was unaware of how they were supplied with such a confidential data and from where. They wanted to deal with it on their own and this intelligence, if wisely used, could change the course of Indian Independence movement and re-establish their grip over the lost territories too.

Not even all the heads of the departments were informed about it. The line of trust was being drawn with a sword that could prove you dead on the other side.

Whatever the consequences might turn out to be, Prudhvi wanted to warn his friend. But also without being caught and he knew a perfect way to do so. There will still be some unimportant words left in the sequence that occurred after feeding today's message with his code. He filled up those spaces with few important words which were obtained from feeding his Acquaintance Key to the spy message. The key he used was 'Nightingale' – the name he always called her with, the name that always made her smile. For him, it was the synonym for Sanjuktha. He knew that Rudhra would take the hint of hyphens and easily guess the key out.

But one couldn't afford to waste a minute. Prudhvi prayed that his friend decoded the information before it got too late for any action to be taken. The rebels should be warned, and this time they had no contact with the outer world to do so. Rudhra had to travel all by himself. That was the only way it could be done and there was no Plan-B left, except for Prudhvi himself being on the team that was supposed to fly on this mission.

"Sir, Mr Beckman can meet you now," said the white lady who seemed like a typist, walking towards him at a pace.

"Thank you," Prudhvi smiled standing from the iron chair.

He was waiting in an office that was filled with temporary cardboard walls, tensed employees and infinite number of files stuffed into infinite number of racks all over the place.

"Please find him in the southern hangar, sir," the typist smiled back, just for courtesy and walked away in the same pace.

Prudhvi combed his crew cut hair with his palms and placed his officer's cap on, adjusting it by the visor. He pulled his uniform straight by its edges before walking in the direction where the hangars stood behind the office.

He knew that Mr Beckman was not so easy to break, but he did not want to leave any chances of Plan-B going completely un-attempted. This was war, and it had a very strong habit of not being on the side of morality.

However, Prudhvi did have his advantage with Beckman. He was the creator of a security system that went past all imaginable levels, rewarding him with a gold medal and the position of the Chief SIGNAT engineer in return. He also had a personal liking too, towards Prudhvi – an Indian who wanted to support the enemy in his need and the phone call from the king that day, which happened in his presence, pushed everything to the next level.

Prudhvi filled his face with a fake professional smile that seemed livelier than any real smile, as he shook hands with the subordinates of Mr Beckman, who opened the gates. The echo of his shoes hitting the concrete floor reverberated in the abundantly widened hangar space. With years that passed by, technology too took its turn at many unexpected edges. Unlike the aircrafts on which he was trained during his first regiment in London, today they could carry machine guns in their wings, heavy missiles in their bellies, extending warranty of destruction and death in the very purpose of their creation. Nothing could speed up the technological advancement like a war does.

Prudhvi walked across thirty to forty upgraded versions of Hawker Hart bomber aircrafts that stood in an arrangement which made him remember the formation of his soldiers when they are ordered to march – stiff and straight, calm but lethal.

"Mr Prudhvi…" exclaimed Beckman, walking out of a conversation with his fellow generals. "So nice to see you after a long time, son."

"Same here, sir," Prudhvi smiled extending his hand.

"Oh come on… Let's hug on this," he laughed out loud, and they both hugged.

As he left him from the hug, Prudhvi turned back to the group of men who went busy in their conversation without Beckman.

"Don't look at them," he warned. "They are boring me to death. Let's get the hell out of here."

* * *

"So… what's that made Mr Chief himself to come looking for me?" smiled Beckman, as both the men in uniform strolled the aerodrome.

"I wanted to join the mission, sir." It was a fearless proposition.

"Mission? Which one?"

"The one that was looking for one last rider," he said making Beckman take a sudden halt.

"I hope you are not referring to what you are referring to."

"But I am, sir. I want in."

"This is not as simple as building a code Prudhvi. This is something more…"

"Something more like me. It too wants to take lives."

"Of whom?"

"You know the answer, sir."

Beckman said nothing but simply stared at him for the next few seconds. Prudhvi too hadn't blinked an eye.

"I wonder why you wanted to," he finally said. "But I can't let you in, son."

"Why can't you, sir? You have every power to."

"But you're an Indian," he said as a matter of fact. "We can't afford an Indian on this mission."

"Don't you think that the one who wanted this mission the most is also an Indian?"

"Gandhi is not behind this, son. Neither was Nehru. It's just a rumor."

"I hadn't taken names, sir."

"Then?" he said starting to get irritated. "What do you say?"

"I wanted in. Please… help me."

"Why do you sound so desperate, Prudhvi?" Beckman took his name and he sensed that the argument was going off track. But he was well prepared for this too.

Prudhvi said nothing in response but just started to act as if he was controlling himself from breaking. His eyes began to fill with tears – the fake ones that a master spy produced in support of his act.

Beckman was shocked to see a young man, who was the head of one of the biggest branches of their army, cry.

"Prudhvi?" he said placing his hand over his shoulder in support.

"I don't know what my mom looks like, sir," he said, sounding like he was crying even harder inside. "She died of an illness even before I knew her. It was my dad who raised me. And I don't know if you can believe this; in my entire life, even for today, I never missed my mom. Never...

My dad was my hero. A human who's so tender at heart, a man who's so dedicated to his job and an officer who's brutally slammed to death for being so. Do you know who did that, sir?"

Beckman moved his head in a 'No,' with his mouth still open a little.

"The one who's being called 'Netaji' these days," he said, now shaking with anger. "With his very own hands, he stabbed a knife into my father's heart. He dragged him down all the way from his office, out of the house, towards the lake and threw him in it like a bag of fish feed.

"His body was swollen all over, by the time they pulled him out. Eaten by fishes, soaked in the mud and cut into pieces by the doctors later on... Could you ever imagine that happening to *your* father, sir?"

"Son..." stopped Mr Beckman unable to produce any sound that seemed meaningful. "Why hadn't you ever told me this?" he finally said.

"Because I saved it for situations like these,' he wanted to say. "Because you make me remember him in a way, sir," he replied instead, wiping his tears off. "I don't know what that makes you call me 'Son.' But it always sounds like you literally mean it. I felt soothing every time I talk to you and I never wanted to disturb it."

Beckman suddenly felt silence gripping him stronger than before. He hated himself for asking him that question, but loved the way the kid respected him all through. Now he understood the motto of Prudhvi in helping them with all that he had over all these years.

"What all that he had?" thought Beckman. "Now it feels like he had nothing. His life seemed meaningless from every point. But maybe it can still find a purpose in the death of the murderer of his father."

"*Sometimes*, life won't be that fair, son," he tried to console.

"Actually, life will never be fair, sir," smiled Prudhvi. "It's we who misinterpret *sometimes*."

That tore his heart to the very last layer.

"Are you a certified pilot?" he said at once.

"It's you who handed me the medal, sir," he smiled again.

"War time training?"

"Cleared all the levels."

"Hmmm…" Beckman started rubbing his neatly shaved chin. He wanted his soldier to have his fair share of revenge. "But I still can't promise you any certainty, son. You need to convince the head of this mission first."

"Who's that, sir?" he enquired with a tone that said he definitely will, at any given cost.

"Gracie Gomes," answered Beckman, in an I-am-really-sorry tone.

***

"So she might be a really good singer then," said Eshwar dressing his nose with some cotton and a small piece of surgical tape. "Or is it just Mr Prudhvi who thinks she is?"

"You should hear her sing kiddo," answered Rudhra, who was in his final iterations. "You'll think twice before you joke again, which I am very sure that you can never do."

Eshwar turned to him in surprise.

"She sings like an angel Eshwar. You'll cry if the right song strikes."

"Oh my god…" he exclaimed, without a smile.

"Paste a longer piece," suggested Rudhra, turning back to his work.

"Is there any possible chance of us tracking her down, sir? Like once all this mess was sorted out, can we find her and meet her?"

He said absolutely nothing. Not even a sound in response and that made Eshwar to turn to him for visual footage.

Rudhra was staring into the paper in his hand like it was playing something on it. Something dangerous, even than the World War… His hands started shuddering in distress and eyes in uncertainty. Eshwar felt danger filling their immediate future.

"Sir?" he tried to make him turn, but Rudhra hadn't. "Sir? Sir, what does it say?"

Still no reply…

Eshwar grabbed the paper from his hands, which remained in their positions. On the extreme left bottom of the paper that was filled with transforms all over, he found the original message.

"*Attacking* Ghagra *3 days*."

"It's the forest camp in Ghagra," Rudhra said, still in trance.

"Another attack?"

"This is not *just* another attack Eshwar." Rudhra was on the edges of blowing off. "How come the British knew about this? Double spies?"

"Sir, it can be-"

"Damn…" he cursed trashing the dashboard with his angry fist, making Eshwar go calm at once. The dashboard came out of its fitting and Rudhra out of his senses. "How on earth they spotted a place which was indefinite even to our own spies? No one at least knows such a camp exists and…"

He stopped at once raging with resentment and helplessness. The inside of the car echoed with his angry intakes of oxygen.

"What's so important about that camp, sir?" enquired Eshwar in a calming tone, after a long silence.

"It was more than a camp," said the Rudhra who was pulling himself together. "It's the place where Bose meets up the heads of rebels every quarter."

"Bose?" exclaimed Eshwar. "Why would Bose be in India? I mean… how could?"

"What how could?"

"There's a shoot-at-sight on him. And he's in Burma right? Being secretive and all… How could he enter India in the first place, sir?"

"We here are talking about a man who built an empire of spies underground the British lands. The Father of the Rebels."

"Then how come the British knew about such a secret camp?"

"Well, that's the bigger question. But for now, the one with more priority is – 'How are we going to warn them?'"

"We can fly right?"

"We can't," he said as it's never going to happen. "Calcutta had a highly secured air space. It's closer to our enemy lands and it's the most used passage into India."

"Then we should plan an alternative, sir," he said seeding a solution into Rudhra's mind. "But it says only three days."

"Eshwar?" Rudhra spoke as calm as he can. "Can I ask you for a favor that I can never repay you with?"

"Yes, sir. Sure…"

His intern sounded ready for helping him with anything he wanted to, but Rudhra started feeling bad to ask him.

"It's ok, sir. Go on…" he said assuring, half expecting what he was going to ask.

"Can you travel to Ghagra?"

"Me?" His eyes widened out when he actually heard it.

"Yes, Eshwar. You... I wanted you to act as a carrier. I can't afford to go missing for days, and return with a good alibi at such a short notice. Chances of getting noticed or caught are more likely."

"But how could I locate them in the forest, sir?"

"I'll write an address and a letter. Go meet the guide in that address and he'll help you reach the spot."

"Where Bose was?" he said as his spine shivered from the very thought of it.

"Yes... But do remember. The letter I write, don't share it to the guide you meet. He knows nothing about who's in there. Hand it only to this man – Drutha. He's the personal security officer for Bose, whom you always find behind him. He's also one of the most wanted... Clear?"

"Yes, sir," he answered taking a deep breath.

"Let's go get your luggage," Rudhra said twisting the key beneath the hanging dashboard and the engine roared to life, as Eshwar shivered to fear.

* * *

"So do you think you can break her?" enquired Beckman, with his consciousness crying out the answer – 'No, he never can.'

"I think I can, sir," replied Prudhvi, though his own consciousness was crying out almost the same.

"You good at these?"

"Yes, sir."

"How good?"

"5 of 5?"

"At least expand the scale to 10," smiled Beckman.

Prudhvi smiled back. "What difference does it make, sir? End of the day, it's 100% anyway… There can be nothing more than that!"

"Yes, there can be," Beckman smiled again bending close to him this time. "But not now. There can be more, when you still hadn't uttered your answer."

"I am confidence, sir. 'Over' is not my surname."

They both laughed aloud as they took a halt in the shade of a jet's wing. But in real, it was only Beckman who was laughing. Prudhvi just faked it, as his mind started turning intolerant to the fact that he had chances to fail.

It was not his mistake that he needed help right now, but it was the reputation to that name – Gracie Gomes. Very few in the SIGNIT department had actually seen her in person, but the name was very well known. 'The Witch of the Royal Air Force' they called her. One of the exceptionally few lady officers who made it to a cadre of such level and the only one who fights men in the boxing ring, in Inter-Air-Force boxing competitions. She had won most of the trophies.

Pushing aside many other such evil qualities, it was also profoundly believed that she had a habit of being flawlessly strict, that she can spot a mark on your sock even with your shoe on, and would reject you for it.

"I hope I can help you on this, son." Beckman tried to sound as if he meant it, and he really did. "But I can only recommend you for the slot. She had all the powers rested in her grip."

"That's fine, sir," he said thinking it over again. "Do we have any areas of advantage? Like the work I have done for SIGNIT?"

"Or you can tell her the same, that why you wanted to kill Bose."

"No, sir," he ruled it off. "I have opened up now because it's *you*. I don't think I can do that with a stranger." It's just the extra butter he was rubbing. But the real reason was, from what he had heard of Gracie Gomes through many years now, she would easily track him down. May be with a background check involving both his previous life and the most recent messages he had transferred. Any spike coming up with the name 'Sanjuktha' from both the ends would ruin everything. He should think of a much better passage – much cleaner and stronger one.

"Ahh... Prudhvi," called out Beckman, as if he was in the process of calling something back. "I just remembered something about Gracie I once heard from her father."

"What's it, sir?" he enquired with all the interest.

"I think she hates Indians..."

* * *

"*Jai Hind*... It's the shout of the Indian National Army," explained Rudhra, as they left the parking lot towards the ticket counter. "They say that it was coined by Mr Subhash himself."

"Do I look nervous, sir?" Eshwar enquired all of a sudden.

"Why do you ask? Are you?"

"I… I don't know, sir. I am not going on a holiday right. I am going to meet… I don't know…if I can really take it when I do see him. I don't think I am qualified enough, sir."

Rudhra smiled as he pushed a ten rupee note with the portrait of King George VI on it, into the ticket counter.

"I personally don't think that there can be someone who's more qualified than you," he said handing him the ticket, which he tucked into the inner pocket of his over coat. "You deserve this, Eshwar. It's not just an accident that you walked in, just when I needed you."

"Thank you, sir," he smiled bright. "But what if something happens to me there?"

It was just a mere question he threw to see his Chief's face take colors. Eshwar wanted something to distract himself with.

Until then it never crossed his mind. It was just the message that he wanted to reach Mr Bose at any cost, but Rudhra never thought of this. He was right. What if something happened to this kid? The blood of a young soldier will soak his hands for the rest of his life.

"Sir, it's just a joke," smiled Eshwar, trying to pull him back to normal. It did distract him now.

Rudhra knew that Eshwar was willing to die for his country. That's what a soldier does, but this one was different. He couldn't imagine that energy die down to zero.

Rudhra moved to ask him something when suddenly the train whistled from the distance and they both turned to it.

It was an old-modelled coal engine that would take at least five more minutes to reach its stop. Rudhra turned back to Eshwar, to raise a question that ensures the chances of his not returning. He wanted to ask him the whereabouts of his parents, so that he could take care of them, in case of…

"Can I ask you something?" It's not Rudhra. It's Eshwar.

"Ya…" blabbered Rudhra. "Go… Go ahead."

"What's in the letter that you handed me, sir? The one I should-"

"A better plan," he said at once.

"To?"

"To keep Bose low after this."

"Underground?" enquired Eshwar.

"Something way better than that."

"Hide him?"

"Kill him."

"What?!" Eshwar sprang out of shock.

"You heard me, Eshwar." Rudhra was not smiling, and it clearly wasn't a joke. "Bose is going to die in an airplane crash soon."

"For what?"

"Simple… How can someone stop who's already dead?"

"Fake death?" Eshwar slowly realised.

"You're asking?"

"But how?"

"The Taiwanese government will help us," he said, as if everything was already set. "We'll get a fake body that's unable to spot if it's really Bose. Make even the doctors believe it's him and treat him before declaring death. We should take care of everything; from the type of blood to the dental dentures; from surgical implants to skeletal injuries. No one who's outside the accident spot should ever know the truth. Then we'll ask them to get a fake name to that body they believed Bose. And try to cremate the body with that name. To the world, it should look like we cremated Bose in secrecy."

"I didn't get it," he said, trying to hold pieces together. "When we wanted them to believe it, why keep it a secret? And that too after covering up every other corner that's left for uncertainty. We can state it as a fact. Why lie?"

"Because facts face doubts, Eshwar. But a secret? They strive harder than their limits to reveal a secret. They knock on every door they can. And when they do crack it, they don't question it. They just believe."

***

"Let's not waste any of our time on this, anymore," Bose argued. "What if they are not providing us with utilities and transport? We can still walk... We can still fight..."

"But our soldiers are not willing to, sir," the general said. "The chain was breaking."

It was the heart of one of the denser and dangerous forest in Rangoon; the base camp of the Number 1 Guerrilla

Regiment. It was full of energetic and patriotic Indian war criminals when it started. But now they are breaking down, as the Japanese government reduced the supplies of food and utilities from the last few months. Even the trucks that are supposed to transport the land soldiers to the boarders and bring them back were on hold.

"Who are not willing Nawaz?" It was more than a question. It seemed like a threat. "Who are not willing to face the odds that shouldn't even matter to a soldier who's fighting for his motherland?"

"Few of... our soldiers... sir," he said trying hard to look at his leader.

"Then throw them out," said Bose walking away from him at once.

"Sir?" It took him by shock. "We'll lose number, sir."

"It's not about *number* anymore Nawaz," said Bose, stopping at the hut's entrance. "Now it's about keeping the chain intact. I think you know the saying. A chain is as strong as?"

"It's weakest link..."

"Cut them out. I need a new chain made, by the time I return," he ordered and walked away into the forest, towards his office.

"Sir, the cargo was ready," Drutha informed him walking into the shelter, as Bose stared at his own reflection in the mirror hanging to the bamboo wall.

Bose said or did nothing. He just stared at his own self, as if the mirror was a portal to some parallel world. It worried Drutha.

"Sir, everything fine?"

"No Drutha." He was still staring into his own eyes. "Something feels wrong."

"Wrong?!" he said walking close.

"Yeah… very wrong…"

"About the trip?" Drutha enquired in a worried tone.

"No…" he said, turning back to him. "It feels like someone is calling me Drutha. Someone… or something…"

"What's that, sir?"

"I don't know… It never felt like this before."

"We are winning, sir" Drutha tried to cheer him. "This meeting will speed it up. Freedom is at our door steps."

"Not just freedom. There was something else."

"Which is?"

"Responsibility…"

"What does it have to make with this trip?"

"You're always concerned with what comes up in the immediate next," smiled Bose.

"Should we stop, sir?"

"Have we ever?"

Bose and Drutha slid themselves into a suit made of polythene covering them all over, and stepped into the empty truck. Once they both adjusted themselves in the cabins made under the wooden floor, their men covered them up with thin but thick planks of wood that suited the floor and started loading the truck with dead bodies of wild boars and forest deer that were to be transported into India.

* * *

The conductor opened doors to their bogie as the engine started throwing thick smoke from the exhausts beneath and the chimney above. Rudhra still wanted to ask him about his parents, but it still felt like he was suggesting his death.

"What if something really happens to him and I don't know where his parents live?" worried Rudhra.

"Eshwar?" he stopped him from hopping into the train.

"Yes, sir?"

"Should I ask you something… Don't take it wrong. But I just want to know where your parents live."

Eshwar smiled as if he knew why Rudhra wanted him not to take it wrong.

"Just in case…" Rudhra turned away his eyes unable to look straight at him.

"I don't know, sir," smiled Eshwar. "I never saw them. I am an orphan."

"What?!" Rudhra let out a cry. "Orphan? What do you mean orphan?"

"It means I am an orphan." He smiled brighter. "I never knew who my parents were, sir. They said that they found me in a… In a carriage that was sent to the Gurdwara before the night our village burned down to ashes in a holocaust."

Rudhra began to battle those tears inside him. How could someone who smiles so bright and could make you smile too in any given situation turn out to be an orphan?

"Don't worry about me, sir," he said with a lump in his throat. "There's no one to cry on my death."

It fell like an even harder blow this time. Rudhra's heart wiggled to bear the sudden pain. Who can he be an orphan? How can Eshwar, be an orphan? Was all that vim and energy he emits; were they to control the grief that was plunging inside his heart for every other second that passes by?

"You're an orphan?"

"Yes, sir… I am an orphan."

"Not anymore Eshwar," Rudhra's voice was quivering, but he was so determined to tell him what he wanted to. "You're not an orphan anymore. You have a brother now."

The tears that rolled inside Eshwar's head until now started filling his eyes at once. It was his childhood fantasy to have someone in this world that he could call with not a name but with a relation.

"Brother?" enquired Eshwar, with that one little word hardly leaving his lips.

"Yes… *Brother.*"

Eshwar smiled and sighed, as he turned back to push his bag into the bogie and hopping in controlling himself from not crying.

The engine emitted huge amounts of smoke again, but this time along with a whistle that echoed into the empty lands behind the station. Eshwar turned back to Rudhra as the conductor who was locking the doors moved towards their bogie. They just stared at each other for moments. It was not just a stare; it was the way a hero sent off another to the field. It was the stare that filled courage, support and strength.

"Brother..." Eshwar called out as the conductor started unbolting the open doors at their bottoms, to close and lock them.

"Yeah?" smiled Rudhra.

Eshwar waited for a moment before spelling it out.

"Jai Hind," he said raising his fist.

Rudhra smiled with pride as he raised his fist in response.

"Jai Hind..." he said, and the doors between them were closed.

* * *

Prudhvi waited in her office, with a brain that was racing like a cheetah on its hunt. His work in SIGNIT was of no use here. He couldn't tell her the same story that broke Mr Beckman. He couldn't plead her to let him join. And on top of everything, she hated Indians.

He wanted a point of his advantage that could impress her and push her to make him a part of her team. But what could it be? What was there with him to sell her?

Prudhvi lifted his head up from the carpet before the visitor's sofa that he sat on, to take a keen look at her office. There could be something that may help him impress her.

There was a huge wooden table which had tactfully tapestried ancient Scottish sculptures on its sides that covered almost the other side of the room. It had few bunches of files, paper weights, a British flag, fountains pens of different-colored inks stashed into a porcelain jar, a rotary dial phone, some photo frames facing towards the rotatable comfy chair, a type writer, some letter heads, an antique lamp and many other items neatly arranged on top of it. There were glass door bookshelves attached to the wall behind the table and they all were filled with countless books, resembling a lawyer's office. There was a four-winged fan, with a long stem, hanging from the roof.

The other side of the room had a three-piece sofa set on which he was sitting and a luxurious table that was made out of a wooden horse resting on its back, balancing a thick and clear glass on its hoofs. The walls on both the sides of the sofa set also had bookshelves attached, and the whole floor was covered with a red floor mat perfecting the office look.

"God… give me something…" he shouted inside his head.

Failure was a second chance to start more intelligently, but this time there was going to be none. No second chance. Prudhvi knew that he couldn't lose now. He couldn't let Bose die at this point. He was almost there and freedom was at the borders of India. Just few more months, or may be a year, Bose was going to break the British from inside so that they couldn't withstand the pressure from outside. All that they wanted now was some time. Just some time, to see his country break free from the crushing claws of the British… Just some time, to escape the army and reach his country safely… Just some time, to hug his love to his heart and live happily ever after…

Prudhvi suddenly heard the commotion outside turn into silence. He turned aside and tried to look through the translucent glass as the silence turned into *absolute* silence.

It's the Witch.

He saw a brown shade of a neither tall nor short woman walking towards the door. The brown color told him that she too was dressed in an officer's uniform and her pace of walking, that she was way more confident than he thought she was. She was going to enter her office and in few more seconds, he was going to stand in front of her.

"The Witch of the Royal Air Force… That's what they call her right," he thought, as he stood up adjusting his cap and the uniform, ready to greet her with a bright and confident smile. "The Witch… So I need a magic now. Any sort of magic that can break her…. Sanju, ask your Krishna to help me. Help me with a miracle. Please…"

The door swung open, and she walked in looking into a file. His file.

Prudhvi could see her barely with her cap on and face bent down, but his heart did skip a beat with his mind processing the fact that she was standing in the same room as his.

"So it's you who wanted in? Mister…" she said, dragging her figure along the 'Name' section in the file, walking to her chair.

Like a flash from nowhere, all at once her figure froze at his name, and so does she at the edge of the table.

Gracie suddenly turned back to look at the man who's waiting for her, and the magic did happened. A miracle…

Prudhvi went into a trance with the very sight of her. It's her… With her eyes struck in between surprise and excitement, and lips in between silence and smile.

"Emily?!" he cried out. But that word barely left his throat

Chapter 12

"When did you come back?" she said, still trying to stop herself from being the old little Emily again.

They were in the canteen, with steaming black coffee in front of them, one for each, and no one touched their cup yet. Their officer hats which held Royal Force emblems on them were placed on the table, on their right hand sides – the official's style.

"I have never been to India actually except for a few weeks," he said staring into her eyes.

"Few weeks! Then why did you leave me in the first place? You would have stayed back and saved me from years of tears," she cried inside.

"It feels strange to see you like this, Emily," he smiled, to which she reciprocated.

She was in the uniform too, but a first grade officer's stitch, with her efforts and services hanging in the form of medals to it along with a formal ascot around her neck, which reflected her cadre again. Emily had changed a lot. Her skin that used to glow with the whitish air once had lost its smile now, and so it's radiance. Her eyes which used to hip-hop once had lost their rhythm and it only reflected a sense of opacity. Her hair that used to dance in the slightest of wind once was now tied in a bun and it really looked funny.

Though he smiled real after a long time, Prudhvi too was still in shock, surprise and pleasure to see her again, his best friend, after all these years. But he picked his words very carefully, as they might turn against him in case of any mistake. He was completely unaware that Emily had no strength left in her anymore to remember or at least completely process what he was saying.

In fact, they both were in the same state. They knew that they were left with no other options but to travel back in time in the very next second or the other. There could be nothing in this entire universe that could question or defeat *Time*. But we humans are fortunate enough to be blessed with a weapon to do so – memories. Though sometimes some of them may not turn out to be complete blessings.

"How's Sanjuktha?" she said. Prudhvi knew that was coming. There was no answer prepared and he should come up with something right now.

"I don't know. I never met her," he said.

"What?" she yelled in surprise.

"She moved to a place far from ours and I never got to see her again."

Emily tried to talk, but remained silent for some reason.

Meanwhile, the soldiers around started to wonder what Madam Gracie was doing in the canteen, chatting with a man who seems to be of a lesser cadre.

Prudhvi too stayed quiet avoiding any further explanations about how he failed to meet Sanju. He could not elaborate trying to make her believe. He couldn't explain her much, because only lies have details.

Emily stared at him in intervals avoiding from getting caught, but it was not working for her. She wanted to fill him in her eyes. Like there will only be her peripheral vision remaining active with the main part entirely filled up with his smile forever. She felt pangs of torture that made her witness hell over all these years get off her shoulders. Emily wanted to throw away the face of a commander as she was and fall into his hands, crying all the pain out of her heart. She wanted to have him right now. But this time, it was not having sex that she wanted. She wanted to make love.

"Now it feels like I am still missing our past," Prudhvi said. He was taking the advantage of Emily being the commander, and hated himself for doing so.

But it was ok. Everything is fair in love and war. And this was war.

"Hope we can go back to where we were once," he said.

"How can we both go back to where one of us had never been to?" she said with a sarcastic smile.

"What? I didn't get you."

"Nothing." She wanted to avoid explanations. "So don't you want to get back to Sanju?"

"I don't know. I think she still hates me. So for now, I just left her to what she wanted." Prudhvi despised the very sound of it though it was a mere lie.

"Then she's going to love you now."

"What? How could you say that?"

"Simple. Love is long-sighted… It could see only those who run away from it."

They both smiled, as they took the first sip from their coffee that already lost half its warmth.

Emily smiled brighter, knowing that she might have a chance with her first love, after all these years. May be she could use the still existing arrogance of Sanjuktha as a means to drag him far enough from the thoughts of her, and make him her own. She hated herself for thinking so.

But it was ok. Everything is fair in love and war. And this was love.

"Why do they call you Gracie," Prudhvi said at once. "Gracie Gomes?"

"That's my name."

"Your name is Emily." He gazed deep at her as if demanding an answer.

"I… I changed my name."

"Why?" It's a question of mixed meanings.

"I hated being called so," she said staring into her cup.

"Or you are a spy," he smiled.

"Spy?" she smiled back at once looking up at him. "For whom?"

"I don't know… Hitler?"

"You haven't changed much," she smiled again, mapping him with the old version of Prudhvi she knew.

He hated to see her smile. It weakens him from cheating her.

"Why 'Gracie'?" he repeated.

Emily sat silent for a moment before she spoke again. "In a language," she finally said. "*Emily* means *Enemy*. May be because some people in my life called me so for years… I lost them."

Prudhvi knew what exactly she was talking about. They did belong to two enemy troops and that couldn't be altered though he was working for them now. Once all this chaos was sorted, their destinies would lead them to different courses all over again.

Emily too knew that Prudhvi understood what she was trying to say. But she couldn't ask or expect him to answer her. It was not his own decision that day to leave for India. He may not have loved her even if he had stayed back.

The coffee lost all its heat, adjusting to the room temperature now, but no one spelled a word again.

Emily prayed that Sanjuktha should never contact him even if the great war ends and Prudhvi should stay back with her, being convinced that Sanjuktha was not made for him, or that she was dead.

"Hope she's really dead," Emily thought.

But that would devastate Prudhvi and break him into pieces, making it impossible to not just Emily but to no one else in this entire universe to bring back at least any two of them together.

"Why do humans do this?" she silently wondered. "Why sometimes, it's our closest ones that we wanted to destroy the most?"

"Isn't it strange that we met like this?" said Prudhvi, breaking the silence. "You and me, with our silly young faces… And these uniforms… It feels like we are in a play."

"Shakespeare's…"

"Definitely Shakespeare's. With all these twists and turns."

"You remember…"

"How can I forget? I still remember you in those girlish-colored gowns, Emily," he grinned.

She smiled at once lowering her head in a leap. Few heads turned in surprise, to see the Witch blush.

"Stop it, Prudhvi," she waved her hand away. "We were just kids then."

"Without the war, we will be still considered kids," Prudhvi started teasing her. "Do you remember the night clubs?"

"Shhh…" she looked up at once, smiling brighter. "They are people around."

Some argued with their mates that it was definitely not Ms Gracie, and some believed it without any argument.

"And the fun we had in skipping lectures?"

"Prudhvi…"

"Are you still eating with your bare hands, Emily?"

"Stop…" She was dying to stop laughing.

"You still watch Cricket?"

"That's it. Not a question more."

"You still love me Emily?"

"Yes I do but…" She halted to stare at him in fear.

* * *

"How did you do that?" exclaimed Beckman over the phone.

"Expanded the scale, sir," smiled Prudhvi.

"No… It's not getting in I am asking about. They are saying that you made her smile. Is that true?"

"Yes, sir. She did smile now and then."

"Then it's not 10 you've expanded to, son… It's 100, and still counting."

Prudhvi smiled again, but a bit louder, so that Mr Beckman could hear it over the phone.

"So, you met your team?"

"Not yet, sir. But we are meeting for lunch tomorrow. Emily's place."

"Who's place?"

"Ahh… Gracie, sir… Madam Gracie's."

"Oh… Great. Do enjoy your time with the team, son. They are the ones you should die for if needed," reminded Beckman. "And I am sure they'll do the same for you."

"Yes… Yes, sir," Prudhvi stammered as a scenario that he never thought of specifically started tingling his brain.

"Ok, son. See you when I see you again."

Prudhvi stared out of the glass with the receiver still to his ear.

"Son? You there?" enquired Beckman, raising his voice.

"Sir… Yes, sir. Have…Have a good night."

"Good night, son."

Still caught in deeper daze, he lowered his hand slowly, placing the receiver down.

When it comes to saving Bose, Prudhvi was well determined and it was way obvious too that he should take down all the other aircrafts even before they locate and lock missiles on him. It was just his basic instinct as an agent that he was going to make kills whenever they were needed. There was nothing special to think or plan on it, but it just happened as it happened over all these years.

"But now it was different…" Prudhvi realised at once. "What if I should kill Emily?"

"You should when you should," the agent said.

"How can he? She's an innocent girl," the friend intruded to argue.

"Oh yes? That's what you're going to do? In the next split second you spare her life, she's going to blow you up and kill Bose too."

"No she will not. I can talk her down. Tell her what I am up to and how my love and life depends on it. She understands…"

"No, she can never understand you. She might be your friend once, but now she's our enemy. Your plan will get us killed." The agent was raging with anger.

They started arguing at a pace.

"No… That's not right," cried the friend. "She loves me. And I know how much. She's going to love 'Us' too."

"Yeah right… It's true what they say. Love can kick senses out of any genius."

"Let's tell her the truth."

"Shut the hell up… She's going to die like the others. I will slit her throat open if I should and-"

"STOP IT…" shouted Prudhvi making them both go silent at once. "LEAVE ME ALONE…" he screamed closing his eyes and ears shut.

Stepping back in helplessness, banging on to the red wooden wall with glass windows from half their height, he slid down, bending his knees close to his chest.

Prudhvi stayed in that public telephone booth until it went dark. Real dark…

* * *

"How could I possibly kill her? Then how am I going to save Bose? Should I talk her down to quit the mission? Or ask her to stay, but help me out? Or… Why am I turning stupid with every question?" Prudhvi started growing even more restless as he neared her house.

He was in a taxi that he took from his quarters – an Austin 12/4 low loader taxi.

Well groomed, neatly dressed in a mat-black tuxedo and carrying a bouquet of some accurately picked flowers that a guest should bring to an English lunch, the accuracy of which was left to the old florist lady; Prudhvi tried to calm himself down staring into the tall and dense forest that had a line of mud drawn cutting it into parts, making road for their vehicle to roll on.

It was not a hill top where the address was located, but the lands were pretty much higher than the sea level when compared to those where the major part of the city lived. It seemed like the country side, where most of the farming and carpentry workers reside.

After a long and curvy journey in the woods, the taxi finally took a halt at the foot of a rock stairway that had weeds peeping out of their gaps. As Prudhvi stepped out, a huge cloud of dust rose, but it luckily flew in the opposite direction along with the forest wind. Prudhvi hopped for it to fly on to him so that at least it could provide him an excuse for his burning red eyes. Last night he hardly slept for an hour. That too filled with dreams of him killing Emily in many painful ways.

"Should I wait, sir?" the driver enquired bending down to look at Prudhvi.

Prudhvi stood there staring back, unable to make a decision of such trivia, with his brain already half-dead with anxiety. As most of the taxis, along with the cabmen were requisitioned by the Auxiliary Fire Service to tow trailer pumps in the war, finding a taxi these days had been really tough. And that too on lands like these, a backup was always a good thing.

"Ahh... yes. If you can-"

"No, you can leave," she shouted and they both turned to her.

It was Emily, standing at the top edge of the stairs. The driver's head was literally on the seat beside him now, but all that he could see was her black leather farm boots.

"Ask him to leave, Prudhvi. I'll drop you."

"Leave…" Prudhvi just uttered the word, as his eyes still stared at such a beauty as she was.

Emily, was back in her gowns.

Though it was not the once used to be single-layered short gown, the multi-layered long one suited her even better. With the cute little puffs over her shoulders, the gown hugging her tight around her chest and waist making the lower portion bulge out, those loose strands of hair that were trying to feel her skin, the flour that was all over her and the baking gloves she was wearing; she seemed like the Kitchen-Version of a princess.

"Wow, I love those flowers," she smiled descending the stairs towards him, as the taxi left them all alone. She actually hated them.

"Thank you." Prudhvi managed a smile. But his heart was still burning with the thoughts of killing her. She looked like she was just born – pure, content and smiling. He hated the idea of seeing her murdered and the thought of him being the murderer.

"Been a hectic ride?" she enquired pulling the right glove off with her teeth, to get hold of the bouquet.

"A little. But the road to a friend's house is never long."

"Ooh," she left a sudden smile. "So we are friends again?"

"No?"

"Maybe we are. Or maybe we are not." That smile was a clear and complete fake.

"If not friends, then what are we? Strangers?"

"Looks like it," she said vaguely. "We are strangers."

"But with memories," he said, and that made her heart laugh on her face.

She looked up to him at once from the flowers, and her eyes glittered with uncontrollable and unclear emotions. She tried to utter any word that seemed meaningful at this point, but found none to her rescue.

"Let's go," she finally managed after a long stare, and pulled him by his shoulder. "You're already late."

"Yeah," he said, jumping out of the wait. "We do that a lot."

When they finally reached the top and started walking in the grass, towards the house, the sudden elegance of that construction took Prudhvi by shock. It was a kind of ancient British architecture, where the domestic houses were built up to the size of a manor house, and usually designed elegantly but simply by local builders or architects, rather than the grand palaces of noble magnates. There would be lots of space allocated to the porch around the house, with a portico that marked the entrance. Most of the portion would be built with long boards of wood framed together and painted. This one was painted white.

"Nice house," Prudhvi said. "It's Queen Anne Style"

"What!"

Prudhvi smiled for the way she exclaimed.

"Queen Anne… She was a 17th century British queen," he explained suppressing the smile somehow. "And an architect herself. She was the one who firstly designed houses of this kind, so that the common man could also afford a house that looked royal."

"Wow," Emily smiled in surprise. "You know much more about our country than we do."

But she was completely unaware that it was not just knowledge, but the kind of preparation he had to melt himself into their mold.

"You know, right, I love England more than India."

"As always," she smiled.

Prudhvi smiled back, but it was as incomplete as hers. "So, we are not friends anymore?"

Emily knew that he would ask again. "We are," she said. "It's whatever you wanted it to be."

"Whatever *I* wanted?" exclaimed Prudhvi.

"Yeah," she nodded, looking up from the grass.

"What's with me? Why the *special* privilege?"

"Because I owe you things."

"Like?"

"Life?" That was a sharp and fast reply.

"Life!" he hated that word.

"You saved my life once. Remember?"

"It was just 'once'. And that's what friends are for. You don't owe me your life, Emily."

"I do, Prudhvi," she said promptly, but in a soft note. "It was not 'once,' if it's effect prevails forever. And owing things need no approval. It just depends on the one who's obliged."

It felt as if she was suggesting him that he could kill her if he wanted to, and that won't be considered wrong, even without the war and all. Prudhvi started turning restless again. All that he wanted now was to pull her back by her shoulder and shout on her face, "YOU DON'T OWE ME ANYTHING".

He knew that all this was nothing but her unending love towards him, and he hated it. She loved him in a way that made Prudhvi jealous.

As they walked towards the house in inquisitive silence, Prudhvi, tearing out of the spy-skin for an uncontrollable instance, wondered if he could tell her the truth instead of dying from inside or ending up killing her. Though she was not foolish enough to stay calm on that, there were chances that she may. Because at one or the other point of our lives, we all may choose to ignore what that should be acted on the greatest. If it was not foolishness, it could be only one thing more; Love.

Chapter 13

The house was a neatly decorated and finely maintained one, with antiques of different kinds all over the place – hunting guns hanging on the walls besides the rugged sofa set, bear skins that carpeted portions of the floor, vintage furniture and wood works, fresh flowers adorning hand-painted vases, roofs that were higher than usual and the inside of the house seemed mostly brown.

As Prudhvi stepped in, taking his blazer off, the warmth that the house was filled with from the burning pit in the fire place welcomed him with a smile that was comforting. The mantel piece was made from the combination of wood and iron. It had many pictures in handmade frames on it and there was a semi-reflecting glass over the chimney. Wondering what it meant for, Prudhvi hung his blazer over the coat stand beside the main door and walked in with Emily, straight into the dining place.

"Hi guys," Emily called walking into the kitchen. "This is Mr Prudhvi Prathap. The one I just told you about."

As Emily walked further into the room, giving way to Prudhvi to enter, he saw two men sitting on the round wooden table in the center, each holding a beer, and they looked like hard-core racers – tall, well-built and brisk. They both had the same textured jeans on, leather jackets of almost the same color and even their physique seemed same. But besides all these, they even looked similar.

'Same' might be a better word than 'Similar.' Prudhvi stared at them alternatively in comparison and surprise.

"Don't get shocked," Emily smiled, as if she half expected the shock. "They are twins," she said moving towards the kitchen counter.

"Oh…" Prudhvi smiled at once realising the trick behind the optical illusion. "I am sorry. Hi, Prudhvi Prathap," he said extending his hand.

"Robert Stigler." The first one shook. "Aston Stigler." And the second one.

Even their handshakes felt the same.

"Great," Prudhvi said, trying not to look stupid anymore, but the question that followed failed him. "Twins… like in 'Twin' brothers right?"

Emily turned to him in surprise from the steak she was attending to.

"Yeah," Aston smiled; though he wanted to laugh out loud. "As per my knowledge, twins would be normally brothers. Or sisters in some cases."

"Or can be brother and sister too sometimes," Robert added with a perky smile. "Nice suspenders, by the way."

"Stop it guys," Emily said placing the bowl of meat on the table, which already had some steaming dishes, few cakes, alcohol and seasonal fruits in a steel bowl on it. "Why would you say something like that?" she said smiling at Prudhvi.

"Ah, actually what I wanted to ask was 'Are you the only children to your parents?'"

"That hadn't covered it up much," Robert said. "But yes. We are the only children."

"Good. I am going to destroy a family then," Prudhvi thought. "God, why am I thinking all this? I never bothered to kill," he wondered in the split second.

But he knew that the answer was in the same room as he was, and it was setting the table now.

"Hey man, come on," Aston said hugging him at once from a side. "We are just joking."

"You don't say," he said patting his back, and they all laughed.

* * *

"Ummmm, the steak was really great," exclaimed Robert, with his mouth full of food. "Lucky husband."

"Thank you," blushed Emily, and her cheeks turned pink. Which made Prudhvi hate her even more.

They were around the table, having their lunch. Eating, laughing, bonding and more eating.

From her Kitchen-Princess attire, Emily had now changed into her usual home wear. A loose blue-denim capris, which was tied way above her waist with a black leather belt around and a tucked in pink cotton shirt with short sleeves and a flower patterned collar – the pattern that matched the strips around the sleeves. Her shinny golden hair was left loose now, and was taking its benchmark curls at the ends.

"The potatoes were really nice too," Prudhvi smiled, lifting his fork that stuck two slices on it. "Good that you fried them."

"But the French style?" Aston shrugged, gulping his wine down his throat.

"That's the way he likes it," Emily said.

"Not exactly. But the word 'Fried' sounds good."

"Actually, that's the only way I can fry potato," winked Emily. "But sorry that I don't remember the other dish. Something that had mango in it…"

"Mango?" It surprised Robert.

"Mango-Dal," answered Prudhvi.

"Yeah right," Emily smiled in recollection.

"Wait a second," Aston said at once. He was in between Emily and Prudhvi, facing his brother. "Why do you guys sound like you know each other already?"

"Because we do," said Prudhvi. "Same college."

"Wow. Really?" It's Robert. "You hadn't mentioned that earlier," he said turning to Emily in surprise.

Aston moved his head in support.

"I totally forgot," she said in what's-the-big-deal tone. "But why would we lie now?"

"So that's the reason you took in an Indian?"

Prudhvi felt awkward being discussed, which just took a turn at the 'He's not one of us' corner.

"No," Emily exclaimed at once. "Not because he's an old friend. But because I know his potential."

"Oowww… Poteeeential," ragged Aston.

"Oh my god," Prudhvi left a sudden shy smile.

"Shut up Aston," Emily too did the same, but after throwing some cutlery on to Aston, from which he dodged. "Even we are friends from school. These two idiots and me," she told Prudhvi. But her look was little different now; like she liked the earlier comment.

"Oh, is it?" That surprised Prudhvi. "Now this looks like more of a reunion team than a… you know."

"A top secret mission," Robert said, with drama in his eyes.

The others laughed, but not Emily. The word 'Mission' actually reminded her where she was and what was the real purpose of this lunch, other than her personal purpose of being with Prudhvi for as much time as she could.

"Guys," Emily said disrupting the moment of humor. "As we finally moved to a place where we can call ourselves a team, can I explain you the plan of our attack now?"

"Sure, go ahead," said Robert, and the professional mode was back on in no time.

"It's simple." Emily explained turning to each at an interval. "We fly in a normal Square pattern. All the rules, same as you know them. But," she said waving her finger as a symbol of 'point to be noted', "the main two, meaning both the Stiglers, one of whom is Aston, the tracker who locks the target's position," she said to Prudhvi. He loved the way she sounded – sharp and hot. "And the other, Robert, the bomber, whose plane contains both the bombs, will stay in the front two corners.

"I know that's not the way a Square pattern goes. The front corners should contain the guarding planes. But in case of getting spotted or tracked, let the enemy think the same – that the bogies at the rear end are the once that should be attacked first. And Prudhvi," she said turning to him again. "All that we should do is this, 'Protect these guys, even at the cost of our own lives'. Aston, you know how less time you'll have to track and lock him, and Robert you'll have less than half the time Aston gets. You know that right?"

"Yeah, we do."

"Great. Aston will be the front left node. Robert you'll be the right. Prudhvi, you'll back up Aston, meaning rare left. And I'll be the rare right. If at all we should face an attack mid-air, we will opt for Thach Weave technique – the Beam Defence Position. The two Stiglers stay put their speed until me and Prudhvi catch you up to form the line. That makes me the A-node, Robert the B, Aston the C and Prudhvi the D. As verbal communication won't be a good option then, my double beep in the intercom will be the signal that we start Thach Weave. And all our planes will be equipped with some minimum weaponry for our self-defence. Like mechanical guns in the wings, flares in our tails and seats that can be ejected... Any doubts?" she said looking at Robert, and moving back as if concluding.

"Clear," Robert said.

"Aston?"

"Same here."

"Prudh-" she stopped at once, as he seemed as if waiting for his name.

"What if?" he said at once, but dragging. "What if we don't find him there?"

That took some of them by surprise.

"We will, Prudhvi," Emily assured, as if she personally knew the movements of Bose. All of a sudden she seemed angry. "Our spy, who left us this information, was killed there and then, and by our very own men. There's no going back of the fact that we knew it or that we are coming for him."

It made the cocoons in the Stiglers stomachs hatch into butterflies at once.

"Then, the day after, we are going to make history. Let's raise him a last toast," Prudhvi said, raising his glass, staring straight and strong at her. "To Bose…"

"To Bose…" all the other glasses rose.

Prudhvi smiled while he drank his share.

"To Bose…" he murmured again.

* * *

"So you finally managed something with mango in it," Prudhvi smiled pressing the opener's beak hard into the containers lid, making a triangular opening.

They were having a post-lunch chat in the backyard, which after the open grass ground and a garden, slowly turned into a forest. The warm noon wind was so light and fresh that it made them feel more alive.

"That was my dad's favorite mango juice."

"Yeah, I was about to ask," he said remembering something. "Do you live alone here?"

"Now I do, after dad too left me last year. Heart failure."

"Oh," he felt difficult to react. The 'Too' she added made him wanting to take blame. "Your mom?"

"She died when I was a girl, remember?" she smiled.

"Yeah I, I do. I am sorry again."

"Don't be," she said pushing her hair around her ear. Prudhvi loved to see her so free again. Unbound and real. "Ah, the second hole?"

"What?"

"Make a second hole," she said pointing at the can. "A smaller one on the other side, so that when the bigger one gets closed while you drink, the pressure from the smaller helps the liquid flow easy. Or else you should suck it out of the can."

"God, you look amazing when you talk science."

"Science?" she exclaimed as if she didn't mean it. "I don't know if we can call this science."

"Anything is science," he said obeying her with the opener. "I know you heard the 'Amazing' part too. Why do you act like you don't?"

It made her feelings suddenly take higher jumps and deeper dives. However, she somehow felt it coming. The cool breeze, open grounds, greenery all around; she knew they would make him talk. Or else she would have.

Emily turned back to have a look at the brothers, as Prudhvi started tasting the juice. They were busy in laughing to their own Stigler jokes, hanging out on an old bench under the bald cypress tree. She wanted to make sure that they are far enough not even to see them.

"Let's walk?" she said, walking towards the garden to the left of the house.

"Sure," he said walking along, leaving the juice on the floral garden table.

"Don't like it?" she enquired looking back at the labelled yellow can.

"Not really," he said making a face.

"You would have smelled it first."

"But you ordered to drink it madam," he said going stiff at once.

"Shut up," she smiled pushing him away, and the push felt strong.

"It seems all these years have made you stronger," he exclaimed walking back.

"What wise?"

"What else? Physically," he said squeezing her bicep. "Oowww."

"Shut up, Prudhvi. I am the same old Emily you knew."

"But with stronger biceps. I know you beat men in the ring."

"You knew?" she said surprised.

"Yeah I knew that Gracie Gomes did. But I never imagined, even in my wildest of wildest dreams that she will turn into an Emily undercover."

"Yeah. Even I never knew."

"How is this even possible Emily?" he said in complete shock. "You used to cry on little things, got beaten up by freaks and cover them up as bathroom-accidents."

But what that he never knew was that behind an every strong and confident grown up girl, there will be a broken little girl.

"I don't know Prudhvi. May be that's the poetry of life," said the grown up girl. "Getting used to what we never expected or wanted."

"Hating Indians, too, was a part of it?" He sounded sarcastic.

"You knew the exact reason," she said turning to him in mockery, making her eyes smaller.

"Yes madam. Charlie-1, over and out," he said walking away, and Emily smiled uncontrollably for the way he walked – as an army clown.

She treasured the fact of being with the Prudhvi she once fell in love with.

They had walked deep enough into the garden and the whole area around was beaming reddish yellow now. The dry leaves are rolling and rustling under their feet and their clothes were waving to their bodies in the direction of the wind. A bunch of new leaves rained from the trees for every harder blow now and then. Only the branches were standing out dark and wet brown, with the leaves covering every inch of the land beneath, along with the trees.

If not Prudhvi was deeply lost in the conversation, he would have been stunned to such a scenic beauty.

Though the garden failed to do so, the shinning black granite statue did. It was the statue of a man who seemed like a hunter from the end of the rock age. He had a long stick with a triangular spear head in a hand and the other hand was rested on his hip in style. The sculpting of the cape he wore was to make it look like it was some animal's skin and he also had a long beard on his high-held chin. He stood on a rock podium right in the middle of the walk, making it hard to miss him. And his size too was not something that escaped your eye even from a corner. He was scaled to double the size of a normal human, or may be humans then had been of that dimensions.

"Nice statue," Prudhvi said lifting his head high.

"It's my great-great-grandfather's."

"Wow. You do look like him a bit," he grinned.

"Mister!" she said placing her hands on her hips, like she once used to. "That's the man who owns this garden, *even now*. Don't you try making fun of his great-great-granddaughter or he'll do what he should."

"You are talking as if he will jump off any minute."

"May be he can," she said making her eyes big. "There won't be a smoke without the fire!"

"I didn't get you!" Prudhvi moved his head parallel to the ground.

"Let me tell you an interesting story then," she smiled, walking past the statue.

Prudhvi followed her, taking another clear look at the great-great-grandfather's face.

"My dad used to tell me this story often," she said, as if thinking back in time. "This man in the statue was the only man who resided in this forest once. He was famous for many things back then, but not as famous as he's now for killing his wife."

"What?" exclaimed Prudhvi.

"Yes. They say that he loved his wife like a mad man. Like he will die when her heart stops. But no one ever knew for what reason he killed her for, stabbing her in her heart with a dagger, while she was out here picking up her clothes as it was raining. Then he sculpted his own statue to place it over the ground where he buried the body. And from that day, it was believed to run in the family."

"What?"

"Killing wives," she said as if to frighten him. "My great grandfather killed his wife with an axe on a thunderous rainy night. Reasons are unknown. They say that it's this man's ghost which took over him that night, as there had never been at least a word fight between them. And twenty years from then, my grandfather got his wife killed in an accident where the carriage he was riding on the edges of a mountain went sliding into the valley as the sand lost its grip from the rain. And then my father. He lost my mom to food poisoning. He cooked her last meal. And you know what? The day my mom died... It was heavily raining."

Prudhvi said nothing but just stared at her with his lower jaw hanging loose, and he hoped that any minute from now she may turn to him in a huge laughter revealing that all this was just a crazy joke she made up. But she seemed like she's not going to.

"Its rains when it happens, Prudhvi. No matter what the season was," she continued. "Legend says that, this man also had an ability to change seasons at will."

"What?" Prudhvi almost freaked out yet another time. "That sounds like some crazy Egyptian fairy tale."

"Oh yeah?" she said as if getting ready to prove him wrong. "You know London better than us. What season was this?"

"Spring," he said as a matter of fact. "What's there to mention in-" and it struck him. He looked around at once, turning directions, to see the entire garden with autumn leaves all over.

He turned back to Emily in bafflement. "How is this even possible?"

"May be some complicated science?" she said smiling, as if she was used to stuff like this.

"It's definitely science," Prudhvi ensured her, and himself. "And it's just a weird story that was created by those all who failed to crack the trick."

He himself was not clear if this is really a trick of science.

"Whatever it is," she smiled. "But this was the reason why no one ever dared to go out with me in school, or in college. They believed that the same curse applies to a girl too. And maybe it will. Like if a guy wants to marry me, he should have a good reason to kill me first."

Suddenly it all felt so related, that Prudhvi was now in serious efforts to control his feelings. It's just now that he slowly came out of the 'I am going to kill her' thoughts and all this had ruthlessly raised the bars to a whole new level of grievance.

"Have a reason first? May be. Orrrrr… maybe not," she said turning to him suddenly, smiling bright and impish. "The guy who kills me… is my husband. Right?"

It fell harder, both on his heart and his brain. But as always, the heart cried louder.

"Then no one's going to marry you," he said, trying to sound normal. "But only if they knew that the price they should pay missing you will be way higher than the value of the memories you make. Yet never mind. Someone how's worth waiting will risk everything for you one day."

That suddenly tore her from inside. It felt like he was insulting her love from implying that he had thoughts of her getting married to someone else.

"Why do you talk like that Prudhvi?" Her tone turned hollow at once.

"What do I talk like?"

"Like you care," she said without any fear.

"But I do. Don't I?"

"I don't know. If you really care, why did you leave me in the first place?"

"Leave you?" he said surprised.

"Yeah. What's there to get shocked? You knew that I love you."

It felt so awkward to both, with the word 'Love' vibrating in the air between them. Prudhvi felt so bad to see her on the side that he had always been.

"I don't know that when I 'left you.' I have been an idiot back then."

Emily smiled sadly. "Then how come you know now?"

"Sanjuktha made me realise." He almost said that out, being carried away from the one little lie he should maintain.

"What?" she said, as if wanting a faster answer.

"I… I slowly realised."

"And you never wanted to come back to me?"

"I can't hurt you more, Emily. Because I can never love you back."

"Yeah," she said moving her head away in despair. "Who knows better than you, how hard it was to not being loved."

Prudhvi felt a storm of tears heading his way. But Emily was already on her edges.

"Don't the wounds of love heal with time?" It was to comfort himself.

"Yours did?"

"My love was much older, Emily. More than a decade," he said trying to explain something that even he never knew. "It will take more time to heal. Yours should have been healed by now."

"Prudhvi…" she said making a halt to turn to him. It felt so hard for her to utter any word. She just stood there staring at him in fear whether she should talk her pain out.

"Speak," he said, after a long session of uncontrollable staring at her.

"Yeah," she said moving her eyes away. "You were saying something."

"I asked if your wound had healed."

"No," she said at once, with her eyes rolling in support to those two letters. Her eyes started filling and her white British skin turned red.

"Why? Why hadn't it healed? It's been years since-"

"It's not about time Prudhvi." She finally found courage. "Some believe that love depreciates with time. And some say that it appreciates. None of it is true. It's simple science again." Her eyes started leaving tears out of them. "Love is definitely a variable. I do agree. But it's neither directly nor inversely proportional to time. It's independent of it."

Prudhvi too was crying now seeing her sob, but still trying to explain him her agony.

"Love is independent of Time, Prudhvi. It's not about the number of days we spend together. It's about the strength of feelings we share. The quality of emotions we exchange. A weak foundation may never last long. But at the same time, a slow start can also make it to the end."

"Can I hug you?" he said at once.

"What!" she literally screamed.

"Can – I – Hug – You?"

"Yeah," she said moving her head as if to wiggle her brain from the sudden extra charge on the neurons. "What's there to ask? It's just a hug." She spread her arms apart, moving towards him, having a very neat idea that it was not 'Just a hug.'

As she neared him, Prudhvi caught hold of her by her hair and pulled her head close to his heart, rolling his arms around her. Hugging him back as tight as she could, Emily took a deep breath to suppress her feelings, but the exhalation turned out to be a loud cry.

She started crying all her pain out and the garden started echoing her sobs. Prudhvi felt weak and helpless at once and found himself sobbing along with her. He hated his own existence like never before. But there was a reason for everything that happens. Whether it happen the right way or the other, it happens for a reason.

For the next few minutes, they just hugged and cried. They say that, if someone hugs us for more than twenty seconds, it releases a chemical called Oxytocin in them that leads them to trust us more. Prudhvi hated the amount of trust that her subconscious was building up on him.

"There's a reason for everything Emily," he said, once she slowly settled. "A reason for everything. A reason we met. A reason we came close. A reason you love me. A reason I never knew. A reason you ignored letting me know. A reason for what you did. A reason for what *I* did. A reason for all this pain. But right now, that reason is beyond us. But someday, when we meet again, where we can treat each other right, cherish and love; then will we know the reason. And then, maybe I will find strength to say that I love you too."

Emily remained silent in his embrace, staring into the infinity, listening to his heart race. Her body suddenly felt the jiggling sensation of a silk cloth being dragged over another silk cloth. Whatever that he just said, was completely out of this world.

"I mean every single word, Emily." And he really did.

For the first time, Emily realised that it's killing him, like it's killing her.

"You're not imagining Sanju right?" she said, trying to smile. "Hugging me like this."

Prudhvi too smiled at once, squeezing his eyes shut. "No, I am not."

She felt his tears dipping on her head.

"Why is Love the only blessing that always comes with a curse, Prudhvi?"

"I don't know. Even I was at the cursed end."

Emily too smiled, wiping her tears off and hugging him back even tighter, before leaving him.

Her face was still red and it was all wet and moist with tears. But he loved the way she looked.

"You know, when I was a girl," she said flickering her eyes to dry, but still looking straight at him, "I used to fear that I can never find my soul mate in this life. Thanks for stopping by."

* * *

It's just silence that they heard, with the engine coming to an abrupt halt and the thinner air around stopped vibrating in no time. Emily turned the keys off in a way that suggested she was open for another big talk. They were in her jeep that she parked in a dark street behind his quarters. The foggy gully was all black from except the far away light post and its freezing cold outside.

Prudhvi too felt that there was a lot more to talk to her on. But this was not the right time, and also not the right amount of preparation he had. He hadn't even considered the cases that he can never even think of. After all, it's a girl that he's going to deal with here, which makes the situation hang on a wire that's made of the world's strongest metal, but with both the ends left free.

"So we are here," she said, just to make any sound.

"Yes, we are," he reciprocated, just to make a reply.

"Can I ask you something, Prudhvi?"

"Sure, go ahead."

"What that just happened back at my place," she said, making her eyes small and clenching her teeth, as if not to sound stupid. "Do you think it's kind of embarrassing?"

"Embarrassing? No, not at all. I even think it's kind of, lucky."

"Lucky?"

"Yeah," he said ensuring. "It made us open up to each other again right?"

She loved the very sound of it. "Yes. It did," she said, smiling inside.

There was only one more day left for the mission and she wanted to make the most of it. "May be a good lunch at a good place? The hotel we first met in?" she fantasized. "And then a long stroll in the reconstructed Imperial King's, so that the then sweet memories can be stirred a little?"

"How abou-"

"Can we have breakfast tomorrow?" he said, at the same time. "I am sorry. I am so sorry, you're saying something?"

"Aaahhh… 'Something' not as important as 'Breakfast'," she said giggling. "Sure. Let's… Let's have breakfast… Tomorrow… 8ish?"

"Yeah," he said moving his head and smiling to see her breaking her sentence all over. "So, good night then."

"Ok. Have a," she said looking at his lips and back at his eyes again, "good night."

Prudhvi knew what that meant. He knew that he could kiss her right away and end up in bed with her. He could use the sex part to make her believe that he was completely off Sanjuktha now and that he wanted to live the remaining life only and only with her. He could break her to the core with this weapon in his hand, tie her by her nose, reveal what he was here for and ask her to elope with him to some place safe. Of course, after helping him with the mission.

"Everything is fair. Every-thing-is-fair," he repeated inside his head like sixty time a minute. "Kiss her, Prudhvi. Just kiss her."

Emily stared in silence, into the eyes that are going deeper with every passing second. She tried to, but as always, hadn't found a way to contemplate the feelings that were leaving his eyes encrypted. She wanted a 'Kiss' to decode them.

After all the deep and passionate staring into each other's eyes for infinity; it just happened in a flash that she hadn't even realised that he actually did it. Prudhvi caught hold of the door handle, opened it and stepped out to close it behind. In a split second, she found him on the waving-goodbye-with-free-hands side.

Prudhvi could really see a smooth way to ride the play towards the end he wanted, but it's not the *right* way. If he really should tell her the truth, he wanted to, but not by taking the side of War. He wanted to take the side of Love, the fairer side. Whatsoever might be the outcome, Prudhvi decided to tell her the truth.

But not today. Today was perfect. A day that they can always look back to. And he planned to let it be that way.

"See you, Emily," he said, buttoning his coat and making it sound like 'I am really sorry'.

"See you," she said turning the keys on, with the most awkward smile ever. She felt like getting off the jeep and kicking him in his gut, shouting out all her pain on him and all that ignorance out of him. But suddenly from nowhere, she felt that he somehow knew what exactly she was going through right now.

"May be he too always wanted to kick Sanjuktha," she wondered, staring at him in the rare view mirror, until she took the last turn she could.

***

"Madam?" the secretary said, shivering with fear that might easily kill her from any second now. "May I come in?"

"Come in, Rosy," Emily said still immersed in her scribbling but she did smile.

A bigger wave of shiver hit her spine, seeing Madam Gracie smile. The Witch never smiles. And if she did, that's pure sarcasm.

Today the smile felt very close to a real smile, meaning that Rosy was in deeper trouble for not getting the files from SIGNIT on time. Or at least she thought she was, completely unaware of the unbelievably surprising fact that the Witch, is no more a Witch.

"Come in," she said looking up from her files and smiling bright. "Why are you struck there?"

Those were the hardest steps Ms Rosy had ever walked.

"The files you asked for madam," she said, handing them from the other side of the table. "The SIGNIT guys took time. I mean..."

"It's ok, Rosy." She smiled again. "May be you should leave. It's been really late and I still had some work to do."

Rosy just stood there her hands loosely hung. "This is definitely some new kind of sadism. Wow it looks damn real. Don't leave Rosy. Say that you are sorry and cry. The sooner, the better."

"Why do look like you had some kind of fever?"

"I am sorry, madam. It's not me. I have been asking them since morning and they-"

"Rosy... Rosy stop," Emily said laughing. She knew what exactly had scared her sweet little secretary. "This is not one of my sarcastic and sadistic smiles ok? This is me, really smiling."

"Ok. Here it comes. The brand new level of sarcasm."

"Don't worry about the files. Just leave them here," she said placing them on the table. "I'll look into them. You may leave for the day. Thank you."

As she walked out of the office, Rosy heard her mam smile again to herself. "Oh my god. I am resigning," she decided shutting her eyes tight, running out of the cubicle.

Emily felt it really soothing that she was actually smiling after years. And the name on the yellow hardboard file that was lying in front of her made her smile turn into a giggle all at once.

"Prudhvi Prathap Raju, you're mine now," she said dragging the file close. "All under my control."

She knew that she just failed really bad in getting a kiss from him, but there was still this hope, that one day she might. And that day, it will be full of love. Even after a life time of grievance, one can never realise that though Love and Hope are the mirror images to each other, they are still on the opposite sides of the mirror. Any question with the exact knowledge of the inevitable answer is fool's hope. And people get to ask them a lot in love.

The same love, out of which Emily just got her eyes blurred and though that she had a good enough look at the information in that file, she missed the last few words that would easily ring a bell, even at the least of a stare.

It was a file consolidating the much deeper details of the candidate. In there, they had the track record of the applicant; his areas of excellences, the missions he led, any hitches in his career that were worth mentioning and at the greatest importance, the most recent activities that are logged in with his name. Meaning, the last three messages he transmitted through his system.

As it was an out of branch information what they provided, there were only the final encrypted messages.

JHS AKN EJA DJI AKW GPA BFO BYJ MAE PHA QRF SIJ HUS – GU JI MA

EBS JIS LDI GFD VPZ NFK CNI SHS MEG SIC HGS JSD FJD – PO SE DE

SAU NSW JUT HJU LAU NHI AHG JUO SHJ OKA AJW EHW SJU – SA-JU-TA

With the last six letters read in the same pace and significance as of the all others, Emily closed the file, to place it on the files of the Stigler brothers. It's just the breakfast the day after that filled her thoughts and she wanted to get back home, as early as possible.

"Should sleep a lot tonight," she thought. "Can't look tired on the big day."

Picking the keys on the table and her coat on the stand, Emily walked out of her room, switching off the last light in her office – the last light on the floor.

And thus the secret, that would have given her a chance to save her life and the mission, stayed in the racks of files, silent and unnoticed forever.

* * *

But only until the light was switched on again.

The door swung open at once, and Emily came running in to her office. She was in terror and doubt of witnessing something that she thought it was, turn into reality. Running to her table form the other side, she literally fell on to the glass surface to get hold of the top most file, with the name of her love on it.

With her hands shivering as if from cold, she opened it from the rare end. Some kind of extra pieces of code made them look different from the others. But it's not the difference that bothered her much. It's the combination of words that was registered in her eyes because of that difference. And it's already in the human nature, to remember most what we had seen lastly. She knew that she had already seen the last six letters somewhere.

When the page finally fluttered in front of her eyes, Emily started turning into what they call her the most, other than her fake name.

"SA-JU-TA" It was a very familiar combination and she just wanted to make it more clear. She took a pencil that fell from the stand when she jumped on to the table, and filled the hyphens with the letters that felt most appropriate.

The filling was done now, and Emily was not the same anymore. She was not Emily, or Gracie. And it was not anger or grief that was making her shake. It was betrayal.

The shell of the poor little girl started shattered off her body, and she started realising that all the love and concern he shoved on her the whole day, all the sudden considering of her feelings and the deceptive hug that made her a bigger fool; they all were just to keep her out of her senses.

"He used the advantage of you being the head of this mission," a voice inside her head whispered. "He used you, yet another time."

Her eyes started filled up with tears that boiled inside her raging eyes. She started going numb from her heart and what that she wanted back was all her tears from the past. Or a revenge in exchange.

By the time she sat in her seat and picked up the handset, her face went all wet with tears rolling nonstop. The fact that Prudhvi was a spy was not sliding down her throat and she was choking to death on it. The crazy stupid lover inside her is still trying to take over and convinced her to accept him for what he was. 'It was just the situation that was making him look bad and maybe he never meant anything he said or did,' it tried to talk her down.

But Emily hadn't yielded the least. She had already decided to take the side of War. It's the only way of being fair. It had just been proved that Love had multiple faces despite of being more ruthless.

Dialling his number on the rotary board of the telephone, she placed the handset to her ear, trying to clean the tears off with her palms. As she heard the rings from the other end, she prepared herself not to sob while talking.

He picked up at almost the last ring, and sounded as if he was sleep talking. It took her some literal physical effort to speak the first few words out.

"Mr Beckman," she said, sniffing pain into her lungs. "We had an emergency..."

Chapter 14

04:36 am

3rd April, 1945

SIGNIT staff quarters. London.

The banging on the door felt like a manual war time alarm – annoyingly loud and irritatingly repetitive. It made Prudhvi jump off from his sleep with a jolt, to see the door to his room trying hard to stay intact to the wall. Someone was trying to knock it down with their bare hands. Prudhvi jumped of the bed at once, throwing his rug away. His eyes were still not completely cooperating.

"Whoever you are, you better have a good enough reason," Prudhvi thought, walking to the door, pulling his t-shirt on.

"What?" he said calming down, knowing that it was his subordinate.

"Sir, a code-red message from General Beckman, sir," he said saluting his chief at the first 'Sir'. "He wants you to meet Ms Gracie Gomes at the Aerodrome-B in less than half an hour. And also wants you to know that "The Mission" was brought forward by a day for some security reasons."

"What?" exclaimed Prudhvi. It felt like one of his weird early-morning dreams. "Who told you this?"

"A call from his office, sir."

Prudhvi tried to comprehend things but all that he could do is to leave an empty sigh. “Sure soldier,” he said, realising that he had no time. “Thank you for the information.”

“Sir,” he saluted again and walked away towards the dorm’s exit.

It hadn’t struck him when he actually heard it, but it did now as he walked back into his room to pick his uniform. Prudhvi shivered with bewilderment at once with the thought of ‘What if Rudhra hadn’t reached them yet?’ He knew that it will take at least two days, as he cannot fly in those airs.

“Damn,” he screamed getting hold of his head with both his hands. “What should I do now?”

* * *

Same day
Same time (10:06 am, Indian time)
A small village near Ghagra.

“There is nothing that we can do now,” the guide whispered. “I can’t lead you anywhere. They got eyes on me.”

“But this is important. Even than our own lives,” cried Eshwar.

“Shhh… Keep your voice down kid. There are guards all over this village. You’ll get us killed.”

“What would you do living afraid? It’s not just your job, sir. It’s your responsibility, to get people in and out of that forest.” He kept his voice down this time, but not the anger in his tone. “Just get me in. I won’t ask you to get me out. Leave me there and just run.”

"Don't you have a mind that can process words?" he said, offended and irritated to his extreme levels. "*They will kill us both.* You can't even be spotted talking to me. How do you think we can intrude into that forest?"

Eshwar sat silent, realising that he can't bring this man down, and he had a point too.

They were in the guide's house – a small hut with nothing but few chairs, a table with handmade maps from carbon black ink and brown oak papers on it and a bed that seemed like one that no human can sleep on. In sync with the whole village, his house too was all brown and there was dust all over the place. The guide was a fifty-something man and was in his almost-torn black suit. He seemed like the one who once fought the intelligence wars. Expert in deceptions, maps and women.

"What if you give me a map?" Eshwar whispered at once. "Something that you hand a beginner?"

"Impossible. You will get lost."

"That's better than getting us killed, right?" There were both sarcasm and pain in his question. "Tell me any other way that may sound better than this and I'll opt for it. And don't you worry, I know how to deal with a compass and count meters in footsteps."

"Why?" he said as if he can never understand even if Eshwar answers. "Why are you so desperate for this kid? Whom do you want to meet in there?"

"Not to meet. I should save someone."

"Save?" he said surprised.

"Yeah."

"Good. One should look after his fellow soldiers. That's what I am trying to do to you. You don't look like you can make it to the end. But by the way you sound from the start, it seems like you are on to save Mr Bose himself."

With the name of Bose popping up, Eshwar got tempted to tell him the truth. So that he can understood the importance of all this and would help him with utmost care. But he couldn't risk it. There was surveillance on this man and it could lead to declassifying of information if he was caught and tortured.

"What if there was really Bose in there, sir? Would you come with me then?"

"No. If that's the case, we should be even more cautious right? I will definitely not escort you."

"Then? What will you do to save Bose?"

Eshwar hated the enthusiasm in the man's bloodshot eyes. One shouldn't see the difference between the leader and the soldier. That's not the way Bose wanted to operate.

"Hmmm," he said rubbing his shabby beard. "I'll right you a map that's as good as me coming along."

"Then, sir," Eshwar said staring deep, "let's say there's a Bose in there."

* * *

"What's happening?" shouted Prudhvi. "Why was the mission moved?"

"I don't know," Robert shouted back. "They won't tell us. May be Emily knows."

They were just few steps apart, but should still shout, as the whole open air around was vibrating to the sound of four 24-cylinder H-type engines running at once. Their propeller blades too were on, covering the higher frequencies. And on top of these, the early-morning fog just started clearing off and the wind started blowing.

"Ok. I'll see you guys," he shouted again, walking away in search of her.

The airdrome staff were cleaning the flaps, testing the engines and filling them with fuel sufficient enough to make two trips to the targeted area.

Prudhvi took slow steps along the beaks of the bombers that were arranged in a row, to see if Emily was in between any of them. It was still dark around, but also bright enough for human eyes to adjust. He searched everywhere, but she was nowhere to be seen. There were only the two Stiglers and the staff along with the sun peeping out from the other side of the air field.

Prudhvi stood to a side after the planes and stared at them, turning restless for every beat his heart was taking. They were the Blackburn Firebrand models, and all of them seemed same. Except that the last one had two heavy loaded missiles hanging side by side on its belly. The front part of the missiles were so smooth and curvy that they seemed like birthday balloons and the later longer body made him remember the miniature version of a submarine. There were small rotary blades attached to their tails, which were used as sensors to activate the trigger. When the missile hit the target and came to a halt, these blades will stop rotating due to the abrupt loss in speed. And when they do, in about nine to ten seconds, the missiles explode, making life around them in at least five hundred meters, impossible.

With the very thought of their explosion, Prudhvi felt shivers down his spine. In few hours from now, one of them is going to head for Bose, and he'll be there standing helpless.

He suddenly wondered where Bose was right now.

* * *

The truck that unloaded some dead bodies of hunted deer and wild boars in the markets of Ghagra early this morning, had headed towards the other side of the Tarafeni River. It took a route that was not the shortest one, but which involved crossing a thin mud road parallel to the forest. Also it was scheduled to stop nowhere until it reaches its destination on the other side, but it did. Near a fencing that was laid by the British from restricting any entry into the woods, the truck took a halt.

Though it was the start of a scorching summer now and one may not stop a lot to urinate, this particular driver had his reasons. He made the truck come to a halt in an angle that made the rare end more inclined towards the fence. And he did take his time in enjoying the unloading that happened at his end.

When the driver finally closed his business there and drove his truck off towards the southern stream of Tarafeni, there was not much difference that occurred to the surroundings, except for the wet ground, and a small piece of polythene hanging to the fence, which might have ripped from a polythene suit.

* * *

"Prudhvi?" screamed Robert from the distance, making him turn away from the missiles he was staring at. It felt like it was definitely not the first time he screamed. Prudhvi already missed the first few.

"What?" he said in his normal tone, but making his body talk.

Robert too felt it the better way to communicate now, so he just raised his hand to point in a direction. Prudhvi turned to it at once, and saw Emily walking towards them.

She was already in her pilot uniform. Black leather jacket on brown pants, which were tucked into her combat shoes. She had a leather cap with large earflaps and chin strap on, the Aviator hat it was called, and a pair of heavy goggles pushed above her forehead.

She seemed upset from the way she looked, but also angry from the way she walked.

"Why did they moved the mission?" he enquired, when he was at the farthest point possible in his run to her, from where she could hear him clearly.

But Emily hadn't answered until he reached her, and also even after he did. She already ran all the possible outcomes of her rage in her head, but what she finally settled to was to keep calm and let the simple plan apply its consequences. However, she was still fighting a war inside, not to give this away to Love. She was not on its side now; neither she wanted to be dragged to.

"Talk," he said shaking her by her shoulders, fighting with his breath.

She hated his hands on her.

"I don't know," she said, as if she was confused too. "Mr Beckman took this decision. All that I can get out of him was that there's going to be some change in plans of Bose's movements and if it's not today, there might not be a next time. And also there was lot of pressure from the Indian government."

"India doesn't have a government. It had only political parties," he said pushing all the idea of change in Bose's activities aside. He knew that there was something much bigger that was happening.

"But India does have leaders right?" She sounded as friendly as ever. "And the world knows that some of them want this very badly. Do you think this is not going to work?"

"No. It will work. It should work." Prudhvi started given away his feelings. Or maybe because she knew the real him now, she could see them. "But do we have the exact information that Bose is going to be there? Like today?"

"Yes, Prudhvi," she said, hating herself for not being able to see him suffer. "We still have people in there."

"Our spies are in there?" he said surprised.

"Yes," she lied. "We had Indians, who are our spies."

"Really?" he was surprised again, and also raged with anger this time, but concealed it. "There were Indians on our side?"

"What! *You* are asking?"

"Ha ha," he faked a smile, "right. I don't have a right to say that."

She too smiled back, but that was not completely fake.

"So, go get dressed, pilot. Bose is running out of his time."

"Let's do it," he said in an affirmative tone and she knew that he had prepared himself to anything that may come. "God speed to us."

"God speed to us."

The four fighter aircrafts took off one at a time on the run way, to form a square at 30,000 ft. above sea level. These fighters were stealth mode ready. They had no radio noise that could be detected, their engines were buried deep inside their bodies to prevent detection of the heat they generated, and, they were headed towards the southern lands of Asia.

* * *

The map the guide handed him was clear and clever, but Eshwar knew that he could fall into the trap of time where he could be led astray into heading the right way but actually ended up screwing everything, and even the point where he made a mistake would be unknown, to go back to it and start fresh from that spot. Also it was going to get real dark by the time he reached the camp even if everything went well, and it was the only day he had. The enemy may attack any time tomorrow.

The guide also taught him an old school technique to get to the camp, in case he was totally screwed. The Tarafeni

River cut the forest into halves, and one could never get out from the other side without crossing it. So if Eshwar could find the river walking towards pure north, checking the soil humidity levels to keep his track right towards it, he could easily reach the river. Once he found the river, he must mark where he met it, and choose a direction, preferably east first, and walk until he finds a wooden bridge to the other side. That was the only bridge over the river inside the forest and the camp was just a couple of kilometers from there.

If he was unable to find one to the east, it was probably because he got too much of east already, and he should head back to the mark he made, and then walk west.

But when he made the map, the guide was completely unaware of this place that was on the other side of the forest, where Eshwar could just walk past the fence unnoticed by any of the British guards. However, it was a very narrow gap that only few agents knew of.

Controlled and driven by the limited knowledge of the guide, Eshwar roamed in the market that sold vegetables, seasonal fruits, hunted deer and boars; with the map and the compass hidden inside his blazer pockets, waiting for his chance to sneak into the forest behind the market, with no eyes witnessing him.

Watching the vendors in the market sell their hard-earned crop and hunt at the prices the British officials sitting in air conditioned offices decide, he felt happy for what he was doing right now. Even if it scared him to death a day back, he was not scared of death anymore. All that he wanted was to reach out to Bose at any cost. Though he did have some time to take out to relax a bit; as Rudhra said, 'In war, 'Now' is all you get.' And also he didn't know why, but it felt like the enemy had already entered the country.

As he walked the lanes lined up with make-shift shops for another impatient hour; in a much crowed place, Eshwar saw a shopkeeper fighting with his custumer over some lame issue. He dismissed the thought of trying to calm them down at first, but when he saw the gap that could help him out, he ran to them at once. Not to settle the issue, but to encourage the shopkeeper from hitting the customer, beginning a street fight.

They both fell into the grip of their egos and started hitting one another in temper. People who were shopping for stuff gathered around them. Some even tried to pull them apart, but no one succeeded. Meanwhile, someone from the group shouted for the guards inspecting the lane behind, and they ran to the crowd straightaway.

That 'someone' was the boy who started the fight himself, and who just walked past the approaching guards to run to the lane after, jumping off the high laid fence taking support of the trash bags laid in a mount in front of it. As he planned for, no one saw him jump, and by the time they can, he vanished into the thickness of the trees.

* * *

Drutha dried his head with a towel that's already half wet, as he walked in his underpants across the camp that was laid around an old wind mill. The mill was not in working condition and it was long gone that it had the cloth around its wings torn and hanging loose. There were tents all around it, and guarding soldiers (the soldiers of Indian National

Army) roaming in vigilance with rifles in their hands and eyes wide open to any suspicious movements. There were horses tied down in a row near a long water tub, a whole tent stuffed with boxes of ammunition, guards hiding in the outer circle of trees around the camp and also a medical center just being set up by their men with a large red cross on the outer side of the tent cloth. This whole setup was rounded by the forest that was cut in the shape of a vast circle and the land they were walking on still had high raised grass that was just above their knee level.

Drutha went into his tent where his new uniform hung against the window cut in the fabric. Bose already had his bath that they needed much, not just to smell good, but also not to catch an infection from all the blood they soaked in. He threw himself into the uniform as fast as he could, and walked out of the tent, towards the medical center, to get some antibiotic shots.

Drutha somehow hadn't liked the idea of Bose hiding in the wind mill that made the center part of all this arrangement. It seemed obvious to guess him in there. But it was the only place that could contain a radio set against the atmospheric odds, and Bose need to transmit messages to the rebels who were reaching for them the next day.

He climbed the old iron stairs on to the rock platform on which the brick mill stood and knocked the wooden door twice in a row, and then twice again.

"Yes, Drutha," Bose said out loud, and he entered in.

In there, there was nothing but just another stair case on to the low lying wooden roof, a small window with two iron grills, a huge set of transceiver that was blinking lights and a pair of folding iron chairs with Mr Bose on one of them, peeping into the frequency meter. He was in his commander uniform.

"Feeling good?" he said still engrossed in setting up the frequencies.

"Yes, sir. Are we going to talk to them today?"

"Yes we are. And I actually want to settle the most important ones on the radio itself. I can't risk their lives."

"Great idea, sir." He nodded while he pulled the other chair close to rest his legs. "You closed the spy frequency, sir," he said pointing to the knob that was turned down.

"I don't want any distractions during this transmission," said Bose, adjusting his glasses, but without batting an eye towards him.

"But what if in case of any emergency, sir?" It started bothering Drutha. "We never turn off the spy channel."

"Oh, cut it Drutha," Bose waved him away. "It's just for an hour."

"But sir it's not-"

"Drutha, I am working," he said cutting him off.

Drutha said nothing in response. What else could he say? This man never even listened to the greatest leaders of this country.

"Yes, sir," he murmured in arrogance, to which Bose's lip took a curve.

* * *

They flew towards the British India, and the sun slowly started moving away from them as the earth started rotating in counter to their movement, trying it's best to conceal the sun from them. Prudhvi felt as if they were chasing it, fighting back with the earth they just flew from.

Emily was so silent all through and it was just Aston who spoke in intervals to update their coordinates. A weird and freaky silence occupied the square even from the start. Prudhvi turned to his right all the time to look at her and he also waved twice or thrice by now. She hadn't turned or noticed him at least once, but she seemed cute in those goggles, and the way she held the steering made him smile. He still wondered how a girl she once used to be had grown up to be a commander flying bomber planes at thousands of feet above the ground and had no glitch of fear in her. Though he wanted to talk to her on the radio, he hated the idea of poking his personal feelings when on the mission. He hated himself for worrying more about her than Bose.

Emily wondered if she should let the other two hear her when she confronts Prudhvi, or maybe they could turn furious and attack him. She was dying to keep her silence, and it made her go all chaotic when she saw Prudhvi waving hands to her. Though she ignored it as if she had never seen him do that, she started wondering why he was not using the radio if he wanted to talk. Maybe he wanted to talk only to her. She could do that. She could cut the other two planes off and talk just with him. She had the controls on her panel, but she was not still under control.

She had already done what she could do. She kept the fact that he was a spy to herself. She moved the mission with the help of Mr Beckman, stating that she got an intelligence report of possible information leak, trying to save the mission too. She also saved Prudhvi from the enemy lands, and now he was headed towards his country where he will be as safe as they were in England. She wanted to ask him to fly off the pattern and never come back. She decided to spare his life, but not yet ready to lose him. She was still acting fair, but standing on the fine line that separated love from war.

"We're in," Aston beeped in at once, making her jump off her dreams. "We are in the Indian airs now. Twenty from the target. To the victory."

"To victory," the others repeated.

"Twenty minutes more," she repeated inside her head. "Maybe I can let him do what he wants to – save Bose. Let him win and report the mission a failure. I can do that… But at what cost?" Her brain started taking control again. "Though all this is a lie… All the words he spelled, all the time we spent… But how good is he at this? Is he prepared to kill me too? Yes, he's worth dying for. But what *I* am worth to him? Nothing? Just a puppet? Or he still wants to find courage and reason to love me back?"

She thought of turning to him, to see if he was still looking at her. If he was, she wanted to talk to him right now. Ask him to leave before anything that could slip out of hands starts slipping.

She took a deep breath in an attempt to fill confidence inside her and slowly turned to him. She had just seen him already stare at her, and he waved again. Emily had no idea why she did that, but she waved back and smiled like a fool. Prudhvi too smiled back and started to move his hands as if to tell her something, and suddenly a clump of clouds blocked their vision.

Emily turned back at once, to see Robert too out of her sight. They had just entered a thick cloud, and it was lasting forever.

"Aston? What altitude we are flying at?" she screamed.

"Guys, ascend 500," he said sounding disrepute.

They all pulled their sticks slow and hard, to resurface the cloud. The four bombers poked themselves out of the clouds at once, making four smoke drags from the surface. As they drove up steadily to settle at a fixed altitude again, a loud thunder clapped in the distance making them shiver with panic.

"What in hell was that?" exclaimed Robert.

"Didn't you heard it?" Prudhvi said, peeping through the glass to take a look at the clouds beneath them. "It's a thunder."

"Guys," Emily said at once, staring deep towards the horizon covered with clouds. "I think we had a serious problem."

The clouds she was staring at were not the usual white and fluffy, calm and cool ones. They were pitch black, with waves of thick precipitation rotating inside, making it look like an angry sea. And there were not just beneath them, there were above them too.

It seemed like a trap someone had set for them. Two layers of furious black clouds waiting to swallow them up.

"Aston," Emily called. Her voice was not stable. "Can we fly any higher?"

"No, madam." Aston too was shivering. "We can't fly higher. But we can fly low."

"No. Not a thought of it. They'll spot us."

"How can we fly through that?" Prudhvi argued. "And why the hell there were two layers of clouds?"

"It's kind of natural," Robert said. "Not a new phenomenon to happen. But the only thing is that we should hope for no cross thunders."

As if they heard him, a huge thunder clapped from the top layer to the bottom, making them go blind for a second. It seemed like an electric charge between the plates of a capacitor. The sound was unbearable, that it started ringing their ears.

"Madam, we can't proceed," Aston screamed. "We're going to get fried."

Emily said nothing. She quivered with anxiety and fear that she may get her team killed. But she can't give up. The inside of their cockpits started going dark. They were entering the layers and the wind started questioning their intrusion, pushing them back by their wings. But there was still no sound to be heard, except their heartbeats.

From a distance, the four bomber planes which emitted beastly fumes down on earth seemed like four tiny flies, entering a huge cave of clouds. They are literally invisible if seen from a little more distance.

Emily lifted her head up, to witness the blackest clouds she had ever seen in her entire life. Even the small ray of light that was beaming from the distant airs through which they entered, started dimming off.

"Madam, please. Let's get out of here. We can still head back."

"Aston, don't push the commander," Robert warned.

"Why not?" Prudhvi said. "We are not going to make it through these waves. We'll get hit. Let's not-"

The wind started blowing hard at once and the planes trembled to the rage of nature. Their wings were quaking unable to stand the pressures. A huge formation of smoke running as a tornado invaded and they lost visuals of one another again. The radio too was just squeaking.

"-put. There's no-" Prudhvi started hearing breaking voice of Emily. "-an order. No one- … -I told you to- …"

"Emily?" he started screaming. "Emily can you hear me? Emily?" But his connection was lost. "Aston? Robert?" he cried still in hope, but no one heard him. Or maybe they did, and called back too. But he couldn't hear them.

The smoke started getting thick and the wind was going to tear his vessel apart in no time. Prudhvi had nothing to do with what happened to the others. He could dive down into the lower layer and pop out from the other end safe. But he couldn't leave Emily in here.

Another thunder clapped and he saw a bright light just over his shoulder. His heart stopped at once in impulse of his brain expecting a shock wave. Nothing happened to his plane, but the radio screamed at once. A loud static made him close his ears though they were already covered.

The plane's beak started lifting up, unable to bear the opposing pressures and the wind was now at the highest of its strength. It was just before Prudhvi decided to dive off into the darkness beneath his feet, the smoke cleared off at once.

He darted out of the mist, into the space between the clouds again. It did give him some visibility to look around. But all that he could see were the vast layers of vapors getting darker and darker, with thunders clapping in the far distances and also few points close to him.

But there were no other planes to be seen around. He was all alone. Just hanging there, looking as small as an electron, floating in between the plates of a huge cloud capacitor.

***

"Is this going to affect the meeting?" enquired Drutha, who just entered with a plate of salad containing boiled potatoes, carrots, beans and sprouts.

"No, Drutha," said Bose, stretching his body to relax himself from hours of sitting near the transceiver. He stood up to stretch. "They are already here," he said cracking his knuckles and sat down again.

"But it's thundering, sir."

"Yeah," he said looking straight at Drutha. "The sky is clapping for what we are striving for here. You hate me right? For turning off the spy frequency."

"Kind of, sir," he said placing the plate on the receiver set. "You never think of your safety."

"Oh c'mon, Drutha. I am a soldier. The purpose of my life is to die."

"And I am your friend, sir. My purpose is to save you."

"Friend?" smiled Bose. "That's a nice word to hear. Now stop the drama and sit. It's going to rain for hours. Happy that my friend brought me something to eat in here," he said picking up a piece of carrot.

* * *

"Prudhvi?" the radio called out at once.

"Oh my god. Emily? Where were you?" he talked in shuddering tone, turning directions to spot her.

"Way ahead of you," she said, and sounded more like his commander than his friend. "Turn back Prudhvi. They think you got lost. Keep it that way."

"What? Who are they?"

"Aston and Robert. They think we lost you. But I just disconnected you from them. We are talking private now."

"But why?" he almost screamed with shock. "And why do you pick up pace without me? Or it's me who missed it because of the bad signal?"

"Prudhvi…" she said as if to calm him down. "I know what you are here for. Who you are and why you wanted to be on this mission. I still remembered the 'Acquaintance Key' you designed."

Prudhvi said nothing in reply. He just sat there, calm and steady, with both his hands holding the steering stick, and his only heart soaking in fear.

"Emily," he finally said, not taking much time. He digested it on war foot basis. "I know how it looks like from your end. But not 1% of it is true. Yes, I did keep some secrets to myself. But-"

"Sorry, Prudhvi," she intruded into his talk. "Bandages don't fix bullet holes. There's no time for all this now. And I don't want to wave a goodbye to you. You'll always be there; where you had always been. I am cutting you off. We are above the target space."

"Emily wait I-" and the radio went dead. "Damn..." Prudhvi cried out loud. "Damn Damn Damn..."

He was shaking with anger for being a total fool for not taking steps to prevent Emily from seeing those messages he transferred lastly. Why did he not remember how good she was at all this?

But there was no time to repent. He couldn't leave them free in the air above Bose. There were no more options left now, but to take all of them down; including Emily.

Chapter 15

"It's ok, Aston. We can do this," she said trying to reinforce their strength. "It's not like we lost him forever right. Once this is done, we can search for him. Ok?"

She also tried not to make the lump in her throat decide how she sounded, but it did give away a little. She knew she was dying to have a big cry out loud, but she wanted herself to be much bigger than that.

"Yes, mam," Aston conformed his approval.

"Robert? You ready?"

"When Aston was."

"I am ready."

"Guys, look for the thunders. We are not letting this depend on our luck anymore. Aston, you're on. Lock the target. I am backing you up."

"Madam," he said taking a sudden dive into the clouds, and Emily left the tail of Robert to join him.

Aston had a huge analog device setup in his lap, between the control board and the steering, which he used for locking the coordinates of the target into the missiles hanging from his brother's plane using low range electromagnetic waves. The analog meter was to keep them at stealth while he locked the target range and the low range waves only traversed between them, not interfering with any enemy devices on land. Once he locked the range, the only thing that would be left was Robert to drop the missile flying over that range. The rest would be taken care of the algorithm inside the rocket board.

Aston could hardly see the circle cut in the trees for the altitude he was flying at, but the eyes of his equipment were quite sharp. It was claimed to be one of the accurate and fastest device available up to date.

"Locked," Aston confirmed his catch in less than two minutes and all at once a rumbling sound occurred from nowhere, following which one of his wings blew off into pieces.

"I am hit," Aston screamed. "I am hit. I am hit."

"What!" Robert said springing out with shock.

"Aston pull up," shouted Emily. "Pull off the course. Robert stay where you are."

She turned to her rear view mirror at once to see the bomber they just lost, fly off into the clouds above them.

"Prudhvi..." she said clenching her teeth.

* * *

"What was that sound?" Drutha cried taking off his headphones.

"Shhh..." Bose said scribbling notes of what his mates from the other side were speaking of.

Drutha said nothing but just left the headphones on the table, to walk out of the wind mill. He was sure that he heard shots.

"Sir, I heard shots," a soldier came running to him as he closed the door behind.

"God, get the guards in row," he said jumping off the stairs and running towards the tent of ammunition. "Surround the mill. Secure the perimeters and look for anything that moves. Aim two machines at the sky."

"Yes, sir," the soldier said running off to his team.

"Hope they are not here for Bose," he prayed as he ran into the tent.

* * *

Aston tried to regulate his plane but it was shaking with loss of his control on it. He pulled it above the clouds but it was not going to stay there anymore.

"What the hell is happening?" Robert cried. "How do they know we are coming?"

"Aston can you maintain?" Emily enquired.

"I think I cannot." All their planes were reverberating with the emergency siren in his pit and the smoke from his wing started covering her path.

Emily searched all around for him, but Prudhvi was to be seen nowhere. "Where are you hiding?" she murmured.

Prudhvi sat down with all his strength as his plane trembled nonstop and uncontrollable to the hits it was taking from the thick formation of condensed water droplets. The turbulence was very high that his head started aching like hell. He was following them from underneath, that is from inside the cloud and when he resurfaced, he wanted to take his first shot on the missiles.

Aston's plane finally gave it up and it lost its ability to fly anymore.

"Oh my…" Robert cried seeing his brother fly off the field.

"Aston," Emily screamed and took an immediate dive to her right to avoid his plane hitting hers. "Aston you there? Aston can you hear me. Eject. Eject right now."

A flash, as if some heavy amount of gun powder was burned, occurred inside the cockpit, blowing off the whole glass above its head and the pilot's seat went flying separate from his plane.

"He's out," Robert shouted in celebration.

Prudhvi heard the blast and he immediately pulled the stick, prepared to take another shot.

***

They all just froze where they were, staring at the sky from which a sudden ball of fire emerged out. It was burning bright in the shade created by the clouds. Drutha got frightened with the thought of how many more were in there, and why were they fighting among themselves. Or if it's just the thunder that knocked it down? Then who took the shots he heard earlier?

"Move move move," he screamed at once bending into the grass and running fast towards Bose. "Take covers. Aim at the skies."

He ran into the wind mill with an extra rifle in his hand.

"What's the noise?" Bose enquired trying to step out.

"Sir, no," Drutha stopped him, handing him the rifle. "You shouldn't step out, sir. We are under attack."

"Attack? No one even knows this part of the world exists."

"But now they do, sir."

"God… This can't happen. Let's shoot those morons down," he said walking out again.

"No, sir," Drutha stood before the door. "I can't allow you out."

"Drutha step aside."

He knew when Bose really meant something he said, and he meant it now as well. He also knew he couldn't stop this man from going out into the field. But he should.

He unlocked his rifle to point the barrel at Bose.

"If you really want to die, die in the hands of your men," he said as if warning him. "Or just step back into your seat, sir."

Bose stared at him in rage. Not for pointing a gun at him, but for not letting him fight.

"You know me, sir. I can do this." But what Drutha didn't know was that he was making him stay at the point on to where the missiles were locked.

"Do it then," he said stepping forward.

"Yeah, I will." Drutha took the barrel off Bose, to place it below his chin. "Go, fight without me."

* * *

Prudhvi emerged out of the clouds in a sharp jump and he was right behind a plane.

But it was Emily's.

Emily saw him in the mirror, flying behind her, ready to fire on Robert. But she was not letting him get any close to him. He should kill her first, to make any other kills.

"Robert, don't ask me anything," she talked into the radio, with her eyes still fixed on Prudhvi. "Prudhvi is a spy. And he's coming for you now."

"What!" he said surprised, unable to stop that word from leaving his mouth.

"Just tell me if you can launch the missile."

"No. No, I cannot. We are too far from the locked range. He's a spy?!"

Another thunder clapped, in a distance very close to them. Three of them sprung out again. After the few next times, they may propably get used to this. Emily feared the thunders as they may hit any of them in any given fraction of time. She prayed for Robert not getting hit, or Prudhvi.

"Then let's turn around," she ordered Robert. "Always keep me in between you and him. He can't shoot me. Ok?"

Robert was still worried about his brother and wanted to ask his commander a hell lot of questions. But he knew that it was just not time.

"I am taking a vertical turn off," he informed her.

"After you," she said getting grip on her steering.

"Emily," Prudhvi called at once. He got back to her frequency. "Get off the line."

"Prudhvi don't do this. Don't make me shoot you."

Robert and Emily were now upside down taking the turn and Prudhvi could literally see them on the exact top of his head. He took an immediate dive to the left, a horizontal one, and turned his beak up towards Robert. When they rotate their birds back to orientation, he could get a gap in between the wings of her plane, through which he could aim at the missiles.

He did get a chance to shoot right at them at the right time he expected, but by the time he took his shoot Emily moved close to Robert at once. If he fired now, both of them would blow.

"Emily..." he screamed. "Don't make *me* shoot you. Get – off – the – line."

He started chasing them again, but now they were in lead towards the range. He knew that they were approaching fast and once they did, Robert would drop the missile. Prudhvi dived low immediately, but still stayed on top of the clouds. He gave the plane a heavy throttle and it picked pace at once. He passed from underneath Emily to reach Robert and stayed below him, maintaining the speed.

He knew that Emily knew what Robert will do now. He had an extra missile to spare, so he would easily drop one on to Prudhvi's plane, and then go off to kill Bose. And as he had expected, Emily too dived at once, picking up speed and settled in between them. They were flying in a vertical row now.

"Emily, what are you doing?" Robert screamed on her. "Slow down."

"Robert you can't kill him. Just kill the one we came for."

Prudhvi smiled, and it echoed in the other two planes.

"Stop that Prudhvi," she said with anger pouring out of every word she spelled. "You know you're taking advantage of me. And I am letting you. Or else you would be dead by now."

"Same here, Emily. It's just because of you this was not over yet."

"Shut the hell up you two," shouted Robert sliding out of his own senses. "Get off my way or I'll kill you both."

"Ah Robert. I think we have already left the 'Range' behind," said Prudhvi, smiling with sarcasm.

Robert boiled with sudden anger. He took of the glass cap over that special button and pressed it with no second thought.

"Robert what did you do?" Emily cried, seeing the locks over the missile pop out.

In the next split second the missile fell free on to her. Emily dogged to her right taking the entire bend her steering can give. Prudhvi killed his throttle and pulled his plane up, taking a cross curve to turn back.

"Damn...." he cursed his actions, knowing that if he took a turn back now, he'll be face to face with them. He would have no advantage of tailing them to shoot.

The missile that Robert left just fell off in control of the gravity but nothing else, as it was already out of the target range.

***

They heard a huge blast from a distance into the forest and it echoed, like forever.

Drutha still had his gun to his own head and Bose hadn't moved yet.

"Heard that, sir?" he said panting. "Please don't make me do this."

It was not breaking Bose at all. He just stood there, as if formulating a plan to talk him out. But Drutha was not giving up on this. He didn't want to see a dead Bose in this life.

* * *

Robert and Emily turned their planes back and Prudhvi did, too. They were now on the opposite sides above Bose, and were closing in towards each other.

Prudhvi knew that nothing could be done. There was one more missile left, and he saw Emily flying in front of him, guarding it. The clouds stopped clapping now but they started going even darker as if getting ready to rain. Prudhvi started losing vision to the darkness.

"Emily," he called her at once, but as if he wanted to talk it out, rather than shooting at each other.

"Yes?" She too maintained the cool.

But Robert was now on his edges, with his finger over the big red button shivering in anxiety. It was the only chance he got and nothing's going to stop him.

"Leave this to me Emily," Prudhvi said. "It's not for me. It's not for this man who can get us our freedom… It's for someone else. And you know how badly I want this."

"I am sorry, Prudhvi. You might have all your reasons. I had mine. Actually I had a million reasons not to let you have this. You know what the least painful of them is? – I hate you."

Her tone was not soft anymore. She sounded like the Witch again, and there was arrogance all over her tone, which made his anger strike back.

Prudhvi was shaking with rage, which emerged from the thought of losing this fight - the one he could not afford to lose. And there was no one who could stop him from winning it. Not even a girl who could do the same for him.

"Have you seen the clouds, Emily?" he said.

"What?" She was surprised.

"This time of year, its summer in India." His grip on his steering went tight. "But it looks like someone had control over the seasons. Maybe someone wants it to rain. Heavily…"

She understood what he's trying to say, but hadn't expected the one simple question that followed.

"Emily?" he said, as if staring straight into her eyes. "Will you marry me?"

That shook her like an earthquake, though she was flying high.

Prudhvi pushed the stick and his plane gained sonic speed.

Emily knew what he meant. She hoped that he didn't mean it metaphorically, but he did.

She too pushed her steering at once and attained speed.

"Yes, Prudhvi. My answer is 'Yes'," she said as her plane started trembling to the velocities. "Bring on what you got. I am dying to see how it ends this time."

They both started approaching in speeds that made the air take bursts, but no one had slowed even a little. Prudhvi had his thumb on the trigger to the machine guns in his wings. So did Emily.

When two fighters approach head on, they were supposed to dodge to their right sides in the last minute, to avoid collision. But they were flying like no one was going to dodge or no one was going to spare the other. Only two things in this entire world could fill a human with courage that surpass the rest. One was Vengeance, and the other, Love. But in both the cases, only the ones on the failed end would get the fruit. Both Emily and Prudhvi already had their parts from Love. And as they neared with warnings of each other's death, there started Vengeance, donating its part.

They were just few nautical meters away now and they could even see each other through the glass. Prudhvi knew that Emily could shoot and Emily believed that Prudhvi won't. He never wanted to see her smile vanish into death and she never wanted to see him ever leave her again. But their eyes burned with anger emerged out of helpless love.

Both the bombers neared with their top speeds that the collision may have leave the least chances of life. But just in that one last second left, they both dodged. They went past each other with their bellies almost rubbing against one another.

Prudhvi bent his plane back and headed towards Robert. "Emily, eject," he screamed.

"What?" she wondered just before she realised that she was hit.

Prudhvi shot her on her left wing and it was tearing apart from the air's friction.

"Not fair Prudhvi…" she cried out with anger and disbelief.

She wanted to turn back and get even with him, but the whole wing flew away at once. Her plane started losing altitude and fell spinning towards the clouds, and through them. Emily pulled the eject lever and in the next second she was flying in a parachute on to the forest. She hated Prudhvi like she never did.

This time, she really wanted to kill him.

Worrying if she had got out safe, Prudhvi went on to Robert. He prayed that she pulled that lever. But what that he had just missed was that Robert was already in the zone.

And there was no missile on his belly.

But then again, there was a pit of smoke that was just upraised from the surface of clouds beneath him. Prudhvi's eyes widened with the very thought of it. Robert had already launched the missile.

He could still dive down to take the missile on to his plane and direct it off the wind mill. It won't blast until the rotor on its tail stopped. So if he caught it at the maximum possible altitude, he could keep it moving and he'd have time to redirect and then eject. But with Robert closing in, who was definitely going to shoot him at the first chance, it was not possible. Prudhvi couldn't lend his time that went limited just now, on an air fight, trying to defend himself.

With only few seconds left for them to enter the space where they could fire at each other, Prudhvi tried to deduce a way by which he could take him in just one shot. No such shot ever existed, but that was the only thing which could help him now. There was a missile falling on to Bose.

As Prudhvi finally decided to dive into the clouds to catch the missile, which was of the higher priority, even if Robert may shoot him after that, a sudden thunder clapped, and it hit Robert's plane right on the face. The vessel suddenly lost its power and it descended at once as if the one who was holding him until now just dropped it.

Prudhvi too was struck, with shock. But without a second's lag, he jumped into the clouds, chasing the missile. He was happy for his luck backing him up.

Robert ejected his seat and flew off his plane safely, as if his duty here was over, though he still wanted to shoot Prudhvi in his head for all the betrayal.

Prudhvi dipped his plane head down and descended with all the speed the machine could. He levelled the speed of the missile seeing the toy come to life. It was not innocent anymore, with the potential destruction it was carrying and the mark of the British Air force by the side gave it a look that was even more dangerous.

Prudhvi made his plane race parallel to the diving death, and in no time he was flying faster than the missile. He knew a technique he could catch it with. He only read it once and it was not even been thought with a dummy on field in his training. But he was way more confident, as he should be. Prudhvi rolled his plane to get right in line with the missile, reduced his speed in an abrupt shutdown of the engine and opened the flaps wide. The plane literally turned ninety degrees in air and the missile hit him, right in the middle.

It went piercing into the plane and the three layered metal bottom was bent to its threshold, but it did contain the impact. Prudhvi closed the flaps and left the plane fall again at once.

But one thing that he hadn't considered was, 'With what part of the plane he should catch a missile with?'

Whatever the part was, but it was definitely not the center-most section, where the main grid lay. The missile's impact killed the control panel. The auxiliary systems too went off and Prudhvi failed to bring the vessel back to life. There was power in it, and the steering was also working, but the throttle was dead.

Luck was such a bitch. It would turn on you any minute it wanted to.

Prudhvi knew he couldn't maintain the speed that kept the missile's rotor on, unless he kept on falling free. But if he did, he'd lose altitude in no time, making it impossible to eject at the required heights. He could only steer the plane to safety, but his getting out of it was not possible. And also there was not much time to waste now. If there was a decision he should make that matters; it had to be made right now.

As he fell off the sky with gravity pulling him close to where he belonged, Prudhvi closed his eyes to silence and darkness. It's been a really long time since he saw her. She hadn't changed much. Same smile, same glow, same love and same dream. Prudhvi smiled in his vision, as he took his decision.

When a man ever took a decision as strong and deep as this over the history, there was definitely a result he hoped for, dreamed for or born for. But not this time…

This one time, this one man, is asked for.

"I want freedom, Prudhvi," she asked him. "I want you to fight for it."

He opened his eyes at once, to see a forest forming in front of him. He could also see a small circle cut in the woods, but he could hardly stare as the plane trembled with a hole at its half. But Prudhvi knew that, somewhere there in that circle, there was a wind mill in which this man stood. The one man, who was already at the gates of freedom. The freedom that she asked for…

Prudhvi felt an urge to talk to that man right now. And there was a way he could. He checked the radio for power. It was on and he knew the frequency on which the spies could contact a camp. He tuned the radio with one hand still on the stick, ready to steer when the required speed was attained.

But all that he could hear was void. The channel was not open. The spy frequency was closed and he wondered why they did that. His want to talk to Bose rose to newer levels, knowing that he couldn't. Tears rolled off his eyes and he wondered why they did. Prudhvi cried like a kid sitting in the pit of a plane that was descending to death.

Out of nowhere, he suddenly remembered a message he once transmitted. The mention of a secret frequency band in which the rebels were found communicating. He cleared off his eyes at once and started adjusting the knobs. Then again he still cried doing that. The orientation he was in was making him sick, but this was definitely not the time to throw up.

The channel was set, and he started talking. He was not sure if someone can hear him, but he just screamed.

* * *

The radio suddenly squeaked and someone called his name. Bose turned back to the set at once from Drutha.

"They were still on?" enquired Drutha.

"No," Bose said in astonishment, walking to it. "They're not."

"BOSE…" the radio spoke again, and the one who's talking is shouting like a mad man "I WANT TO TALK TO BOSE."

"Bose speaking," he said at once. "Who are you? How did you know that-"

"SHUT UP AND LISTEN," he cried.

Drutha sprung out with unexpected shock. Someone knew that he's talking to Bose and he just said 'Shut up.'

"DO YOU REMEMBER SAYING 'GIVE ME YOUR BLOOD AND I WILL GIVE YOU FREEDOM?'"

"Yes," he answered turning to Drutha in surprise, and back. "Yes I remember."

"THEN REMEMBER THIS TOO OLD MAN. I AM GIVING YOU SOMETHING MORE THAN JUST BLOOD, AND THAT'S TO SAVE YOU." His voice was trembling and Bose could feel him sob while he talked.

Prudhvi rubbed his face again to stop the tears from falling on to the radio. "Please do remember this, sir," he said pulling himself together. "You are my *last* hope."

Bose said nothing but just went silent, not knowing who this kid was, why he was asking for all this, and how was he saving his life.

"By the way, sir," he said. "I am Prudhvi. We once met in a hanger."

"Prudhvi?" Bose went bewildered having not a clue of what he was doing here. "Where are you talking from? What's all this?"

"You'll come to know, sir," he said realising that it was time. "Don't forget that you owe me India. Jai Hind."

"Prudhvi… Prudhvi? Prudhvi…" Bose screamed to the radio that went dead.

* * *

Switching off the set, he took hold of the stick with both his hands and pulled the plane into the forest.

Emily ran to a small opening in the trees from where she landed, to see Prudhvi taking the missile. She waited for him to eject until it reached half the distance and took a sudden turn there. Then she came to know what might have happened and what he was trying to do. She cursed herself for bringing this on to him, as she ran between the woods in the direction the plane flew.

Prudhvi knew that these may be his last few minutes and he was failing to see her in his thoughts. The shouting alarm on his head, the missile that was sitting on his back, the mixture of feelings that were flowing down his heart; they all were failing him from seeing her.

"One last time. God dammit, show her for one last time," he shouted inside his head.

The plane lost all its altitude and it was flying just above the trees now. The upper layer of the forest was getting trimmed by the blades on its nose, and the sliced pieces were flying on to him but being protected by the glass around. Prudhvi couldn't see the camp from this angle but he somehow knew that this can be the point. But in real, he was way farther than the safe spot.

He finally pulled the lever and the seat was ejected at once. It threw him off the plane and the world started rotating in the next minute. Prudhvi saw the plane jump on the trees in a flash and he lost it. He flew away from the plane and the parachute that just opened up got struck to a tree pulling him back with a jolt. Few of his ribs broke to the sudden impact and he fell face first on a branch. His lower jaw was dislocated to the blow and he bumped off the tree. The branches tore the chute and it got caught in hanging him along with it at a height that may break his legs if he falls.

Prudhvi groaned in pain, oscillating like a pendulum tied to the trees. He felt all dead suddenly. His nose started bleeding, his eyes were almost blurred and he could hardly move his limbs. He felt blood dripping off his face on to the land below.

But pushing all the pain aside, the plane crashed into the forest and what that he heard was not an echo. It's the direst sound, which was from a point not so far. Hanging there, swinging slow, he wondered if the impact will hit him.

He had never imagined, even in the wildest of his dreams, that he will see a day like this. It all happened so fast that it felt like a kind of reverie. Prudhvi stared deep into the forest, with his eyelids giving some way to the light into his eyes. The woods were as calm as they would have been without the blast, but the sudden wind that started to pick up speed felt really strange. It blew in a concentrated direction, and the leaves stared giving up their trees.

As he still stared into the gaps between the trees, they stared filling with a light that was colored bright yellow. The fill was so fast that just over a few seconds it reached him. A huge wave of flames came his way from every direction he could see, burning everything that was in their vicinity. The blast hit him hard and threw him off the tree just like another leaf.

* * *

Emily ran into the forest, towards the huge clouds of black and thick smoke that was getting upraised, turning the sky even darker. As she almost neared it, she started hearing the sound of water flowing rigorously nearby. She prayed that he fell into that river, saving himself from the blast.

As she kept on rambling and trekking in the woods without stopping even she wanted to, the formation of trees started getting less dense. At the end of a landscape that suddenly took a sudden steep, she confronted a river that was slicing the forest. The blast seemed not more than few meters from the river and she could also see few trees burning from here. Emily turned direction unable to find a way to the other end, as swimming across a river that was flowing this fast was almost impossible. She panted, getting hold of a tree for support, and suddenly saw something from in between the high raised plants. It was an old wooden suspension bridge.

Emily ran again at once and didn't stop until she reached the other side. The bridge was as strong as a newly laid one. She ran straight into the burned area, but took a sudden halt when the fumes from the blast started burning her skin. The black powdery soot that filled the air went into her lungs and she started coughing heavily. She took of her leather jacket and folded her sleeves up to feel some air, but it was not working. The whole air around was burning her even deeper.

Realising that she could not proceed any further and she'd lose her eyes to the soot and the heat, Emily turned back to call for help from the camp that might be just few kilometers from here. As she tried to close her nostrils and eyes with her palms and run, she almost fell over a hump in the ground. She took a way around it just before she lost control, only to think of it while she ran. Something about the hump bothered her. It's not just a hump. It felt like… like it once lived.

She took an abrupt halt, as still as a rock that had been there for centuries.

"God," she said leaving a sigh. "God, please don't."

She hoped that she's just hallucinating and it's nothing but just a hump. She walked back to it in slow and suspicious steps.

"It's not him," she assured herself. "It's not him. Not at all."

But it was him. It was a man who closed his legs on to his heart before he burned.

* * *

Eshwar saw her from the other side while she was roaming the forest, losing tracks of the camp. From her uniform and the color of her skin, there was not a doubt that she was one of the assassins they sent to kill Bose. But Eshwar was very determined not to let her find him. He followed her in silent steps, to attack her from the back. These paid assassins were edgy and all their senses worked together in any situations and atmospheres. So he waited for his moment from a long time, and it had finally come.

He made the grip on his hand knife much tighter as he slowly walked to her without the dry leaves making any sound. At first she seemed like she was staring at something, but as she hadn't moved for a while, Eshwar doubted that if she had heard or seen him and it was just a trap she was framing to make him come closer.

But at this point, Eshwar had an advantage. Both her hands were free and she held nothing. Also he was already in a position to take control of her if he made a move right now. And he took it. Eshwar jumped on to her, twisting her hand back and placing the sharp edge of the knife on her throat.

"Don't move or you'll die," he warned her, twisting her hand even harder.

Emily said nothing but started sobbing. She had no concern for the one who had a blade to her neck. She just cried, closing her eyes with the other hand.

Eshwar was shocked to see her sob. Her cry felt so painful that he left her at once. Emily fell on the ground and started taking deeper sobs.

"Prudhvi..." she cried his name out, crawling to him. She didn't know if she could touch him. His flesh seemed like burned wax that was just adjusting.

"Wha... What did you say?" Eshwar cried for that name he knew. He sat near her, realising that there was a burned man lying before them. He hoped that he just heard a wrong name.

"What had you just said?" he said, shaking her by her shoulders. "Hey... You... What's his name?"

Emily looked up at him with her eyes burning and wet. She seemed like there will be no more life remaining in her if she kept on crying like this for few more minutes.

"What name did you take?" he repeated as calm and caring as he can.

"Prudhvi," she said and started sobbing again. "His name is Prudhvi."

"Prudhvi?" he repeated. "The chief of SIGNIT?"

Emily nodded, and it took all his pain away at once, to provide him with a brand new batch of torture. Eshwar turned to look at the burned man, and he knew that he can never believe that this was the same Prudhvi he thought he was. He just stared at the hump not knowing what to do or how to react. And suddenly from nowhere, the hump took a huge breath making him fall back with a shudder.

* * *

The soldiers slowly carried his body into the medical center, in a gunny cloth. They laid him on the iron bed that they use as the operation table, and walked out the tent to give them some space. The doctor, who was also dressed in the brown uniform, entered in as they left. He had his stethoscope in his hand, and a nurse in her gown and white apron with a red cross on it followed him with a tray of scissors, blades and a pot of hot water.

He hadn't taken much time in examining Prudhvi. He had already seen cases like these, and the inevitable outcome had always been the same.

"I am sorry to say this," he said turning to Eshwar, who stood beside him. "He can't make it."

Emily clenched her fist to stop her tears from breaking out again. She stepped back to fall on to a chair near the table on which the nurse was arranging the bandages. The nurse turned to look at the white lady go red and wondered what a British girl was doing in Bose's camp.

Eshwar too found himself wordless. He just nodded to what the doctor said.

But between all these, Prudhvi wanted to talk. He wanted to tell them that he could hear what the doctor just said, and it was not going to happen. However, for some unknown reasons, he failed to move, talk or even breathe properly.

"Nurse," the doctor called out. "Clean the burns and cover him with a blanket. Mr Bose will see him shortly."

Ordering her with few more instructions on treatment, the doctor left the tent, to join his mates in making arrangement for an immediate evacuation. The camp should move now, even before another wave of attack occurs.

As the doctor left, the nurse started cleaning him with some solutions. Emily said nothing but stared at him from her chair. Eshwar stood aside with his hands folded and he just looked at the ground all through.

"The dressing is done," the nurse informed when she had finally finished. "We'll see if we should leave him to die, or maybe we can induce something that can save him from the pain."

Emily shut her eyes tight unable to bear those words. Tears started rolling off again.

"Should we leave him, or…?" she enquired turning to Eshwar and Emily.

"Do what you think is the best," Eshwar responded.

Emily prayed for every god she ever knew, for that one last miracle. She wanted to hear something like 'This is a miracle in medical history.' But she also knew that it could never happen. She knew that no one could ever make through something like this, but she kept on praying.

Don't know who among all those gods heard her. But the miracle did happen.

"Ok. I'll go call Sanjuktha," the nurse said. "She'll take care of this."

"Who?" Emily and Eshwar both screamed at once.

Prudhvi took a deep breath suddenly freaking out the nurse.

"Don't panic," Emily talked in fast formation of words and running to Prudhvi. "Who did you say? Sanjuktha?"

"Yes. Our head nurse."

"Does this Sanjuktha …" Emily tried to ask for her details but found none to enquire.

The nurse waited for another second and just took off in haste, to call up on her head.

"Prudhvi?" Emily talked low, bending towards him. "You heard that?"

He nodded his head, in a very little movement.

"Oh my god. Will that be your Sanjuktha?" she said taking deep breaths. "Can you open your eyes?"

He tried. But the flesh over them was burned, forming a seal.

"Do you want me to tell her it's you?"

"No," he nodded again. But he lost it half way through the second nod going numb. Emily tried to remember anything else she could ask him, and someone suddenly pulled the cloth at the entrance to walk in.

It was her. Sanjuktha. She too was in her nurse gown, white apron, a red cross and a rifle in her hand. Emily stood up at once seeing her.

She had her hair tied in a simple Indian braid, had no earrings, bangles or any ornaments on, but yet seemed like an angel who just landed earth. As she walked in, Emily watched her with her eyes bulging out of her skull. She wondered how in the hell could she be here. How could god sometimes compose such great screenplays? All at once, she felt like they were in the world's wildest play.

Emily hadn't believed her existence in there while Eshwar, on the other hand, was just awestruck to her aura that filled the space around. He was sure that it was the same Sanjuktha. No one could set the description that Rudhra gave him, as exact as this girl did.

Placing the rifle on the desk at the entrance, Sanjuktha came in to another day of her work. Without much ado, she just walked straight to him and took his hand into hers checking for his pulse.

Prudhvi's eyelids started leaving tears out of the small gaps that remained. All that he could see was darkness, but he could surely tell that it was her who touched him. He wanted to talk to her, but couldn't feel his tongue. His soul trembled with pain and helplessness. He wanted Emily to ask more questions, so he could nod. But even his neck was numb now. More tears fell of his eyes unable to move any of his body parts. He realised that he was going to pass out with the most unbearable pain ever.

"He is in lots of pain," Sanjuktha said, cleaning his eyes with a cloth. "And all his flesh is lost."

She could even see his nerves on his neck, and few of them lost their connection too. She examined him for few more minutes before stating: "He won't make it past ten to fifteen minutes."

Emily was still in shock and grief to respond in any ways.

"You are?"

"His…" Emily tried to answer. "His friend. We fight for… Bose."

"Same," answered Eshwar as she turned to him.

"I am so sorry for your loss. Such a brave soldier he was."

"Yeah," said Eshwar, leaving a sigh. He hated himself for witnessing all this. He cried inside for the loss *she* was facing. And what should he tell Rudhra? That he had seen his friend killed by his love?

"We can't let Bose out until we clear all the fields around. There can be assassins still out there. So let's wait this out," she said sitting on the long wooden table next to him on the opposite side as Emily.

"There is no one but us," Emily wanted to say. But she remained silent on that part. "Do you work for Bose?" she said instead.

Prudhvi hated her questions. Sanjuktha was telling them that he was going to die in fifteen minutes when he felt all fit and fine, except for just the pain and the immobility. And in situations like these, Emily was eating up his time, if Sanjuktha was really true.

"Yeah," Sanjuktha said. "I am the head nurse here. I am a part of his secret team that moves along with him when required."

"Great," Emily nodded. She silently hated the fact that she was talking to Sanjuktha with Prudhvi dying on a table between them. To her, it felt like he was not dying totally hopeless. He got Sanjuktha here and he always-

It struck her from nowhere all at once. "His last wish," she told herself.

"What?" enquired Sanjuktha, hearing her mumble something.

"Ahh… My friend here," she tried to make it look as normal as possible, "had a habit of listening to songs while he slept. So… if you can sing."

"Me?" Sanjuktha exclaimed.

"Yeah. I can't sing so well. If it's ok with you," she said convincing her slowly. "After all, he's having his last sleep right?"

"Yeah," she agreed.

"I love you, Emily," Prudhvi wanted to shout out.

"So…" Emily pushed her, who was immersed in sudden deep thoughts.

It had been years since she last sang and that too when she was asked by Prudhvi. She found no reason to sing till date, but her request now seemed worth singing for. However, it reminded her of Prudhvi and that made her sad. But that was not to compare. A man was dying here.

"If you have a favorite one," Emily pushed her further more.

To Sanjuktha it felt like even Prudhvi may want the same. She wondered what he was doing right now and where he might have been.

She took a deep breath and adjusted herself on the table. She decided to sing, and it's the song he called 'Our song.' But she knew that this was going to be so hard on her when it was over. She cleared her throat, tried to remember the verses as they were and started singing.

One morning, one morning, one morning in May,
I spied a young couple, just making their way.
Now, one was a soldier, and a brave one was he,
And the other was a lady, and a fine one was she.

And it's "Where are you going?" said the soldier, so free.
'I'm going to yon river; it's flowing for me.
Going down to yon river, and sit by that spring,
And watch the water gliding, hear the nightingale sing."

Watch the water gliding, hear the nightingale sing.

And, "May I go with you as you journey along?
If I'm to go with you, I'll sing you a song.
I'll sing the old Concordance, and I'll make my fiddle ring.
Then we'll watch the water glide and hear the nightingale sing."

Said the lady to the soldier, "I'm lonesome and blue,
And I think from your actions that you're lonesome, too.
We'll just walk together, then we'll sit by that spring,
And we'll watch the water glide and hear the nightingale sing."

Now after they'd been there for an hour or two,
Out from his satchel a violin he drew.
He played the old Concordance; oh, he made that fiddle ring,
Then he'd watch the water glide and hear the nightingale sing.

Said the soldier to the lady, "It's time I should go."
"Oh, no," cried the lady, "Play me just one tune more,
For I had rather hear your fiddle, or just tap a string,
Than to watch the water gliding and hear the nightingale sing."

So he tuned his old fiddle to a much higher key.
He played the Shamrock of Erin—oh, he played it so free.
He played the Shamrock of Erin, and he made his fiddle ring.
Then they watched the water gliding, hear the nightingale sing.

Said the lady to the soldier, "Will you marry me?"
"Oh, no, my fair lady, this never could be.
I have a wife in England with children twice three,
And that, with the army, is plenty for me."

"Goodbye," said the soldier, with a parting caress.
"Tomorrow I must be at the throne of Queen Bess,
But when I come back, it will be to this spring,
Then we'll watch the water glide and hear the nightingale sing."

"Goodbye," said the lady, and she gave him her hand.
"I'll think of you often in Indian fair land,
For I had rather hear your fiddle, or just tap a string,
Than to watch the water glide and hear the nightingale sing."

Than to watch the water glide, And hear the nightingale sing...

She took a slow halt with the song marking its end, and she felt really strange singing their song after such a long time. It sounded so new, even to her ears.

It happened when she was in the middle of the song. When she was immersed in the mellowness of those lines, singing as if she was singing for someone who meant life to her, Prudhvi took his last breath; just as he wished it to be.

But... he did hear the whole song. Every word of it. Because when a human dies, it's his ears that are the last to go. For a small instance of time and space, all the life, creation, planets and even the entire universe bowed to the one who created man, and for making the hearing sense the sense he left lastly. May be this was the reason why he planned it so.

But unable to bare the loss that just occurred, the birds that were around flew to far away parts of the forest. The wind that stayed calm until now stared taking mad circles. The sun who just witnessed the death of a martyr dipped himself into the horizon, and it all went dark at once.

"You'll cry if the right song strikes," Rudhra told him. And it was indeed right. Eshwar found himself in tears by the time she stopped singing. Her voice carried a command along, which can make any heart bow to her feet.

Along with Sanjuktha, Emily too knew that Prudhvi was no more. She saw him slide into the bed of death, and he stopped taking in any more air. But Sanjuktha hadn't stopped until it was done as if to keep him calm for eternity.

It was just silence that filled the tent now, and no one made a sound.

Emily never heard a silence that was this loud.

One was dying from the pain to see her love die while his love sang to him. One was trying hard to control himself from crying the truth out loud. And one was fighting a war inside her own self, with the cyclone of some unknown and unseen emotions started taking their turn on her heart.

Finding no point in sitting ideal, Sanjuktha thought it would be better to make arrangements to his cremation, as they were to move as early as possible. And it may also help her take her thoughts off these mixed feelings that were killing her. So she stood up, and pulled the blanket on him, that went wet with blood and serum, to cover his face.

Emily and Eshwar witnessed the end of an era.

It started pulling her again. "I am the one responsible off all this. Just because of me," Emily cursed herself, and those words – 'Prudhvi was no more,' reverberating her ears felt like someone started filling her heart with pieces of burning coal.

She too stood up to walk out, when Sanjuktha just picked up her rifle to leave. They both walked out of the tent at once. Sanjuktha took right, towards her tent, while Emily took the opposite, towards the forest.

* * *

Her legs couldn't handle the speed in which she ran. If it was not out of helplessness her pain caused, if would be out of the pain her helplessness caused. She didn't know where she was headed, but Emily just ran. She ran like a wild horse that was gone wilder – rash, angry and tireless. She ran so fast that the trees she went past started making whimpering sounds of the air being cut. She ran deep and directionless into the woods and her senses started giving away. She wondered how today would have been ended if they stayed back in London and went out on a date. He may not have been hers, but he would definitely have been alive. They would have been smiling over a joke he just cracked during a walk in the park.

All of a sudden she came to an abrupt halt and fell on to her knees. All the memories of Prudhvi started flashing before her eyes. The first day they met in that restaurant, how they have been so close in no time, that one great year they spent their college together, those matches they attended, those plays they went to, all the laughs they shared, that kiss she had with him, the way they drifted off, the day when he saved her life, how he left her all alone at that port, their reunion as soldiers at war, that beautiful walk in the garden the day before, that timeless hug they shared, those beautiful feelings they cherished and the way it all just ended.

She closed her face in her hands and started sobbing loud. Emily screamed his name to the heights of her tone and the woods echoed to her cries. Her cry was so loud and shallow that it felt like she's calling him back.

That one word, "Prudhvi", it touched every stem and every leaf in the forest.

Finally losing all her energy, she fell off on to the ground and started curling like her body was in pain. Just the way she found him. Burying her face in the soil, Emily cried, not because she lost her love. She had just realised that she had lost something much more than that. She lost a friend.

* * *

"Sir?" said Drutha entering in slowly, making Bose spring up from his chair with nervousness.

"What?" he enquired getting hold of him by his shoulders. "What happened?"

"I am sorry, sir." Drutha lowered his head in pain. "We lost him."

Bose left him slowly, to step back. He remembered this kid from the one time he met him. That kid who seemed like he can change things to the way they are supposed to be had proved him right. He hadn't just said that he would fight until his last breath, but he actually did. And died saving his life.

"I can never forget the way he looked at me that day," Bose said taking his specs off. "Do you remember, Drutha? How vibrant his eyes were?"

It came as a sudden shock to Drutha when he lifted his head up to look at him. He found Bose in tears. Netaji Subhash Chandra Bose, in literal tears.

"Sir? You're crying?" he said floundering with his sudden feelings.

"What? I shouldn't cry?" sniffed Bose.

"You hadn't cried even when Mr Rabindranath died, sir. He's your best friend as I know. But why now?"

"What was Tagore's age, Drutha?" he said, as more tears left his eyes. "What's the age of this kid? Give me a number at least above 30."

Drutha went silent, and he found himself fighting tears now. "23, sir," he said, even without looking back.

"God…" Bose turned directions to cope with it. "Do you hear that Drutha? 23?" He sobbed for this child of his motherland. "23? Is that an age to die?"

"What a land our country is, Drutha. What a land. No other country can ever give birth to heroes like this country did. Let's give him back to the land he's named after. The land he fought for. Let's cremate him as an officer of the highest cadre. We move only once it's done."

* * *

With all the chaos that just occurred, people trying to kill Bose, a spy among them trying to save him, a man dying on the operation table; it was definitely not a normal day for her. But it sure was a completely different day, in a completely different way. She was not the same today, as she had been all these days. That song she sang, and after *this* long time, made her remember something. Someone, to be precise.

As Sanjuktha sat in her tent, folding her clothes, arranging them into her bag, preparing to make a move; she suddenly started missing him. It had been years since he left, but she had never missed him this much.

The wind outside was testing the tension in the ropes with which the tent was laid, and the cloth above her head fluttered to withstand. Few things inside the tent fell on the ground, and the sheet she laid on her bed went flying off it, making her iron luggage box as visible as it was in the open. The very sight of it made her consider something that she always controlled herself from not doing. But today the control just flew from her hands.

Sanjuktha suddenly left what she was doing to go sit near the bed and pulled the box out. When she had left her camp that day, she took absolutely nothing with her, except for this one thing. No one but only her, not even Prudhvi knew that she still had it. From between the piles of her old clothes, she pulled it out for the first time in years again.

It was her mangalsutra that she always kept safe. The only souvenir she was left with that made her remember him as he was with her right at that moment. It reminded her how much a guy, who was somewhere out there, trying to make her dream come true, love and cherish her as his wife.

But she never wore it for some unknown reasons.

Running her fingers slow and smooth over the texture of the gold, she wondered why she wanted to wear it now, and what that one thing that was stopping her again was. She always had this doubt that was never fulfilled. Even from the day she knew and remembered him, she always wondered if they were really meant for each other, or it was just the feasibility that made them so. But what Sanjuktha never understood was that fate would always have its very own suspicious ways of stating a fact.

As she wondered sitting on the ground in her tent, staring at the chain in her hand and smiled at some flashing memories; a thunder clapped in the clouds. Sanjuktha looked up at once and turned back to the petrichor that filled the air. The smell of first rain after a long period of gap felt good. She stood up at once to run out of her tent. She stared up at the clouds that formed the second sky, and it made her smile again. The wind was so strong that it made her wanting to fly.

As Sanjuktha stared at the sky that was trying to tell her something, it started raining at once. She closed her eyes tight to the impact of the cold water droplets, smiling like a child. She enjoyed the way the wind was touching her and the way the rain was feeling her. But suddenly form nowhere she had a flash of Prudhvi smiling, looking deep into her eyes.

"I love you, Sanju," he said. And she heard it like he just uttered it.

Sanjuktha opened back his eyes at once bending her head down panting. The wind and the rain started making it hard for her to breath now. She cleared the water from her face and slowly stepped away into her tent, wondering what she had just seen.

She knew that this all was just going out of her hand, and the only way to stop this was to hide away things to where they belonged. As she pulled the clothes to place the mangalsutra between them, she remembered something else that she once read. Those lines form his last letter to her…

"*…keep singing whenever you get a chance to. And you'll see me whenever you sing. I'll touch you as the wind, feel you like the rain and reach you like a dream,*" he told her.

Sanjuktha ran back out of the tent at once to look up to the sky, and it really felt like he was watching her from somewhere. Deep down from her heart, she suddenly realised why she got to sing today. Why she got to pull the mangalsutra out. And why it was raining as he promised.

Sometimes you got to ask no complex questions to get to know the simple answer. This was the day she would realise how pure his love was towards her.

Sanjuktha took a look at the chain in her hand again. It was clean from the rain, and it was shining now, as clear as her feelings for him. With no second thought, she wore it on. For the first time in her entire life, she felt like she belonged to someone. This was the first day to her, as his wife.

With the weight that just got on to her heart and the weight that just left, she turned up to the sky again, to spell those words that she always wanted to find the courage to utter. As she at last did, she dreamed of the day when they are going to meet, and when she was going to cook him his favorite dishes again.

"Prudhvi," she called out with a bright and happy smile on her face. "I love you too."

Almost two years from that day, on the midnight of 15th August, 1947, India had finally become independent from the wounding chains of British; taking lives, dreams and sacrifices of many freedom fighters, most of whose names were never written on the walls of our history, but still reverberate in the hymns of our independence.

Hail them all.

Jai Hind

Epilogue

An extract from a letter written by Mr P. V. Chakraborty, former chief justice of Calcutta High Court on 30th March, 1976.

The Tribune of Sunday, 12 Feb, 2006 *'Spectrum,' p. 11.*

"When I was acting as Governor of Bengal in 1956. Lord Clement Attlee, who was the British Prime Minister in post-war years and who was responsible for India's freedom, visited India and stayed in Raj Bhawan, *Calcutta for two days..." I put it straight to him like this: "The Quit India Movement of Gandhi practically died out long before 1947 and there was nothing in the Indian situation at that time, which made it necessary for the British to leave India in a hurry. Why then did they do so?"*

In reply, Attlee cited several reasons, the most important of which were the I.N.A. activities of Netaji Subhash Chandra Bose, which weakened the very foundation of the British Empire in India and the RIN Mutiny which made the British realise *that the Indian armed forces could no longer be trusted to prop up the British. When asked about the extent to which the British decision to quit India was influenced by Mahatma Gandhi's 1942 movement, Mr Attlee's lips widened in smile of disdain and he uttered slowly, "Minimal."*

References

1. "Bose The Forgotten Hero" – By Shyam Benegal.
2. "Bapu and a Spoilt child" – By Swarnava Bera.
3. "India's Biggest Cover Up" – By Anuj Chatterjee.
4. "Gandhi" – By Richard Attenburough.
5. "Gandhi was No Saint" – An exclusive interview with Anita Bose on rediff.com.
6. The Nightingale Song may also be found in: Randolph, Vol. I, #58, "One Morning in May"; Brown, Vol. III, #13, "One Morning in May"; Belden, p. 239, "The Nightingale."

Up Next

Sambhavami

A Space Odyssey in Hunt of an Alien Called God